VANISHING DAY

VANISHING DAY
By Valerie Davisson
Copyright © 2019 Valerie Davisson

VANISHING DAY is a work of fiction. Names, characters, places, and incidents are the product of the author's imagination or are used fictitiously. Any resemblance to actual events, locales, businesses, or persons, living or dead, is coincidental.

Published by Vaughn House Publishing, Depoe Bay, OR
Second Edition
Previously Published by Hauser Publishing in 2018
Print ISBN - 978-0-9838696-8-9
Ebook ISBN - 978-0-9838696-9-6

Cover and Interior Design by Kimberly Peticolas, www.kimpeticolas.com

Library of Congress Control Number: 2019912518

10 9 8 7 6 5 4 3 2 1

VANISHING DAY

A Logan McKenna Novel

VALERIE DAVISSON

To Ron,
You may be our little brother, but we've
always looked up to you. You are the
man many others aspire to be.

"If you can't fly then run,
if you can't run then walk,
if you can't walk then crawl,
but whatever you do,
you have to
keep
moving
forward."

Martin Luther King, Jr.

PROLOGUE

"She's here."

"Where?"

"She and Shannon are across the street, sharing an ice cream cone. There are benches along the boardwalk."

Neal Everly adjusted his sunglasses. He continued to speak softly, even though there was plenty of cover noise in the coffee shop. It was a good spot. Traffic wasn't heavy, and he could keep an eye on them without being seen.

"They're sharing," he added, smiling. Shannon loved chocolate. So did her mom. "I mean what *town*, Neal."

He knew what his boss meant, but right now they looked so happy. Lauren looked good. Sun-streaked hair pulled back from her face, tan, relaxed. She was laughing at something Shannon said. He never knew what that cute, dimpled little kid jabbered about, but she kept up a steady stream of excited chatter from her car seat all the way home from preschool every day.

1

Neal relented. "Jasper, They're in Jasper, California," he said. The moment's hesitation was not lost on his boss.

○ ○ ○ ○ ○

Garrett knew he'd have to remind Neal who held his leash. One phone call is all it would take. But at least he found her. For now, he was still useful. Once he had Lauren and Shannon back home he'd decide what to do about Neal.

When she took off this time, in July, Garrett assumed she'd come home on her own in a few weeks like every other time. Or he'd find her.

But this time, she disappeared into thin air. No credit card receipts, no phone calls, no calls to friends. Not that she had many. But he knew she couldn't resist calling dear old Mom. Mrs. Stanton, Shannon's grandmother. It's the one tie he hadn't been able to break, and Lauren couldn't resist keeping.

Even though Lauren had been intentionally vague with her mom on the phone, saying only that she and Shannon were in a "little artsy town" along the Southern California coast, she'd slipped up. Trying to reassure her mother that she and Shannon were okay, Lauren said she'd taken her daughter to a marine animal center and Shannon had fallen in love with the sea otters. The little girl loved watching a young otter, the star of the show named Sadie, crack her seafood dinner open with a rock as she floated on her back in the pool.

Yes, she was happy. Everything was okay. This wasn't forever. No, she couldn't tell her exactly where they were, but she'd find a way to call her again soon. Maybe even FaceTime.

Thrilled down to his marrow, Garrett listened to every damning word. He'd been bugging grandma's phone. Stupid bitch. Lauren, still tied to her mama instead of her husband. What had her mother done for her? He'd given her everything, and she didn't appreciate it.

He had her now.

It didn't take him long to figure out that there were only three Southern California towns with sea otter exhibits. Long Beach and San Diego had sea otter exhibits but didn't qualify as small towns. Jasper, however, fit the bill. It was small. It was artsy. And it had a Sea Otter Center of its very own.

"She see you?"

"No."

"Good. Keep it that way. She driving the same car?"

"Yeah, I can see it from here. The Corolla. It's parked out front, about a block away."

"Piece of crap. I gave her a brand new GLC and she's driving that. Did you get the tracker on?"

"Not yet. Too many people around. Labor Day weekend coming up."

"Well, when do you think that might happen, Neal?"

"Tonight, once it gets dark and things quiet down. There's enough holiday traffic and tourists around. I should be able to follow them then. If she lives in town, it'll be easy. If she's staying someplace more remote, it will be tougher—fewer cars on the road. She'll recognize the Volvo if she sees it."

○ ○ ○ ○ ○

Neal waited as instructed. He almost wished Lauren would see him and get away, but he did his job. Garrett owned him. Garrett hired him when no one else would. And he could send him back at any time. All he had to do was call up his PO and tell him Neal was out of state. But this was the last job he'd do for him. He'd find a way. He only had ten days left on his parole.

Keeping one eye on his quarry, Neal got up and paid his bill. Lauren was a big girl. She should have left Garrett years ago.

"Do you want me to call you?" he asked.

Silence filled the line for a few more seconds. Then, as if storm clouds had blown over, Garrett wrapped up the call.

"I'll call you. Have your phone on around 11:00 o'clock. That give you enough time?"

"Yeah. She has to get Shannon to bed early, right?" Neal said.

"She should. But who knows what she's doing now. And when I call, I want to hear you got that tracker on that junk heap she's driving my daughter in. Okay, Neal?"

"This is important," Garrett added.

Neal sighed. As if he didn't know.

Waiting until Lauren and Shannon started walking back to their car, Neal left the coffee shop and got into the Volvo. It was a tank. Garrett got it, supposedly to keep them safe, but after a week or so of being their driver, he realized his main job was to keep tabs on the boss's wife.

The engine started right up. Might as well get this over with.

o o o o o

Tossing his phone back on his desk, Garrett Delaney leaned back in his chair, squeezing his eyes shut. Opening them, he scanned the opposite wall, not really seeing the muted, gray wallpaper or the brushed steel sculpture in the corner, blazing orange in the slanting rays of a late, Seattle summer sun.

He reached inside his desk drawer, deftly removing a small, round white tablet from the blister pack stored there, downing it with the leftover coffee in his mug.

Double shot.

He flicked the drawer shut.

Taking a deep breath, he swiveled his chair around to look

out the window at Elliot Bay. Steepling his long fingers, he thought about next steps. The Adderall helped him focus.

He found her. He always did. It was only a matter of time. She always gave in, but this time she almost made it. This time it had been very inconvenient—and expensive—to locate his own wife. That would not happen again.

Once Neal secured the tracker, he'd have him lay low and monitor their movements until he could get there. He couldn't risk Lauren spotting her former driver and getting spooked. Although, with the electronics in place, at least he could find her easily if she sensed something was up. If Neal got the damn thing on tonight. His Ferragamo-clad foot shot out and kicked the wall. This was not a good time. He needed to be here, not a thousand miles away in some little tourist town in Southern California, fetching an ungrateful wife. He had business to take care of. Things were happening fast, and not in his favor.

Even if he could borrow Steve's Cessna, the trip would probably eat up at least four days. Four days lost. A friend from college, Steve was the one who talked him into getting his pilot's license five years ago. And if he took the Cessna to California, he wouldn't even have to rent a car when he got there. Steve's wife was from Oceanside; he always had an extra vehicle or two stored with one of the small Fixed Base Operators, or FBOs, at Carlsbad Airport nearby. He checked on Google maps. Carlsbad was about an hour south of Jasper, CA. Doable.

Garrett combed his fingers through the tight, black waves he gelled into submission every morning, tugging hard at the roots until it started to hurt. For some reason, this helped.

Why did Lauren have to do this to him now? She was so selfish!

He had to hand it to her, she'd made it pretty far this time.

He'd take her back, but she wasn't going to like the new rules. He might have to hire two Neals.

○ ○ ○ ○ ○

A young woman with smooth, honey blonde hair, secured at the nape of her neck with a large barrette, knocked lightly, opening the office door a few inches. Sheaf of papers in hand, she peered around the door and raised her eyebrows for permission to enter. Garrett swung his chair back around and leaned forward, arranging his face around a laser-whitened smile.

Pale blue-gray eyes pierced her soft, brown ones.

"Hello, Gorgeous!" he said, hands folded in front of him on the desk. He had all the time in the world.

"Hi, Mr. Delaney, sorry to bother you again," she said.

It had been a busy day. The phone hadn't stopped ringing. One of Mr. Delaney's clients had been particularly insistent. Didn't they realize he had more than one client? How was he supposed to get any work done if they kept badgering him to see how their money was doing? She entered and placed the papers on his desk, indicating the precisely placed, yellow tabs on the edge of each page requiring his signature.

"The mail guy comes at four o'clock now, Mr. Delaney, instead of 4:30 p.m. If you want these to go out today I can come back to pick them up in a few minutes, or I could drop them off on my way home," she told him.

"Not necessary, Patricia, you work too hard already. Here," he said, pulling the papers toward him, "I'll take care of these now."

Patricia watched as he skimmed the documents and signed in the designated places quickly and efficiently. She loved the way his gold pen flashed in the light, and his shirt sleeves rolled back several times to display very sexy forearms. Everything about him was sexy. Clean and sharp. Dark hair against white skin.

"The Black Irish, I am!" he told her one day, with a wink.

An indigo sweater contrasted nicely with his white shirt sporting faint, indigo stripes. The raw silk, blue tie brought out his eyes.

Straightening the papers briskly on all sides before handing them back to her and recapping his Mont Blanc pen, he looked up, flashing her another brilliant smile.

"Signed, sealed, delivered!"

. . . I'm yours!

Mr. Delaney was so nice, taking time to take care of these so she wouldn't have to make an extra stop on the way home. They just didn't make men like him anymore. He remembered everyone's birthdays and even sent her mother a card when she was sick last year. His wife was a lucky woman.

"Thanks, Mr. Delaney!" she said, hurrying back to her desk to get them in the envelope she already addressed and stamped.

Garrett watched his assistant's attractive backside move from side to side as she walked away, keeping the smile plastered on his face until the door closed behind her.

Why do they insist on being called administrative assistants? They're secretaries.

Dismissing both secretaries and administrative assistants from his mind, he swiveled around to look out his window, pupils dilated, heart slightly racing, capping and recapping his pen.

1

7:30 a.m.

A small shiver of joy ran up Logan's spine. Bare feet splashing in and out of the incoming tide, she turned up the power, lengthened her stride, and sprinted the last forty yards.

Strong and toned after a summer of beach runs and kayaking, she hadn't felt this good since the car accident that took her husband's life four years ago. It almost took hers, too, but with time and consistent effort, her body, and for the most part, her soul, had healed. She sometimes still reeled from discovering Jack was unfaithful to her for much of their marriage, but kept those feelings pushed to the back of her mind.

When she got to Main Beach, she started her cool down, dragging her feet deliciously through the cool water. Pulling her hair up into a loose knot at the top of her head, she looked out to sea. The Pacific was gentle this morning. Glassy, almost. Glad she got her run in early. The sun was already hot on the back of her neck.

The new life she'd forged for herself was taking root. And it was good. She was luckier than most. After the accident, she sold her and Jack's computer business, bought a fixer-upper, and with a few nudges from her friend, Bonnie, embarked on a career in education. At least, indirectly.

Logan hadn't lasted long as a classroom teacher. But merging her two passions, math and music, she created an integrated program based on exciting developments in brain research. Put simply, the program not only helped build students' neural pathways and learning capacity, but measurably increased retention across all subject areas.

The best part, as far as Logan was concerned, was that it verified what she knew in her gut. Kids learn more when they're having fun and allowed to flex their creative muscles. The kids dubbed the new program Fractals.

Originally funded mainly by a generous octogenarian donor, Mrs. Houser, who passed away last year, Fractals was saved from an untimely demise by the efforts and connections of Rita Wolfe, principal of the New School up near Portland, Oregon.

In return for Logan bringing her program to Oregon, which required being on campus two or three times a school year, Rita arranged for the continued collaboration and support of Huey Le, her technology guru. He flew down to attend the CUE conference in March with Logan, and their latest project was integrating music mapping software into the program. CUE originally stood for Computer Using Educators, when that was a new thing.

Logan felt lucky to be working with Huey. She trusted his intelligence, skill and character. They met a couple of years ago, on her first trip to see the New School. When his sister's Vietnamese food truck, Thanh's Pho, was blown up right outside Logan's downtown Portland hotel window, killing her mother-in-law, Huey asked for Logan's help.

VANISHING DAY

Only recently had Thanh been able to reopen. Just the thought of the fragrant Vietnamese rice noodle soup, pho, made Logan's mouth water. She hadn't had breakfast yet.

Luckily, Tava'e's was on the way home.

Motivated by the thought of one their gigantic cinnamon rolls and strong, hot coffee, Logan hiked up the beach and across the sandy scrap of lawn separating the boardwalk from PCH, the Pacific Coast Highway. There was hardly any traffic this early, so she jaywalked at the corner without waiting for the light. What Rick didn't know wouldn't hurt him. Her little brother was a cop in town.

Nodding to one of the regulars anchoring the bench, soaking up the morning sun, Logan opened the door and went inside. Immediately enveloped by the rich aromas of cinnamon and freshly roasted coffee beans, she couldn't help but smile. Life was good.

Tava'e, the owner, was holding court in her booth in the back. Usually, the large, Samoan woman greeted Logan with a booming "Talofa!" and a huge hug, but today her attention was on the chess board in front of her and the move her opponent just made. Logan didn't recognize the newcomer. Maybe Jasper's reigning chess queen finally found someone who could give her a good game. All the better, because no one else could. Tava'e had given her lessons, but Logan was a novice, and knew in all likelihood she would remain so.

After a satisfying infusion of sugar and caffeine, providing absolutely no essential vitamins or minerals, Logan waved in Tava'e's direction, exited the coffee shop, and started home. Her 1940s beach bungalow was just a few houses up the hill. Nicknamed Killer Hill, due to its murderous effect on manual transmissions, it rose at a sharp 45-degree angle. On a full stomach, it felt more like 180 degrees.

Almost there.

Up ahead, Lola, her sapphire blue '58 Corvette, lolled in the shade like a southern belle on the short gravel drive between her house and the converted studio/garage. Logan reminded herself she needed to take her into Mr. Delgado for a tune-up and wax. The salt air was murder on Lola's complexion.

Just before she turned in, movement at the window of the last house on her right caught Logan's eye. A little girl, about three years old, waved furiously at her, jumping up and down on what must have been a chair underneath the open living room window.

Her head was haloed by bouncing, dark curls. "Hi!" she trilled.

Logan returned the little girl's wave. "Hi, yourself!" she said, smiling back.

A young woman, presumably the mother, materialized at the little girl's side. Without looking at Logan, she scooped her daughter up and said something about not bothering the nice lady, then closed the window.

Logan wasn't bothered, but neither did she want to intrude. Maybe the woman didn't think she liked children. Her new neighbors moved in a couple of weeks ago, but Logan still hadn't made it over to say hello. She'd have to remedy that.

Tomorrow, she'd put on her welcome wagon hat. She couldn't bake, but she could bring over a goodie bag from Tava'e's. No one could turn down one of Jean's cinnamon rolls. It's how she and Ben met when she was the new kid on the block.

Time to pay it forward.

2

That plan made, Logan turned toward her front door.

"Mornin', Glories!" she greeted the profusion of purple flowers tangled along a low, white fence running between the street and the narrow patch of yard in front of her house. The sun warmed the slate flagstones. She loved the herbal aroma that drifted up whenever she stepped on the French thyme she'd planted between them.

Digging her key out of her pocket, she opened the door and let herself in. Her cell phone was ringing. Even though Rick wanted her to keep it with her at all times, she preferred not to be constantly tethered. Locking the front door was already a concession to safety.

Kicking off her shoes at the door, Logan did a sock slide down the hall, coming to a perfect stop at the edge of the Persian rug she'd picked up for a song last year. Being a home owner never got old!

Plucking her cell off the coffee table on the way, she pushed open the French doors that took up most of the back wall, and stepped outside, looking at her phone to see who called. Sally. Logan put her phone in her pocket. She'd call her back in a minute. First, she wanted to enjoy her garden.

Ben, her landscape architect neighbor and the man she'd been seeing the last few years, had taken the neglected patch of scrub grass and turned it into her very own, private, Japanese garden complete with meditation bench and stone Buddha.

This was wishful thinking on his part as Logan rarely sat still. She'd tried meditating, but moving meditation in the form of running or yoga was as close as she could get.

Visible through the French doors, the garden extended the living space of her tiny house. At one end, a small stand of bamboo provided the perfect backdrop for a rounded, granite boulder, softened by sea grasses and a stream meandering around an ornamental plum tree.

Most of her yard was around the corner, on the back side of her house, like Ben's. Neither were fond of fences, so Ben installed a small foot bridge over the stream. The connecting path had gotten a lot of use the last couple of years.

Just then, her phone burred in her pocket. It was Sally, so she pulled it out and took the call.

Sally and her husband, Ned, were old friends. Logan was playing with her and Ned every weekend during the summer at the Otter Festival, having a blast. Tomorrow was their final show. The sheer joy of fiddling, getting back in her old grooves, had done wonders. Muscles long stiff and knotted loosened up and unfurled.

"Hey, Logan," Sally began, "glad you're home! Is Amy coming tomorrow?"

"She's planning on it, why?"

"Well, I hate to ask, but can she keep an eye on Quinn?" He's turned into a handful—terrible twos turning into the terrible threes, and all that.

"Of course. I'm sure she won't mind. Amy loves kids."

"Okay, great! He'll probably be fine, but just in case."

Logan laughed. She'd witnessed a couple of Quinn's melt-downs this summer. Her friend was wise to call for more troops.

"How are she and Liam doing?" Sally asked.

"They're doing great," Logan said, "Just celebrated their first anniversary."

"No way! I can't believe it's been a year already. How does Amy like her new job?"

"She's in seventh heaven. What's not to like about getting paid to play with sea otters? Of course, it's not all play, but she still loves it."

Looking back, Logan still had a hard time believing that only a year ago, her daughter, Amy, then twenty-four, home from Africa, recuperating from a bad bout of malaria, had been chased into the Pacific Ocean during a raging storm to escape a murderer.

Today, Amy glowed with health and happiness. She and Liam, her Scottish botanist husband, were a perfect match.

Promising to come in a few minutes early tomorrow to help set up, Logan ended the call and headed upstairs to change. She had a full day of shopping, cleaning, and ugh . . . paying bills.

But after that, the rest of the weekend was hers. She added a note to pick up candles and her new favorite summer wine, a Pinot Blanc.

Tonight was a Ben night!

3

Nights like last night were something to write home about. After dinner, she and Ben took the rest of the wine up to her rooftop deck to watch the sunset. Once the sun went down, the air cooled quickly. They hunkered down into teak lounge chairs under wool blankets, warming their feet on the fire pit. Ben built the fire pit as a surprise for her their first year together, simply because she liked the one at Juan's, a local Mexican restaurant in town. Ben was a keeper.

When Logan decided to set up shop at home for the Fractals program, she enlisted Ben's crew to do the remodel. They'd converted the stand-alone, single garage into a sound studio downstairs and an upstairs office. The only thing she insisted on was not losing the ocean view from the deck. Ben happily complied and she enjoyed it almost every night since.

Logan wished her father was still alive, so he could meet Ben and see what a wonderful man she found, and how she'd rediscovered her music and so many other things. Her dad never liked Jack, but accepted and welcomed him into the family because Logan loved him. And she had loved Jack. But Ben was better. Whether it was because she was older and better able to give love, or whether Ben was simply a better man, she wasn't sure.

What her mother would think of Ben she had no idea. The woman left both her and her father years ago. No one knew where she was now, or even if she was still alive.

Shaking off these thoughts, Logan turned into her neighbor's walkway. Like most of the houses on the street, this one was a Craftsman. Probably less than 1100 square feet, the house was fronted by a generous porch with long, shallow steps. The young couple who bought the place a year ago, quickly put it up for sale when the baby they were expecting turned out to be triplets and her mother moved in to help. There just wasn't enough room for all of them.

Logan didn't know if the new resident bought the place or was renting. Either way, she might as well get things off to a good start. Balancing the to-go coffees and one hot chocolate for the little girl, along with the bag of warm rolls, she knocked on the door. For a minute she was greeted only with silence, but then she heard footsteps and the woman she'd seen in the window yesterday opened the door halfway. Dressed in yoga pants and a long t-shirt, light-brown hair pulled back in a loose ponytail, she looked out at Logan.

"Hello," she said, "Can I help you?"

Yesterday's exuberant window jumper peered shyly around her mother's legs. Thumb anchored securely in her mouth, shiny, dark curls springing out at all angles from her head, she looked up at Logan with large, blue eyes.

Before the mom could shut the door on her, which she looked about ready to do, Logan beamed her best welcoming committee smile and held up the cardboard tray.

"Hi, I'm Logan McKenna, your neighbor," she said, indicating her home next door with a nod to her left. "Thought you might like some coffee this morning. And . . ." she added, looking down at the little girl with a wink, "if it's okay with your Mom, some cinnamon rolls. Didn't know if you'd had breakfast yet or not."

For a few seconds, the woman just stood there, like some feral animal, trapped and ready to run. Instinctively, Logan diverted her eyes, held her elbows in, and looked as small and nonthreatening as possible. Finally, the little girl broke the ice, nodding excitedly, jumping out from behind her mom's legs to reach for the proffered treat.

After a moment's hesitation, the woman seemed to make up her mind. Visibly relaxing, she smiled, stepped back, and opened the door, inviting Logan in.

"That was very thoughtful. Thanks. I'm Lori and this is my little munchkin, Shannon. Why don't you join us? We can all eat in here."

Relieved her friendly overture had been accepted, Logan followed her host inside. The house was tiny as expected, but cozy. Lots of dark wood. To the left was a green, speckled Formica kitchen table with three chairs. After a pass-through to a kitchen, a short hallway led to what must be a bedroom on the right, ending in a back door. Across from the dining room, to the right of the front door, was the living room. A serviceable, if slightly sunken, old-fashioned sofa sat atop carved wooden legs from a graceful past, next to one end table and a lamp. Under the large, picture window facing the porch, sat a matching, oversized chair in the same faded rose fabric. This must have served as Shannon's trampoline yesterday. In the corner were some toys.

"I saw you had a little girl and got her some hot chocolate. Is that okay?"

"Absolutely, she loves cocoa, right Shannon?"

Apparently having decided to trust Logan, Lori shed her former reserve. It was like watching a different person than the one who'd cautiously opened the door.

"Cocoa!" Shannon said.

4

Shannon began jumping up and down gleefully, sans benefit of her trampoline, then looked up at Logan. "Marmarrows?"

Logan looked at Lori for a translation.

"She means marshmallows," Lori said, then turned to her daughter.

"No, honey, not this time, I don't think we have any right now, but it's really good," she said.

Shannon shrugged it off and reached for the cocoa.

Logan was relieved her new neighbor wasn't one of those parents who lived on kale and seaweed and never allowed their children to have sugar. She was all for broccoli and salad to accompany her rib eye steak, but that was as far as she was prepared to go on the health food front.

"I'll just get some milk to cool it down for her," she said, after helping her daughter onto one of the chairs. "And some plates."

She returned in a few minutes with some '70s stoneware plates and soon they were all enjoying their impromptu meal. Logan brought extra napkins, which was good, because within seconds, Shannon's face was smeared with frosting.

"How do you like your roll, Shannon?" Logan asked, digging into her own. Even though Lori brought forks out, they all ate with their fingers. Tasted much better that way.

"Good!" Shannon said.

"Tava'e's down the street is our go–to coffee place, if you haven't been there already," Logan said.

"I can see why . . . this is really good," Lori said, licking her fingers.

Just in case there was a husband or roommate in the picture she hadn't seen, Logan brought an extra coffee, but Lori suggested splitting it when they neared the bottom of theirs, so she didn't think anyone else lived with them.

After everyone finished and Lori took the plates into the kitchen, Shannon grabbed Logan by the hand and dragged her new friend into the living room to see her play tent. Although she didn't have as many toys as Bonnie's kids had, all of Shannon's toys seemed to be new. Logan dutifully crawled in and out of the flimsy tent while her energetic tour guide jabbered enthusiastically, introducing her to all the dolls and stuffed animals. They all had to have 'ciminon rolls' too.

Lori came in and offered to rescue her, but Logan figured the mom probably needed the break, so said she was fine. Lori finally stopped apologizing for Shannon monopolizing Logan's time, sat back on the sofa and curled her feet under her. She was a small woman. Not delicate, but evenly proportioned. Maybe five feet five. Her outstanding feature was that she had none.

Shannon's sugar high proved to be short-lived. She quickly wound down, crawling up in her mother's lap with her favorite stuffed animal, Egee, a caramel–colored puppy, and promptly fell asleep. Lori stroked her daughter's soft curls.

"Man, I wish I could do that," Logan said. She'd always been a light sleeper.

"Where did you guys move from?" Logan asked, straightening her clothes, sitting down on the other end of the couch.

"Mid-west," Lori said, "Fly-over state. Lots of cows."

"Why California?"

Logan would have guessed a job transfer, but with the limited furniture, she didn't get the sense her new neighbor had a job that would ship household goods, or maybe a job at all. Besides, this furniture didn't look like something she would have picked out for herself, and the girls' toys were too new to have been purchased even a few months ago.

Lori straightened up and looked confidently into Logan's eyes. "Always wanted to live here. Sunny California. The beach. Wanted to move before Shannon started kindergarten. She's three and a half, now. Gives me time to get settled, check on schools."

Lori spieled this off as if she'd memorized her answer, daring Logan to question it. Logan let the topic drop and took another sip of the last of her coffee.

"What do you do?" Lori asked, changing the subject, "I hear music sometimes from your place."

She shifted on the couch a little more, adjusting Shannon on her lap.

"I run a Math/Music program for the school district and sometimes the students record there," Logan said, "The studio is supposed to be soundproof, so, if you hear music, it might be me. I sometimes play on the roof or out back. Let me know if it's ever too loud."

"Oh no, I like it," Lori said, "What a great job, how'd you get it?"

That was a longer story than Logan expected to tell, but after the awkward start at the door, she was warming to her new neighbor and began to open up as she did with few other women, even her best friend, Bonnie. She found herself sharing her passion for bringing music into the lives of her students, and even telling her about her life, the accident, her new career, the loss of one of her students last year, even her budding romance with Ben.

"Wow! You've been through so much. But you're so strong. It sounds like it's all working out for you. That's awesome. And Ben sounds great," Lori said, "I haven't had very good luck."

She was about to say more, but Shannon started waking up.

Logan checked her pocket for her house keys and got up to go. "I'm so glad I finally got over here to say hello. Sorry it took me so long. Thanks for letting me drop in like this,"

"No, it's been really great for me—it's great having another woman to talk to," Lori said, "I've been so busy working—I work mostly with guys at the restaurant—and taking care of Shannon. Not much time to get out and meet people."

So, she did have a job. "What restaurant?"

"Juan's . . . have you heard of it?"

"Yeah, Juan's is one of our favorite places," Logan said. "Best Mexican food in Jasper."

Wonder what she does with Shannon when she's working? Logan never saw a babysitter at the house. But then again, she hadn't really looked, either. She really hadn't been a very good neighbor. She decided to fix that.

"Hey, if you like live music, why don't you come down to the Otter Festival tomorrow? I can introduce you to some of my friends, you can meet some new people," Logan said.

"What's the Otter Festival?"

"It's actually called the Otter Arts Festival, we just shorten it. It's a local arts festival that's been here forever. We all worked there summers, growing up, and it's still going strong. It's been upgraded and expanded over the years. Still has sawdust on the ground, though. Very laid back. Some friends and I are playing tomorrow—last concert this summer. You should come."

"Well . . . it sounds like fun, but I've got Shannon, and . . ."

"You can bring Shannon. There are always lots of kids running around. In fact, Sally's son, Quinn, will be there. He's about Shannon's age. And it doesn't run late. If you need a ride, I'll have Amy and Liam swing by and pick you up. They're meeting us there."

"That's okay. I have a car," Lori said, "It's in the garage. Not as pretty as your car, but it runs."

"All right. And thanks—my dad gave me that car. She is a beaut and knows it. I'll have Ben save you guys a seat. Everyone should be there by 4:00 p.m."

Lori started to get up, but Shannon had fallen back asleep, so Logan bent down to hug them both briefly. Looking down at the sleeping little girl, Logan was surprised by a sudden, strong, maternal pull, reminiscent of when Amy was that age. Although Amy's hair had been wispy blonde, not black, she felt the same protective instincts toward this sleeping whirl-wind of little-girl energy, as she had for her own child.

"Do you need directions?" she asked.

"No, I can just GPS it," Lori said, then stopped herself, "On second thought, give me the address. My phone's not working great right now."

Lori pointed to a notepad on the end table. Logan tore a sheet off, jotted the address down and drew a map.

"It's not far, maybe ten minutes away at the most. Two lefts and a right. Easy to find," she said as she handed her the piece of paper. See you tomorrow."

Letting herself out the front door, Logan wondered again where this little family came from and what really brought them to the sleepy town of Jasper, CA.

5

The afternoon set was in full swing. The third day of the Labor Day weekend and everyone was there to soak up the last of the sun, art, beer, wine, and music. They'd caught a break with the weather. Instead of the stifling triple digits they were battling inland, Jasper was enjoying idyllic temperatures in the mid-seventies, with a cooling, ocean breeze.

Shane's Regret, Ned & Sally's bluegrass band, was on stage. Originally, they roped Logan back into playing with them to coax her out of her depression after Jack died. Since then, she wound up not only enjoying it, but returned the favor by convincing them to help her out with Fractals. With Rita Wolfe's new funding, she'd been able to bring both of them on full time for the 2016/2017 school year.

There were three entertainment stages scattered throughout the festival. Even though Main was the largest, Logan was glad they got the Tavern Deck this summer. Tucked out of the way, a curve in the rock wall created great acoustics and formed a natural, mini outdoor arena. Cafe tables in front, open bench seating in back. A long, wooden counter ran the length of a small food court on the left. All Logan's fast food favorites at the fair were here.

With the glassblowing demonstration ending nearby, the tables in front of the stage began to fill. Ned on banjo and Logan on fiddle, they completed a rambling duet of Cripple Creek a la Bela Fleck. When they started the Celtic Medley, Sally temporarily abandoned her guitar to come down and keep time on some of the percussion instruments arranged on the edge of the stage, with her four-year-old, Quinn, and anyone who wanted to jam with the band. Quinn favored the tambourine. It was almost time for their break.

The last number of the set was always a rousing one. As Sally found her way back on stage, someone cleared away the sawdust from a small area up front, and an old man placed several flat, parquet flooring pieces down. Each was just a few feet square. Standing on one, he left the others open.

When Logan hit the first note, keeping his upper body straight, the old man began to clog. Expertly tapping and shuffling on the platform, he gestured toward some teenagers at a nearby table, inviting them to take the other squares, which, after much laughing, pushing, and daring, two of them did.

Everyone loved Slim Jim. He was eighty if he was a day and never missed an afternoon concert. This was part of what Logan loved about bluegrass. It brought all ages together. A combination of Scottish, Native American, and African dance styles formed in the Appalachian Mountains, clogging was a tough dance to learn, but she noticed one of the girls was picking up the shuffle-step-stomp sequence pretty well. She must have taken tap. Logan never had gotten the hang of it. She'd stick to the fiddle.

Ending the medley with a dramatic flair, Ned announced a short break and went to help Sally with Quinn. Logan looked around for Ben or the kids, or even Lori, her new neighbor, but no one was there yet. She'd thrown her jacket over a couple of chairs and strapped her purse over the backs of another two, so they'd have somewhere to sit.

Hmmm . . . she took one look at the crowd forming in front of the hamburger place and almost gave up, when one of the cooks she knew waved her back to a side door.

"Two orders, right? Where's Ben?" he asked.

"Yes, thanks, Terry. Definitely two! Ben should be here any minute," Logan said, "and two of those IPAs Ben likes, if you've got any."

She didn't have time for a burger, but she could wet her whistle and grab a few carbs so she'd have energy to finish their show. She didn't know if Ben was on a diet this week, but if he was, he could always get a Greek salad at Athena's next door. Either way, with Amy and Liam coming for sure, the Fire Fries wouldn't go to waste.

Terry came around the side, handing her two huge, red, plastic baskets heaping with hot, crispy French fries smothered in firehouse chili, brushing her off when she tried to pay.

"I'm getting a free concert," he grinned, before going back inside, letting the screen door bang. "You guys sound great. Always love it when you play."

"Hi, Logan. Want some help?"

6

Hands full, Logan turned around. "Lori! Hey, glad you could make it. Sure, take this one," she said, handing her one of the baskets.

With her free hand, she plucked a chili-free fry out and bent down to offer it to Lori's daughter. "Hi, Shannon! Do you like French fries?" Shannon nodded, taking it politely from her hand. "Okay, then, you're in luck. There's plenty to share."

Logan led them back to the band's table in the front corner, introduced Lori to Ned and Sally.

"Did you have any trouble finding us?"

"No, your map was perfect. Two lefts and a right, right Shannon?"

But Quinn had already commandeered Shannon to find new places to stick his new collection of colorful Squigz (pronounced Squijeez), the suction cup toys Logan got him for his birthday. He had more at home, but Sally limited him to one bag for the festival. They stuck to the table, each other, even Shannon's forehead.

When Sally asked where she was from, Lori proved just as adept at not answering her friendly questions as she had been with Logan. She delivered the same pat answers about loving sunny California and always wanting to move here, never revealing the town, let alone, the state she and her daughter were from.

Maybe Lori was just a private person. She and Sally talked pre-school kid stuff while Logan filled Ned in about her upcoming trip to Oregon. Ben arrived and gratefully accepted the beer. Too late for the fries, he said he had a late lunch, so was okay for now. Logan knew he'd go get an order as soon as they started back up.

All too quickly, the break was over and it was time to do their last set. Normally, it was her favorite, but Logan felt apprehensive. Somehow, this felt like the last time they'd play together at the Otter Festival. How much longer could her life be blessed with such good friends and good fortune? She knew her feelings weren't based on anything concrete, but somehow, Logan couldn't shake the uneasy feeling. Maybe she just wasn't used to being happy.

After satisfying the crowd with some favorites, Ned nodded at Logan and Sally with a wicked smile. Ned had taken a bit darker turn recently, experimenting with some music from an Alternative Bluegrass Folk band called "The Dead South." Tipping his hat at the crowd so they knew something different was coming, Logan did the intro and then Ned growled through a number called "In Hell I'll Be In Good Company." Logan closed her eyes. She liked the sound, but not the lyrics. Luckily, with Ned's enunciation, no one knew what he was saying anyway. Sally just played her guitar.

A younger crowd was coming in and they seemed to like it. It was definitely different.

When she opened her eyes again, Logan saw Ben's friend, Taylor, a forty-something studio musician and sometimes carpenter, was enjoying it too. He had joined their group at the table, sitting next to Ben, who was now allowing Shannon to stick Squigz's on his forehead and pretend to be surprised. Lori was across from Taylor. Logan's matchmaking brain went into high gear. *Hmmmm . . .*

Iona Slatterly, head of security at the Otter Arts Festival since back when Logan worked there as a kid, stopped by as she sometimes did at the end of her shift, and sat in the only chair left, next to Taylor.

Cool. Maybe Taylor will be interested in Lori. They're both about the same age. He's only a few years older than her. Lori likes live music . . .

Taylor stretched his arm up and over, landing casually across Iona's shoulders, missing her towering platinum beehive by less than an inch. Logan thought for sure Iona'd deck him—Iona didn't suffer fools gladly—but she didn't bat an eye. In fact, she snuggled in closer under his arm, smiling up into his face.

Taylor's next move almost knocked Logan off the stage. The quiet, long-haired bass player leaned down and tenderly kissed the tiny, sixty-something Iona squarely on her Candy Apple lips. Luckily, she'd removed her ever-present cigarette just moments before.

Really?

Logan looked to see if Ben had noticed. If he did, he didn't show it. He was watching the show on stage.

Iona and Taylor? She was old enough to be his mother! Iona Slatterly wore spray on jeans, high-heeled boots, western shirts, pointy bras, penciled in her eyebrows, and sprayed her beehive into submission with enough ozone-depleting spray to create its own separate hole in the atmosphere.

Soft-spoken Taylor was into jazz and goat's milk yogurt. Iona was truck stops and chicken fried steak. Taylor was vegan and contemplated joining a monastery at one time. What could they possibly have in common?

The sun wouldn't set for another few hours, but something in the softening of the air, hung with the scent of warm, pungent sage, gently indicated the waning of the day. Logan was up. She always started the final number, a slow, Nova Scotia aire some called "Neil Gow's Lament." It was sad, and yet not. All temporal thoughts flew and she lived in the music. Ned came in with a few soft beats of his Irish Bodhran drum. Sally had spirited her cello on stage and the music spiraled up and over the canyon walls.

As always, the music floated past some, touched some, and broke open at least a few hearts.

7

Taylor and Ben helped Ned load the last of the large gear into a rolling cart to take out to the van in the employee parking lot. Another band started at five o'clock. Everyone used their own equipment. The vendor gate normally stayed closed until the end of the night when the Festival shut down at 9:00 p.m., but Iona had keys, so she went along to help.

Lori stood, chatting with Sally, jiggling a fussy Shannon up and down.

"Time to get this little one home. I've got to get some laundry done so I can work tomorrow night."

"Who watches Shannon?" Sally asked, "I'm looking for someone reliable for Quinn once school starts. Now that I'm going to be working full time with Fractals, I can't keep an eye on him well enough—he's into everything and interrupts my lessons."

Lori's face took on a worried look.

"I wish I could help, but I have the same problem. I'm going to have to find someone to watch Shannon. They were letting me bring her to work. Shelly, the day manager, was helping me watch her, but she switched shifts and the new guy's not into kids. I'm going to have to find some kind of day care three or four shifts a week," she said.

Logan jumped down off the stage, wrapping the last of the power cords, packing them into their case with the percussion instruments. Overhearing the last of their conversation, she said, "Haley's doing some babysitting this year, you should give her a call."

To Lori she added, "Haley's the sixteen-year old daughter of a friend of mine. She's paying her parents back for a loan they gave her. She's a really sharp kid. She's doing Independent Study this semester, so her schedule is flexible.

"Haley's babysitting again?" Sally asked. "Yep!" Logan said.

"Awesome! Quinn loves her! I thought she thought she was too grown up to babysit anymore."

"Pride goeth before a fall . . . ," Logan laughed. Lori looked doubtful.

"Could she handle both Quinn and Shannon at the same time? I'm going to be working mostly days from now on. I mean . . . they're pretty active," she said.

"Oh, absolutely," Logan said, "I've known Haley since she was born. She's helped her mom with her younger brothers and sisters and is everyone's favorite babysitter. Besides, you saw how the kids got along tonight. It will give them someone to play with."

Logan saw the hesitation on Lori's face and added, "If you'd feel more comfortable, Lori, I'm right next door. I can always stop over and see how they're doing the first few days."

This seemed to reassure the young mother, and she gratefully accepted the referral. It's not like she had a lot of other options. It was that or lose her job. They had been patient, but when she left work on Saturday, they'd made it clear she'd better have a sitter sooner rather than later.

VANISHING DAY

Lori said she didn't work until tomorrow night, so she would call Haley first thing. If she was interested, she would drive over and meet her tomorrow morning. Logan gave her Haley and her mom's contact information. She'd let them work out the details. Ben and Ned came back sans cart.

"Where's Taylor and . . . Iona?" Logan asked.

"They said they were going down to Swallows," Ben said. "Swallows?" Logan repeated.

Swallows was an old-school bar in San Juan Capistrano boasting bikers and warped, wooden floors, but great live music every weekend.

"Yeah, Iona's teaching Taylor how to two-step," Ben said with a straight face.

Hands on hips, Logan looked at Ned and Sally, then back at Ben, "Am I the only one who thinks this is a little odd? Are they really dating? Going out? Whatever?"

"Friends with benefits?" Sally deadpanned.

Ignoring this comment, Logan asked, "When did this start?"

If Ben knew, he wasn't saying.

He seemed kind of irritated with her on the ride home in the truck, which gave Logan time to mull all of this over. She knew nothing about Iona's personal life. How old was she? Hard to tell with the dyed hair and makeup. Iona was just Iona. Like the rest of the local kids who worked at the Festival every summer, Logan just assumed all adults fit into some vague 'old' category. Iona could have been in her twenties or thirties when they were all in high school, which didn't seem old at all, now. That would make her . . . in her sixties now??! And Taylor was in his forties? Twenty-year age difference?

Ben's truck idled at the light.

Men did it all the time, so why not an older woman with a young man?

As they walked out to their cars, Sally had brought up Cher, Demi Moore, and Susan Sarandon in that baseball movie.

"She wound up marrying that younger guy in real life," she'd pointed out.

Well, yeah, but Iona didn't look like Cher or Susan Sarandon. She didn't think either of them dyed and teased their hair into straw or had smoker's lines around their lips.

She tried to think of other, more current, examples.

There was the guy running for President in France. Logan just read where Emmanuel Macron, only twenty-nine, was married to a woman in her early sixties. They seemed happy. Not much in the way of romantic arrangements ruffled the French.

Her brain hurt.

They were almost home. *C'est la guerre!*

Logan mentally shrugged, leaving the mysteries of life unsolved, and leaned over to take Ben's attention off his driving.

The world it was a changin'. . . .

8

Lori Wright felt light, happy, and a little giddy—all at once. The music, the food, the wine! She'd allowed herself to enjoy the glass Sally brought back for her, but no more than one. She was driving.

Such nice people. And Shannon had such a good time. This is how normal people behaved, had fun, laughed! There were dogs and kids, old people, young people. Everyone just being themselves. When was the last time she had been herself? Did she even remember who that person was? The last time she felt such vivid, muscular joy was when she used to ride her horse back in high school. Whatever happened to that confident young girl?

Maybe this time it would stick. Maybe this time they'd be safe and Shannon would have a chance. She still couldn't hope that much for herself. After the choices she made, she didn't deserve it.

Shannon wanted to stop at the beach to say hello to Sadie the sea otter, but when Lori told her the aquarium was closed, the little girl settled for shrieking and laughing as she chased the waves, splashing in the shallow water that drifted onto the sand on Main Beach.

Tired to her little core by the time they got home, Shannon ate a few bites of macaroni and cheese, then obediently took a bath and allowed herself to be dried off, dressed in her PJs and tucked into bed. Lori only made it through half of Goodnight Moon before Shannon fell into a solid sleep.

Placing the book back in the cardboard box that served as her daughter's new bookshelf, Lori turned off the light, left the door open a bit, and tiptoed into the kitchen for her own meal, the rest of the mac and cheese. Taking her plate into the living room, she sank onto the lumpy couch, absently ate her late dinner, and enjoyed the quiet.

She'd have to thank Logan tomorrow for inviting her to join her and her friends at the Otter Festival. She'd been so busy planning and executing their escape and then surviving the last few months, she hadn't allowed herself to let down her guard or have any fun.

With a sudden stab, Lori missed her mom. She'd risked it once, did she dare call again? She wanted to tell her she and Shannon were okay, that they made it, but not contacting friends or family was number one on every "how to leave your life behind" checklist. That's how you got caught.

But, she reasoned with herself, she'd been careful. She had followed every other item on the list: no credit cards, she'd destroyed the cell phone Garrett bought her, she hadn't taken any items of clothing or toys she hadn't checked and rechecked for tracking devices. She told no one of her plans. She left early on a day and time no one would miss her right away—Neal's day off. She'd even gone as far as carefully selecting her new name. Lori and Lauren both started with the same letter, to make it easier for her to respond to, and her new last name, Wright, was unrelated to anything or anyone. She picked it off the internet.

VANISHING DAY

The helpers told her she could get a whole new social security number as well as a new name, legally, from the Social Security office in Seattle. But when she checked into it, she discovered that would have involved getting proof of the abuse—hospital records and signed statements from neighbors, friends, or family, then a long wait for approval. She couldn't afford to wait. Things were escalating. Garrett was more and more on edge. There just wasn't time. Besides, Garrett insisted Neal drove her and Shannon everywhere. With no time to herself, there was no way she could go to the hospital or the Social Security office without having to explain why to Garrett.

She would need a name change in order to use her accounting degree and get a better job, one that could support her and Shannon better than being a dishwasher at Juan's, but that would have to wait. She didn't have the resources right now.

When her mind started doing its hamster-wheel worry thing, she shut it down. One day at a time. That's what her helpers said. Don't look too far down the road, or your journey will seem impossible and you'll give up.

Again, Lori thought of her mom. Her lifeline. The one tie Garrett had not been able to sever. Widowed for many years, Shannon's only living grandparent, her mom insisted on being part of her granddaughter's life. Mrs. Stanton was the only person she knew who could stand up to Garrett.

Why hadn't she been able to?

She racked her brain. There was no way Garrett could trace a call if she made it with her burner phone. She even replaced those every couple of weeks, just to make sure. She could keep it short and not tell her where they were.

Lori rose from the couch and walked over to get her back-pack, which she kept hung out of Sadie's reach in the hall. Quietly lifting it off the peg so as not to wake Shannon, she brought it back to the living room and rummaged in an interior, zippered pocket until her fingertips found it. Lifting out a small, silver flash drive, she placed it in her palm and sat back on the couch, letting the backpack fall to the side.

Good, it was still there.

Lori rubbed her thumb back and forth across the smooth surface. The repetitious movement was soothing, like worry beads. If push came to shove, this is what would keep them safe. It was her insurance. The only question was whether to let Garrett know she had it. She wasn't sure how he would react. He'd be furious, of course. Of that she had no doubt, but what would he do?

Would he act in his own best interests and leave them alone, or would he simply not be able to control himself and explode? Was he more afraid of his clients, prison, or losing her?

There was a third option.

If he knew she had this kind of evidence against him, he might try to win both wars and come and get it and her and Shannon, as well as the proof she had against him. That sounded more like Garrett. He would want to win on all fronts. Keep his criminal clients happy, the money rolling in, and get his 'property' back. Because Lori knew that to Garrett, that's all she and Shannon were.

She'd kept the flash drive with her at all times so far, but she'd have to find someplace safer than her backpack for this little insurance policy.

Lori tucked the small device deep into its pocket, zipped it, and went to put her backpack carefully on its peg in the hall. She checked on Shannon, who was still deeply asleep, and returned to the living room to do her evening security routine, testing each door and window, before heading to her own bedroom behind the kitchen. It had been a long day.

VANISHING DAY

Thoughts of the wonderful afternoon she and Shannon had enjoyed came back, and Lori decided. Her mom had been so good to them and she'd be worried sick by now. She deserved to know they were okay. Things were going well.

Just one, short call.

9

Finally dark. Not too many streetlights. Garrett wasn't fond of the dark, but at least it gave him some cover so he could sit there and watch. He was across the street and one house down the hill. In the Jeep, not Steve's nicest car, but the one that was available. If Lauren looked out, she wouldn't recognize it. It also had the advantage of not leaving a trail. No car rental record. If he timed it right, there wouldn't be a flight record either. Both Snohomish and Carlsbad Airports were small. They were uncontrolled airports, which meant they had towers, but they weren't manned 24/7.

Almost as old as he was, with over five thousand hours on the airframe, the Cessna 210 Centurian was in superb condition. It got him in early enough to have some dinner at El Torito's across the street from the airport while he waited for the sun to go down. No rush. He didn't want to get to Jasper until after dark.

Lauren hadn't been hard to find. Neal did his job and was back in Seattle now, doing whatever it was Neal did on his nights off. Garrett went back to watching. On the right of the house, light seeped around the edges of living room curtains, burnishing the railings on a long, low porch that ran along the front. He couldn't tell if any lights were on in the back rooms, but the entire left of the house, inside and out, was steeped in deep, gray shadows.

What a piece of crap. Granted, it was a block from the beach, but it was a dump. He took in the scraggly lawn. No gardener, obviously. The worst cracker box on the street. Nothing like the huge, comfortable home he had given her in their safe, gated community. This whole house wouldn't even fit in their garage.

It was all he could do to remain in the car. But he'd waited this long. He could wait a little longer. He needed to plan this carefully. No neighbors on the right—it was some kind of used clothing store. Windows were dark. Owners must have locked up and gone home already. Someone lived on the left, but there was a garage between the two houses. This worked for Garrett. No one in that house could see what was happening in this one. And the house directly across the street was for sale. Unoccupied.

What he couldn't tell was if anyone else was in the house. He needed to get Lauren and Shannon alone. He started up the Jeep. Putting it in gear, he pulled away from the curb and headed toward a grittier neighborhood in nearby Santa Ana. An island of illegal immigrants—excuse me—undocumented workers, Santa Ana had some cash only motels with Wi-Fi so he could check in on grandma. He didn't want to drive all the way back to Oceanside tonight. Neal said the battery on the tracking device was good for a week. He'd set a notification bell on his laptop to go off if the car moved during the night. She wouldn't escape this time. Tomorrow he'd buy a baseball hat and get into position at dusk, to make sure she was truly alone before he made his move.

Make a plan and execute his plan. Later, checked into his

motel, Garrett yanked off his tie and flipped open his MacBook Air, logging into the monitoring software. Good. Lauren's clunker hadn't moved and dear old grandma's Lexus had been in her garage for hours. Everyone present and accounted for.

While half-heartedly watching the news, Garrett clicked on the audio files from grandma's phone that had recorded that day. Most were of the potluck-at-the-church, or your-car-is-ready variety. He quickly deleted those. He almost deleted the rest but decided to listen to them all. His patience paid off.

Gotcha! Garrett immediately turned off the TV and turned up the volume.

"Hi, Mom."

"Lauren, are you okay? How's Shannon? I'm so glad you called, but should you? I mean, is it safe?" she asked.

Mrs. Stanton spoke in low tones, as if someone nearby could hear. No one was nearby, but someone was definitely listening.

"Yes, I'm okay—we're okay—I'm using one of those prepaid phones, so I think we're okay. But, just to be on the safe side, don't ask where we are or anything. I just wanted to hear your voice."

Lori's voice cracked.

"Yours, too, honey. What can you tell me? How are you getting by? Can I send anything?"

"No, not yet. They say not ever, but I'm working on it. I don't want to live like this forever. I don't want Shannon to grow up without her grandmother."

"I know, honey, I miss you terribly, but you do what you have to do for now. I'm fine as long as I know you're safe."

Attempting to sound cheerful and introduce normalcy back into the conversation, Mrs. Stanton asked, "So, what can you tell me?"

"Well, I have a job—it's just a job, job, but we have food on the table, Shannon has some books and toys, we're in a nice town. I have some very nice neighbors. I may not call again for a while."

"That's okay honey. It's more important for you to be safe." Garrett smiled.

Perfect.

If all went well, by Wednesday, they'd all be home where they belonged. He'd keep them safe.

10

After giving her the short tour of the house and the rundown of her daughter's routines, Lori gave Haley the phone numbers for Juan's and her cell, then taped them on the refrigerator. Finally, she went to work, saying she'd be home by 9:30 or 10:00 p.m.

You'd think she never had a babysitter before.

Haley didn't know how close to the truth that was. From the day Shannon was born, the only time Lori had a sitter was on the rare occasions Garrett needed her on his arm for a client dinner.

Sally needed Haley to watch Quinn only in the morning, so Haley had a few hours off before she got here. Kind of chopped up the day, but Haley didn't mind. Quinn didn't get cranky until late afternoon, and Ms. Wright said Shannon usually took an afternoon nap. It looked like a steady job she could work around her schedule. She'd have her parents paid off by Christmas. Then she could start saving money for a car.

Just like her mom predicted, Shannon was asleep when Haley arrived. An hour later, not quite awake yet, she came out of her room and reached her arms up to be carried into the kitchen for lunch.

"Mommy, home?"

"Mommy's at work, Shannon, she'll be home soon," Haley said.

Accepting Haley's nonchalant proclamation, Shannon lay her head on Haley's shoulder and sucked her thumb.

Her mom said she could have a late lunch or early dinner. "You hungry? What would you like to eat?" Haley asked.

No surprise what she wanted to eat. Shannon immediately pointed at a stack of ready-to-make dinners on the counter. The three-year-old wanted what every kid she every babysat wanted: macaroni and cheese. Crack for the pre-school set. What was it about this orange powder that, when combined with water and butter, made the blandest little dried pasta pieces explode with flavor?

Luckily, it only took three minutes to make and she could do it one-handed. Might as well make two. It was her favorite, too.

Shannon, sitting up in her booster chair, kept up a steady stream of chatter between bites, most of which Haley could not interpret. She did a lot of "Wow! Really?!" and open-eyed wonder, interspersed with laughter, which seemed to satisfy Shannon that she was understood.

She could just not get over those curls. And her dimples. When Shannon smiled, she smiled with her whole, little body. The epitome of joy.

Epitome: a person or thing that is the perfect example of a particular quality or type.

Having fallen behind in a couple of her classes last year, Haley was playing catch-up with an SAT vocabulary building program. From the minute Ms. Wright brought her daughter over to meet her at her mom's house this morning, Haley was hooked. She would have babysat this little angel for free.

VANISHING DAY

Shannon made her entrance by letting herself out of her car seat and out of the car, bouncing up the driveway, throwing her arms around Haley's knees when introduced. What a cutie pie!

After lunch, Haley cleaned up the kitchen, took Shannon in to use the potty, praised her, and took her back in her room to get dressed. Next, Shannon solemnly handed her a soft-bristle brush laying next to the soap on the bathroom counter. Haley attempted to brush her hair smooth, but after every stroke, Shannon's stubborn curls bounced right back, forming her usual halo. Kind of like her mom's, Haley thought, except her mom's were light blonde and Shannon's were dark.

Afternoon ablutions attended to, Shannon led Haley by the hand to the front room to play in the tent. Shannon didn't have very many toys. She would have to ask her mom if she could bring some of the twins' older ones. They were still in good shape.

Even with the ceiling fan going, the living room started getting warm, so Haley suggested to her charge they bring the dolls and her favorite stuffed animal, a soft, floppy-eared, brown and white dog she inexplicably called Eegee, outside on the porch and have a tea party with them. It was in the shade and there was always something of a breeze at the beach.

"Stay here a minute, I'm going to go get the tea, okay? Stay on the porch," Haley said.

She quickly went inside to get the cranberry juice she'd seen when she made lunch. That would make a good 'tea' for the party. She hoped it was okay for them to have some. She forgot to ask if any food items were off limits.

When she got back with the juice, Shannon was right where she left her, but stood frozen and terrified, clutching Puppy to her chest as a clear pool of liquid grew in a spreading pool around her feet.

Putting the juice quickly down on the porch, Haley reached down to scoop the little girl up in her arms.

"That's okay, Shannon, it's no big deal, let's get you cleaned up, okay? Come on, you can have your bath early. We'll use those bath crayons. Which one is your favorite color?"

Even the thought of using her bath crayons, which her mother said she always begged for, didn't get Shannon to say anything. She'd never seen a kid get so upset about wetting her pants. The mom didn't seem like the type to get super mad at her kid for having an accident, so it seemed strange she'd be so upset. Shannon burrowed her face into Haley's shoulder.

Maybe a dog or something scared her. As she carried Shannon inside, Haley looked over her shoulder to the front yard. No dog. In fact, no one in the yard at all, or on the sidewalk. Just a black Jeep coming down the street. When it reached the front of the house, the driver turned to look straight ahead, putting his sunglasses on in one smooth move, but before that, she could have sworn he was staring right at them.

Creepy.

11

Shannon was still awake when her mom got home, but she'd settled down. The bath crayons finally did the trick. Blue was her favorite. She wasn't as bubbly as before, but had no more accidents, and played with her toys after Haley got her pajamas on her. But the little girl definitely did not want to go outside again.

Haley always updated the parents when they got home. What their kids ate, what they drank, how long they napped. An experienced sitter, she knew moms and dads appreciated knowing this information. She almost didn't tell Ms. Wright about the incident on the front porch, but decided the mom needed to know. She started with the positive.

"Shannon did really well, Ms. Wright. She ate a good lunch, took a bath, showed me her toys. Just had one, little a-c-c-i-d-e-n-t on the porch. It was no big deal, I got her cleaned up right away. I rinsed out her pants and top and hung them over the shower rod to dry," Haley said.

She hadn't seen any washer or dryer.

"Thanks for letting me know, Haley. And please, call me Lori. Ms. Wright makes me sound ancient!" Lori said.

Haley nodded. Car keys in hand, she hesitated at the door. "You know, it's probably nothing, but just after Shannon had—you know—there was a guy in a car that kind of stared at us as he drove by. I thought maybe he scared her," Haley added, "but I didn't see him do anything. He was just driving by. He just looked creepy."

Lori got very still.

"What did he look like?" she asked, keeping her voice level.

"Hard to tell. Dark hair, super pale skin. Wearing sort of a polo shirt, he was sitting up straight. Kinda tall. Must not be from around here, nobody's that white in the summer around here."

She wanted to add that she might want to check those websites that tell you if a pedophile or registered sex offender moved into your neighborhood, but didn't think now was a good time.

Lori figured out what she owed her and gave her a little extra for gas, then told her she was off tomorrow, but needed her the rest of the week same time as tonight. She watched until the teenage girl was safely buckled in and her car started, then waved before closing the front door.

Immediately, Lori locked the deadbolt she'd installed and leaned her head against the door. No! This couldn't be happening. But Shannon hadn't wet her pants in weeks. Haley's description matched Garrett perfectly. Shannon was terrified of Garrett. If she saw him drive by, that definitely would explain her wetting her pants.

Shannon used to run to her father with unrestrained glee when he came home from work, but now she got very quiet when she heard his car pull up in the driveway. Even at three and a half, she knew enough to be afraid of him. She hated her father's yelling. So far, Garrett hadn't beat her in front of Shannon, but it was only a matter of time. He was losing control and the violence was becoming more frequent. He told Lori if she left again, he'd kill her.

Going back was not an option.

Checking and rechecking the rest of the windows as well as the back door, Lori finally climbed into her own bed, but she kept bouncing up to check on Shannon. Finally, around 2:00 a.m., she gave in. Getting up, she grabbed her pillow and a blanket and went into Shannon's room. Scooching her sleeping daughter over a few inches, she lay down next to her, and stared at the ceiling.

Their wonderful afternoon with new friends at the Otter Festival seemed a very distant dream.

If it was Garrett in that Jeep, he'd be back. Of that, Lori was very sure. Anger slowly began to inch out despair. She had the flash drive. Maybe it was time to use it. She couldn't predict what Garrett would do, but she wasn't just going to go home with her tail tucked between her legs. Not this time. Shannon deserved better. So did she.

She must have drifted off to sleep for an hour or two, because the room was beginning to get light when she opened her eyes. Her unconscious mind must have put in some overtime. A plan of action began to take form. The first thing she needed to do was find a safer place for the flash drive.

12

Not having been awake most of the night like her mother, Shannon was up and ready for breakfast at her usual 6:30 a.m. Dragging her stuffed puppy behind her, she asked for a nana. After two bananas and a bowl of dry Cheerios—she'd run out of milk—Lori managed to fit in a shower, keeping one eye on Shannon, who was brushing what was left of Eegee's fur, with great concentration.

"Goodog, Eegee! Goodog!"

Towel dried and more awake now, Lori pulled on a loose sun dress and pushed her feet into a pair of sandals. She asked Shannon for the brush and sectioned her hair into a loose French braid. With the sun out and no black Jeeps in sight, they walked down to the coffee shop where Logan said she got the cinnamon roll.

The place was called Tava'e's. The large, Polynesian woman playing chess in the back booth must be the owner. Nice place. Warm, inviting. No sea breeze this morning, though. Burning hot already by the time they hiked back up the hill, Shannon made it about halfway before begging to be carried.

As soon as Shannon went down for her nap, Lori took one of the new burner phones off the top shelf of Shannon's closet.

All morning she'd been deciding what to say. Now that the house was quiet, she just had to work up the nerve to say it. Taking one last look at Shannon's innocent, vulnerable face solidified her resolve. She closed the bedroom door softly behind her, walked into the living room and dialed.

"Hello?"

"Hello, Garrett. It's Lauren."

He may know where she lived, but she didn't have to tell him her new name.

If he was surprised to hear from her, his voice didn't show it.

"Have you come to your senses yet?" he said.

"Yes, as a matter of fact, I have."

"Good."

He didn't sound surprised at that. Obviously, he misunderstood. Lori took a deep breath.

"I don't know how you found us, but I know you were here. Shannon saw you yesterday. You frightened her."

"If my daughter is afraid of me, it's only because of the lies you've told her," he said.

"I'm not going to argue with you, Garrett," she said.

She thought very carefully about how she said this next part. "I'm not coming back," she said, then added, "and this time you're going to leave us alone," before he could interrupt.

Garrett barked a laugh.

Lori pictured him, wheeling around in his office chair, looking out over Elliot Bay. Powerful man with powerful trappings. She had no idea he was still in Orange County, just a few miles away.

"And why would I do that?" he said.

"Because I have evidence, Garrett. Names, dates, bank accounts. I have it all."

"You're bluffing," he said. But he wasn't laughing anymore. Lori took a steadying breath.

"The Cayman accounts, for one. The IRS would be very interested in these records, Garrett. So would Mr. Yoshimoto."

Silence.

Lori gathered her courage.

"I gather your number one client is a man who likes his privacy and wouldn't want you exposing him or his friends. "

"How . . . ?" he sputtered.

"I'm not stupid, Garrett. You don't hide your tracks as well as you think you do. I was an accountant when you met me, remember? Back when I had a life."

She was on a roll now, feeling powerful.

"Are you threatening me?" Garrett growled.

"No, Garrett. I'm just telling you how it is this time," she said, "I don't have the energy or desire to hurt you. I just want you to leave us alone. Let us go, Garrett. Just let us go. As long as you leave us alone, this information won't go anywhere."

Click.

He hung up.

That went well.

Hands shaking only slightly, Lori dialed again. No matter what Garrett did now, she knew what her next step had to be.

First, she called the babysitter and asked if she could watch Shannon over at her house with her other charge, Quinn. Sort of a play date. Haley checked with her mom and said, sure, bring her over anytime.

"Quinn's already here. He'd love to have someone to play with," she said.

That gave her a couple of hours. Next, she dialed Logan, who answered on the first ring.

"Hello?"

"Hi, Logan, this is Lori."

"Hi, Lori, what's up?" Logan said.

Grateful for the interruption, Logan stood up from her desk and stretched, looking out of the studio windows toward the ocean. The first couple of days in the school year she spent in the classroom giving her welcome speech to each new class of students starting the Fractals program. This morning she was back in the office, catching up on paperwork before her Oregon trip.

Lori plowed ahead, "I just wanted to tell you again what a great time Shannon and I had Sunday. Thanks for inviting us."

"No need to thank me," Logan said, "Everyone enjoyed meeting you. Shannon is adorable. Glad the babysitting thing worked out. Bonnie said Haley loves watching Shannon."

"Shannon likes her, too. In fact, I dropped her off over there about an hour ago. She's having a play date with Quinn. Bonnie said it was okay," Lori said.

"I had another reason for calling . . . am I interrupting anything?"

"No, go ahead," Logan said.

'Well, this is going to seem like an off-the-wall question, but I wanted to ask if you knew where a good pet store was in town. Shannon's birthday is coming up in a few weeks and I'm thinking of getting her a real dog to replace that stuffed one she drags around. She loves dogs and I always had one growing up." Lori said. "I figured you might know because you have a cat. That big, tortoise-shell cat is yours, right?"

"Yes, he's mine. That's Dimebox," Logan answered, "He's napping on my desk as we speak. I get his food and litter from Chewy.com, but if I run out I use Pet Emporium. They've got most everything you need. It's over off Geranium, north end of town. They don't sell any animals there, though, except maybe some fish."

"Oh, that's okay, I wouldn't buy the dog there. Pet store puppies are usually taken from the mom way too early. They can have lots of health and behavior problems later on," Lori said.

Logan didn't know much about dogs, but it was obvious Lori did.

"I was just about ready to drive over to the district office," Logan said. "I can show you where it is. I want to get one of those little balls with the bells inside for Dimebox. He keeps losing them. He entertains himself for hours batting those things around. If you want to follow me over there. It's kind of hard to find. GPS takes you the wrong way on that street. If I lose you, it's behind the Chevron station."

"Sure, if it's not too much trouble," Lori said.

She wanted to trust Logan completely, tell her everything, but she didn't dare. Not yet.

"And if you're hungry, there's a little place across the street, ocean side, where we can grab lunch before I have to get back to work," Logan said.

"What time do you want to go?" Lori asked.

"Now is good . . . meet you downstairs in ten?" Logan said, "Just need to straighten my desk up."

Lori hated to use her new friend, but she really didn't have any other options. Besides, Garrett didn't know Logan, so she didn't think what she had in mind would put her in any danger.

13

Garrett fumed.

Bitch! How dare she!

How could she be so cruel? After all he'd done for her! Everything he did was for her and Shannon. This was simply intolerable. He hadn't done anything wrong. Mr. Yoshimoto was the crook, not him. Not really. Until Mr. Yoshimoto came along, all his clients were just regular clients. His hedge fund made them money. No huge ups, but then, no huge downs either.

Garrett was proud of the fact that with only an MBA from a marginal state school, he beat the odds and found his niche early in his career. Finance came naturally to him. He saw the big picture. He saw trends. After working on Wall Street for only a few years, he opened his own hedge fund company. Without too much effort, he made good money.

About that time, he met Lauren. She worked for one of his clients, Jim. Tucker Medical Supplies. They took a short-cut through accounting on the way to his office. Garrett passed by and Lauren looked up from her work. She had the perfect look and demeanor—sort of a quiet, competent type. He learned she was from a good family, a little higher up the social ladder than his. Good wife material.

Not taking any chances, he gave her the full-court press. He'd even paid a guy to give him a crash course in horseback riding lessons, so he wouldn't embarrass himself the weekend her family invited him up to the house. The happiest day of his life was when she said yes. Which made her current treachery even tougher to take.

When Shannon came along, she quit her job to stay home with the baby, like she should. He gave Shannon everything. For a while, everything was perfect. Then Lauren started acting up, so he had to hire Neal. She wasn't happy about it, but he convinced her. He was important now. They needed protection. He just wanted to keep his family safe.

Over time, expenditures started outstripping income, no matter how much the hedge fund made. He had to get the downtown Seattle office. The Beemer. You didn't attract big clients with a shared office and receptionist in Everett, driving a Toyota. All the extra expenses would have been manageable, but he took too many risks in 2008.

In 2009, his hedge fund started looking pretty anemic. So, when Yoshimoto's people first approached him with a healthy infusion of cash, he'd readily accepted.

After exhausting the usual instruments, he put his new client's money in real estate, hotels, and restaurants. When even that couldn't handle the mounting cash flow, he recommended crypto-currency. Specifically, Monero, and a little in ZCash, the most untraceable of the crypto-currencies out there. The man's money wasn't going to stay in those invisible accounts long, so it didn't matter if crypto lasted or not. It was just a temporary stop in the laundering process. Since neither the purchases or sales of Monero could be traced to any individual, it was the perfect vehicle through which to funnel his new client's funds. Garrett prided himself with always being a step ahead of the curve.

Mr. Yoshimoto was very pleased. Garrett never asked where the cash came from.

Not used to such riches, Garrett splurged. And why not?

Growing up, his family wasn't poorest on the block, but he never felt he had what his friends had. And it was fun. Lauren sure enjoyed all the perks. She didn't ask where all this money was coming from. He bought the estate out in Cambria Hills. Took Lauren and Shannon to Aruba, business trips to Asia and Europe, got the membership at Cedar Falls. Golf wasn't something anyone in his Irish, working-class neighborhood ever took up, but he quickly had an under 15 handicap and a set of personalized golf clubs.

As fast as the spigot flowed, they sucked up the water.

In this new world of plenty, Garrett started neglecting his other clients, some of whom started to complain—vociferously. One even threatened to report him to the SEC. He'd started taking some of Yoshimoto's money to keep his other clients happy, reporting returns that didn't exist. He knew he couldn't keep this up forever. That's why he'd been sweating bullets. If Yoshimoto had any inkling Garrett's business might come under the scrutiny of the SEC, he'd pull every yen and dollar in a heartbeat.

And it was all Lauren's fault! He was forced to deal with her when he should be figuring out how to keep the lid on everything. His whole business was unbalanced. If Mr. Yoshimoto ever pulled his money, it would collapse.

Even this catastrophic possibility would be the least of his worries. He'd never asked what Mr. Yoshimoto did, but from the looks of his drivers, and the ridiculous amount of money he was trusting Garrett to funnel through whatever creative avenues he could come up with, he had a good idea what would happen to him if his number one client was ever unsatisfied. In any way.

He needed to get whatever records Lauren had. Yesterday.

14

Her car engine almost didn't turn over, but finally it caught. She had no trouble following Logan's cute convertible to the pet store. Lori hoped they'd have what she needed inside.

Located in a small, stand-alone building behind the Chevron station, the Pet Emporium's hand-painted, wooden sign welcomed four-legged customers with a water bowl to the right of the front door and a rubber paw-print mat. Logan pushed open the door and Lori followed.

"Dog stuff on the left, cat stuff on the right," a passing employee said, over the top of a huge bag of dog food they were carrying up to the front counter for a customer. "If you need help finding anything, I'll be right back."

Logan went to the right to find a jingle ball for Dimebox. Lori turned left.

"KONG toys?" she asked the cashier, who just finished ringing up her customer.

"Halfway down the second aisle," she said, "You want me to show you?"

"No, I'll find it, thanks," Lori said.

It didn't take her long to find what she was looking for, a

shrink-wrapped package housing a lumpy, blue, hard-rubber dog toy. She selected one for puppies. It looked kind of like a headless Michelin man . . . or maybe a decapitated snowman.

Logan came around the corner, jingling a package of balls with bells inside, waving what looked like a fishing pole with several feathers on the end.

"Found 'em! Couldn't decide, so I'm getting both. Did you find anything?"

"KONG Classic," Lori said, holding up the package. "They're virtually indestructible. You hide dog treats inside and they have to work to get them out—awesome when they're teething."

"Excellent choice!" the cashier said from the front of the store. After gathering a few more items, then spending an inordinate amount of time picking out a puppy collar and leash, the two women took their purchases to the front, paid, and put them in their respective cars.

"We still have time for lunch," Logan said, pointing across the street to the sandwich shop. "We can walk."

Excited about finally taking some positive steps in her plan to deal with Garrett, Lori realized she was hungry.

Logan agreed to hide everything at her place until Shannon's birthday. Lori had no idea how she was going to explain there was no puppy in Shannon's immediate future, but she'd cross that bridge when she came to it. Logan offered to put everything in her car now, but Lori said she wanted to wrap them first. That meant she would have to spend more of her dwindling money to buy some gift bags and ribbon, but it was important.

She had one more item to add before taking it over to Logan's house for safekeeping. Logan said her meetings should be over by 5:00 p.m. or so. Lori could come over any time after she saw her car in the driveway. Ben was coming over later, but they weren't going anywhere tonight.

She'd be home.

Lori thanked her and got into her own car. She didn't like lying, but she didn't see any other way. She hoped Logan wouldn't slip up and mention a puppy to Shannon. She would be so disappointed when no puppy arrived. Someday, she would get Shannon a dog for real.

With about an hour to spare before she had to pick up Shannon, Lori still had time. Laying her supplies out on the dining room table, she got started. First, with a pair of sharp scissors and some muscle, she removed the KONG Classic toy from its package.

Why do they make these so hard to get into?

Holding the bulbous toy small end up, she checked to make sure the design hadn't changed. It hadn't. Through the center of the hard, rubber toy was drilled a 1-inch wide hole. The idea was to hide dog treats in there, or stuff it with peanut butter, to give your teething puppy a workout. Great idea, and perfect for what she had in mind.

Scotch tape . . . did I remember to get tape? Yes!

Tearing off a small section with her teeth, Lori picked up the silver flash drive she just retrieved from her back pack, taping it deep inside the hole. She hoped this particular KONG would never be chewed on by a puppy.

Good.

Unless you knew to look inside, you wouldn't know anything was in there. Still . . . if you turn it sideways, it showed. Grabbing a small, green bag, she ripped open the top and pulled out a few dog treats to stuff on top. Checking it from all angles, it passed the test. No flash drive in view. Even if for some reason someone peeked inside, all they would see would be toy and treats.

Quickly placing the KONG Classic with some other toys in the large, stainless steel dog dish the fictitious puppy would have to grow into, along with the collar and leash, she placed it all in a large gift bag and tied the handles together with blue ribbon. Apparently, this was going to be a boy dog.

Satisfied with her work, she hid the bag on the top shelf of her closet. Once Shannon was asleep, she'd run it over to Logan's house. She sighed, suddenly tired after the expenditure of optimistic energy after only a few hours of sleep.

Someday, Shannon. Life will be normal again . . . someday.

At least the flash drive would be safe. As soon as she had some more money or was able to establish a new identity and open a bank account, she could put it in a safe deposit box, but in the meantime, this would have to do.

Garrett didn't know in what form she'd stored the evidence, and even if he did, he would never think to look for it at Logan's house.

15

Logan seemed really excited to be part of the surprise for Shannon. She'd even tossed in a doggy bed to line the crate at the last minute. She was a soft touch. Sally's son, Quinn, called her Auntie Ogan. She fit the bill. She could see Logan as being everyone's favorite Aunt.

All of which made Lori feel guilty. She'd like to have a friend like Logan, someday. Maybe someday she could explain her reasons for lying.

Lori waited until Shannon was asleep before lifting the bulky bag off the top shelf of her closet and tiptoeing out the back door. The last thing she wanted was for Shannon to wake up and start asking questions. She took the shortest route, a narrow, grassy path that ran behind the studio garage, adjoining the two properties.

Logan answered her back door with a soapy sponge in one hand.

"Come on in," she said, turning back toward the sink. She tossed the sponge back in the sink and dried her hands on a flour-sack dishtowel hanging on the refrigerator door handle.

"Looks like fun," Lori said, as she stepped inside, bag in hand, closing the door behind her.

"I don't mind—Ben and I have an arrangement. He cooks fabulous food, I clean," she said, smiling.

"Speaking of cooking, Ben made brownies. He just went to get them. He likes to serve them hot, and his oven works better than mine. He'll be back in a minute if you want to stick around."

"No, I need to get back, but thank you so much for helping me out with this," Lori said, handing the bag to Logan by the handles.

"No problem, happy to help," she said, taking it from her. "I can't wait to see Shannon's face when you give it to her."

Placing the bag on the kitchen counter for now, she added, "Do you know what kind of puppy you want, yet? Big, small?"

"Not yet, still researching," Lori said, opening the back door. "I really should get back. Shannon's a sound sleeper, but still . . ."

"Okay, I'll bring some over tomorrow if Ben doesn't eat them all." Logan said.

Lori laughed, "Okay, night then," letting herself out.

It seemed darker now—the moon must have gone behind a cloud. Feeling with her feet, Lori picked her way over uneven clumps of crab grass and weeds. The night was soft, but she felt an increasing sense of anxiety, bordering on panic, and ran the last few feet. She shouldn't have left Shannon alone—even for a minute!

Relief flooded through her as she opened the door to Shannon's bedroom and saw her daughter's peacefully sleeping form. Sitting on the edge of the bed, Lori sat there for a few minutes, enjoying watching her daughter breathe. Everything was going to be okay. The world was not an evil place. That was her old life. This was her new one. She had to stop living in the past.

"Assume the positive," her mother always said. Normal people could run next door for a minute without panicking. Normal was going to take some practice. A sharp knock on the front door interrupted her reverie.

Wow, that was quick. Logan must have decided to deliver a couple of brownies before temptation struck. Wishing she had remembered to pick up milk, Lori went to let her in.

"Now, this is what I call service . . ." Lori said, sliding back the deadbolt on the front door, swinging it wide open.

Her heart sank.

Garrett's darkened form loomed in the doorway, only the planes of his face lit sharply by the porch light. Before she could slam and re-bolt the door, he pushed his way in.

Placing his finger on her lips, he forestalled her crying out, "Shhh . . . you don't want to wake Shannon, do you?"

Reflexively, she started to jerk back, expecting a blow, but caught herself. This was the new Lori, not the old Lauren. Lori didn't flinch.

Taking in the Spartan decor in one disparaging glance, Garrett strolled into the living room and plopped himself down on the couch.

"Nice place you've got here," he said.

It was much easier to be brave with Garrett on the phone than when he was sitting two feet away. She had to think of a way to get him out of here before Shannon woke up.

Keeping her voice as steady as she could, she said, "You can't be here, Garrett. I'll talk with you. Tomorrow. I'll meet you anywhere you want, in town."

"You're my wife and I can talk to you wherever I want," he said. "Get your things. I'm taking you and Shannon home tonight."

From somewhere in her gut, Lori found the strength she

needed. If she didn't stand up to him now, she'd be running the rest of her life, or worse.

"No, I'm not going back," she said, "I meant what I said."

Without missing a beat, he went from threatening to pleading. "You know this is wrong, don't you? We're good—things are good when you're home. If you didn't keep pulling these stunts, everything would be fine."

As if someone let the air out of him, Garrett's shoulder's sagged and his face crumpled.

"I love you, Lauren. I'll do whatever you want," he said, getting up to pace the floor. "You want to go to counseling? We'll go to counseling. I know I've been working too much. I can take some time off. We can get away, just the two of us."

If she hadn't seen this hundreds of times before, she'd be impressed. Then he added the one thing that may have worked—in fact, had worked in the past.

"We got Shannon into Darwood, right? Best pre-school in Seattle. That took a lot, Lauren. I called in some favors for our daughter. Kindergarten at Wharton starts soon and they only take kids from Darwood, you know that. Just come home, Lauren. Everything will be all right—if you'll just stop all this. I promise."

Lori looked at the man she married, the man she fell in love with. Part of her still loved him, in spite of everything. She remembered running her hands through those thick curls, kissing his brow, his eyelids, making love. Thrilling to his touch. Now, she recoiled from it.

She knew he believed everything he was saying. He could flip a switch that fast. She also knew he would never keep his promises. She used to agonize over whether he was incapable of change, or simply chose not to make the effort, but it didn't matter anymore. The results to her and Shannon were the same.

She remained standing.

"We're not going back, Garrett," she said. "Like I said on the phone, it's over."

16

Something in her voice must have made Garrett realize she meant what she said. For a moment there was only silence.

Then, looking past her, he said, "Fine, then give me what you've got, or I'll just take my daughter."

Rising from the couch in one fluid motion, he added, "It's obvious you don't care about what's best for her." Stopping only to glare at her on his way past, he said, "You're selfish, Lauren. You've always been selfish. I just didn't see it until now."

Reaching out, he flipped her nose up sharply with his index finger, snapping her head back. Dialed back, it may have been a playful gesture, endearing and flirty even, if it didn't have such venom behind it. Lori knew the signs. Garrett wasn't going to be able to contain himself much longer.

He'd almost reached the hall.

"Where's her room, down here?" he asked, heading for the narrow hallway.

"No!" Lori said, throwing herself in front of him, blocking the entrance with her outstretched arms.

"Then where is it? On your computer? Where's your computer?"

"I don't have one! It's not here," she whispered urgently.

"Then go find it. In the meantime, I'll just get Shannon. You can have her back when I get whatever it is, wherever it is," he said.

Lori stayed where she was. "Just go, Garrett. Leave us alone, please!" she begged.

Garrett bored a look of pure hate into her eyes. "Get out of my way!" he growled.

Grabbing her wrist, he twisted her around, jamming her right arm up between her shoulder blades until her shoulder popped, making her cry out at the pain. Pushing her away, he shoved past her toward Shannon's bedroom door.

Lori scrambled up, launching herself onto his back. Grabbing a fist full of hair with her good hand, she yanked his head back, trying to flip him onto his back, or at least stop his forward movement. She didn't care if he landed on her, as long as he didn't get to Shannon.

"Bitch!"

Throwing her off like a wet raincoat, Garrett turned and came after her. He wasn't a large man, but he was tall, sinewy, and fueled by rage. She knew she had no chance against him.

Looking desperately for anything she could use to even the playing field, Lori ran back in the living room for the lamp, but Garrett, right behind her, reached over the back of the couch, lifting it out of her reach, holding it in the air.

"Is this what you wanted, Lori? You're going to attack your own husband?" he said.

Lori stopped, her whole body tensed, eyes laser focused on his. Placing the lamp back on the end table, he calmly lowered his arm. Hidden behind the couch, Garrett's right hand curled into a tight fist. Lightning fast, he slammed it into her face, knocking her back onto the coffee table, then took his time walking around the couch.

Blood spurting from her nose, dazed, Lori roused herself enough to roll onto her side, away from him. Blinking her eyes repeatedly, she tried to focus. If she could only make it to the front door, she could get help.

It was just steps away, but it might as well have been miles. Garrett stood between her and any escape.

Easily lifting his 120-pound wife up off the floor by her t-shirt, he threw her against the wall. She literally bounced off like a rag doll, landing in a heap next to Shannon's play tent. Instinctively, Lori curled into the fetal position, using her arms to protect her face, resigning herself to what she knew was coming.

Then, starting with a swift kick to her ribs, he began the beating in earnest. Soon, either unconscious or dead, she no longer moved.

◊ ◊ ◊ ◊ ◊

"Mommy!"

Garrett whirled around.

Eyes wide, mouth opened, chubby legs rooted to the floor, Shannon stared at her father. Eegee dangled from her left hand, long ears grazing the ground.

"Shannon . . . !" Garrett faltered, pulling himself back from his murderous rage.

Within seconds, he switched gears smoothly and started helping the limp body of his wife off the floor.

"It's okay, Shannon," he said, in as calm a voice as he could manage, "Mommy fell and hit her head. Come help me take care of Mommy."

Shannon dug her chin farther into her chest, slowly shaking her head. Then, after one last look, she let out a strangled animal cry, turned and fled down the hall, her bare feet thumping a staccato rhythm on the hardwood floor.

Before he could recover himself completely, Garrett heard her fumbling with a doorknob.

"Shannon!" Garrett called, running after her.

Cool air whooshed in and he heard the back door bang against the wall.

Shit!

Directly behind the house was a hill.

Which way did she . . . ?

Quickly patting the inside wall for a switch, he found one, but no porch light came on when he flipped it. Piece of crap!

He saw a flash of white to his left, the bottom of Shannon's bare foot as she rounded the corner of a detached garage next to the neighbor's house. The woman he'd seen Lauren with earlier.

Moving as quickly as he could without making any noise, Garrett followed his daughter. Maybe he could still catch her.

"Shannon," he whispered, crouching down when he got to the corner around which she disappeared.

No answer. Then a loud crash as someone, probably Shannon, banged into some metal trash cans against the woman's house. Within seconds, bright light flooded out, silhouetting a woman in the doorway. Seeing Shannon run into the woman's arms made the rage rise within him again, but he forced himself to stay where he was. He needed time to think but didn't have much.

If the woman lived alone and had any sense, she wouldn't chase after him, but she might call the police. If she knew Lauren, she might try to call her first. When no one answered, her next move would probably be to call the cops. He had three or four, maybe five minutes tops.

VANISHING DAY

Running low, he used one of those minutes to get back to Lauren's house. He did not check on her to see if she was okay. Instead, he looked around quickly for her backpack, dumped it on the floor and searched all the compartments.

Nothing.

He looked back at his wife. She was wearing yoga pants, so no pockets. Skin tight yoga pants. He'd never allow her to wear those.

Whore.

Aiming another satisfying kick at her stomach, Garrett was on his way to the kitchen next, when he heard someone opening the back door. Before whoever it was got inside and saw him, he turned left and bolted out the front. Quiet was no longer necessary. His whole focus was to make it to his car and get the hell out of there. As usual, Lauren ruined everything!

17

Something crashed into the trashcans outside.

Ben? Maybe carrying brownies in the dark wasn't such a good idea. Why was he coming in that way? The shortest path from his house to hers led through the garden. He usually came in through the French doors.

Preparing to give him lots of grief, Logan opened the kitchen door and looked out. Instead of a handsome Norwegian bearing chocolate, a tiny whirlwind propelled on short little legs threw herself inside and latched onto Logan's knees. She found herself looking at the top of a mop of wild, black curls.

"Shannon?"

The little girl, eyes screwed tight shut, thumb in mouth, was shaking all over. It wasn't that cold outside.

Automatically going into mom mode, Logan picked her up. "Hey, hey there . . . what's wrong, little one?"

She looked around in the back yard, but couldn't see anything, so shut and locked the door, carrying her little leech into the living room.

"Where's your mommy, Shannon? Is your mommy at home?" No answer.

Wrapping her up in the knit throw she kept on the couch, Logan decided her questions could wait. Moving from the couch to the rocking chair, Logan lowered herself into it, holding the frightened little girl's head gently on her shoulder. Pushing off lightly with one foot, she soothed her with a gentle, rocking motion.

"It's okay, Shannon, I've got you," Logan said softly, "I've got you." She'd held her own daughter many a night over skinned knees or bad dreams, but this was different.

What happened? Where was her mom?

Just then, Ben arrived. Through the French doors as expected.

"Hey, Girls," Ben said, raising a questioning brow at the little girl in Logan's arms. Ben's dog, Purgatory, padded faithfully in at Ben's heels and immediately plodded over to the girls and sat down.

"We're just taking a little rest," Logan said, hoping she sounded calmer than she felt. "Shannon had a bit of a scare, I think."

Directing her comments to the top of Shannon's head, Logan turned her charge a bit so she could see the dog.

"Look who came to visit you, Shannon. It's Purgatory, Ben's dog. Do you remember Purgatory? You played with him the other day."

As if knowing his job, Purgatory then lifted his head and nuzzled Shannon, licking her bare feet, then her arm and cheek. Being a Greater Swiss Mountain dog, his head came to Logan's shoulder, right at Shannon's level. Shannon opened her eyes, reached out a hand and grabbed onto his neck, pulling the big dog in closer. He allowed this without protest.

"Babysitting?" Ben asked, putting the brownies down on the counter along with his phone. "I thought her mom didn't have to work tonight."

"No, we're just visiting, aren't we Shannon?" Logan said, then mouthed, "I don't know," and looked in the direction of the kitchen door. "I have her number, but maybe we should check."

The look of concern on her face was all Ben needed to see.

"Flashlight?" he asked.

"I think there's one in the junk drawer."

There was.

With a nod back to Logan, Ben stepped out the back door, scanning the path with the beam from the flashlight as he picked his way past the trash cans. Maybe Lori had tripped in the dark and fallen on the way over. But the little girl was barefoot and in her pajamas. He doubted any mother would let her out of the house without shoes. Unless she'd been carrying her.

"Have you got your cell?" Logan whispered.

He'd already left, so she didn't know if he heard her or not. Nothing for it but to wait until he got back.

For a few minutes, Logan heard nothing. Then, someone running from the direction of Lori's house, loudly crunching gravel in her driveway with each sprinting step, followed by the sound of a car door being yanked open.

Ben must have scared them off. If it was whoever frightened Shannon, they were getting away. Haley's pedophile-next-door theory started sounding more real, but if it was someone from the neighborhood, why would they use a car?

Killer Hill had no streetlights, but Logan kept a security light on in the front of the studio. She wasn't stupid enough to try to stop him herself, not with a preschooler in her arms, but maybe she could catch a glimpse of the license plate before he took off.

Keeping a firm hold on Shannon, Logan strode across the

living room, whipped open her front door—just in time to see a tall man get into a Jeep and start the engine. If the Jeep had a color, she couldn't see it clearly—just that it was dark and looked fairly new.

She clearly saw the back of the man's head and shoulders for a second or two before he shut off the overhead light. Short curly hair, black, broad-shouldered, lean. Collared, knit shirt. Fit the description Haley gave of the creep spying on her and Shannon the other day.

The Jeep's engine leaped to life as he gunned the gas and peeled away from the curb, making a hard left u-turn. Squinting, she tried to make out the license plate, but saw mostly tail lights and exhaust. She didn't know who was getting away or why, but nobody peeled out like that if they were just a neighbor going to the all-night market for some ice cream.

Who was he and what did he want? Had Shannon interrupted a burglary, gotten scared, and ran over here? Why not go to her mom? Where was her mom? She wished Ben would get back and tell her what was going on.

TZ2 . . . TZ2 . . .

Before she could get back inside to write the partial plate down, Logan's right foot caught on a tree root, sending her flying. Turning her shoulder to the ground just before she hit gravel, she managed to protect Shannon as she fell, landing with a thud on her arm, wrenching her knee as she went down.

18

"It's okay, it's okay," Logan whispered, kissing the top of her head. Purgatory came bounding up right behind her, ready to assist.

Gingerly getting up onto her good knee, leaning on Purgatory's massive shoulders, she gradually raised herself to a standing position and hobbled back to the house. Once inside, she sank gratefully onto the couch. Relinquishing her hold from around Logan's neck, Shannon threw her arms around Purgatory. Guardianship transferred, Logan rubbed her right arm.

"TZ2, TZ2 . . ." she kept whispering to herself. No paper in sight, she got her phone out of her pocket to send herself a text.

A minute later, Ben came in the same way Shannon had, looking very relieved when he saw them sitting there.

"Is Lori okay? Did you see that guy?" Logan asked, trying to keep her voice calm for Shannon's sake. Ben took her cue.

"No, just heard someone run out," he said, "You okay?"

"I'm fine, just tripped. I got part of his license plate," she added, indicating her cell phone, "TZ2 . . . something," I couldn't get it all."

Ben picked up his phone off the counter and dialed 911, giving in the universal "Wait" signal as he stepped into the kitchen and spoke in low tones so Shannon couldn't hear him. Logan heard the operator answer just before he lowered the volume.

"911 . . . What is your emergency?"

"There is a seriously injured woman in the house next door. Her name is Lori, Lori . . ." Ben answered, looking back to Logan for Lori's last name.

"Wright," Logan supplied.

"Wright," Ben said, "My name is Ben, Ben Halvard." He gave them Logan's name and address. "I don't know the address of Lori Wright's home, but they're the next house down the hill, west of here, toward the ocean. . . . We'll show them when they get here . . . I don't know, she was unconscious . . . No . . . we didn't move her," he said, then lowered his voice so Shannon couldn't hear, "she looks bad."

"No," Ben said in answer to the operator's next question, "there's no one else in the house as far as I can tell. A guy ran out when I got there. He must have been the man who attacked her, but I didn't get a good look at him. Her daughter, Shannon, ran over here. Yeah . . . hold on . . ."

Walking back into the living room, Ben sat on the couch next to Shannon and Purgatory. He gently looked through Shannon's curls.

"I don't think so. She looks okay . . . I don't know exactly," he looked at Logan, eyebrows raised, "maybe three or four?"

Logan nodded. She remembered Shannon telling her she was three when Logan asked the standard meet-a-kid questions.

"I'm putting you on speaker for a minute," he said, pressing the appropriate button and laying his phone on the coffee table.

Then, as naturally as if she were his own daughter, Ben reached his arms out for her to climb in his lap. Without hesitation, Shannon let go of Purgatory and complied. Both Logan and Ben did visual checks as she went over. No blood, hers or her mother's.

Logan hoped that meant she hadn't been anywhere near her mom when she was attacked.

"No, looks good," Ben said, settling Shannon into his lap, warming her bare feet by rubbing them between his large hands.

"Okay," Ben said, "We'll wait until the police get here."

Logan reached over and disconnected the call for him.

When Ben tried to gently disentangle himself from Shannon's hold, she let out a heart-breaking cry.

"That's okay," Logan said, motioning for him to stay where he was.

Not very good at waiting, Logan started pacing. "I'm going to go wait with Lori," she said.

"No, Logan, she said the police are on their way. That guy could come back," Ben objected.

"I'll be fine . . . that guy is long gone and we haven't heard anything. You stay with Shannon. I promise I'll be careful. If she's conscious, she's probably worried sick about Shannon. Someone should be there with her," Logan said.

Not liking this arrangement, but knowing it was useless to argue with her once her mind was made up, Ben nodded and sat back in the couch, letting Shannon snuggle against his chest. Purgatory lay at his feet. Logan knew he didn't like the idea of her going over there alone.

"I'll be fine," she said, "the guy already left and the cops are on their way. Ambulance, too. If he does come back, he'll be seriously outnumbered."

"Pepper spray?"

Rick bought her a gazillion cans of pepper spray to keep in every pocket, jacket, and purse she owned. The only time she actually had to use it, she sprayed the wrong guy. Not her best moment.

Trying not to wince as she put weight on her damaged knee, Logan grabbed the flashlight from the counter and retrieved the pepper spray from her jacket. She held it aloft and wiggled it for Ben to see, then tucked it into her pants pocket before exiting the house. Being careful not to trip over another tree root, Logan stepped around the fallen trash can. So far, her knee was holding, but not without complaint.

A silvered sliver of moon watched her steady progress to Lori's back door. Such a peaceful night. No violence could have been committed on a night like this. Like an undiscovered Edward Hopper painting, dim, yellow light reached out from the open door, creating a triangle of illumination on a small square of cement. Logan checked her pocket for the pepper spray, stepped into the hallway, and listened.

It was silent as a morgue.

19

Hoping Lori wasn't dead, she made her way to the living room. Only two days ago she and Shannon played on the floor in this living room. Now she dreaded going in.

Steeling herself for the sight, at first she saw nothing. Maybe Lori wasn't hurt as bad as Ben thought she was. Maybe she was cleaning herself up in the bathroom.

Then, on the outside curve of the circle of sick, lemon light created by the living room lamp, she saw Lori's foot, sticking out from behind Shannon's play tent. Covering the short distance in a few long strides, Logan lifted the play tent out of the way, and almost threw up.

Lori, or a person who used to look like the healthy, young mother laughing and talking at the Otter Festival two days ago, lay completely still. Curved into a horizontal C, only the front of her body was visible.

Logan never saw anyone beaten this badly. Every inch of Lori's distorted and swollen face was either red, ripped, or covered in blood—a physical record of each blow received. Rivulets of blood, some already beginning to dry, ran from her smashed nose, over a torn lip, down her chin and onto her t-shirt. The whole front of her chest was drenched. Left eye swollen shut. A few inches above the brow, where her hairline used to begin, showed only a roughly two-inch square of white scalp. Blood pooled around her head, like a deep, crimson halo. Her right ear, filled with blood, black in shadow, had begun to crust over.

Logan sank to the floor, kneeling beside Lori, afraid to touch her. One hand on the floor to steady herself, she reached carefully forward with the other and placed two fingers on the side of Lori's neck, trying to find a pulse.

Every inch of her wanted to do something—mop up the blood, clean the wounds, put Neosporin everywhere and bandage everything up neatly. But with injuries this severe on the outside, Logan knew Lori must have even more serious ones internally. If there were any broken ribs, moving her even an inch in the wrong direction could puncture a lung or some other vital organ. She would bleed out before the EMTs could get here. She'd just have to wait.

At least she reassured herself Lori was still alive. Pulse was faint, but still there. Rocking back on her heels, Logan began taking deep, even yoga breaths, willing the woman to hang on. *Where is that ambulance?*

While she was waiting, Logan looked around the room for anything that would explain what happened here. The front door was open but didn't look damaged. No broken windows. At least not in this room. So, not a random, interrupted burglary. Unless the guy had a key, Lori must have let him in. Someone she knew? Had she ordered pizza and thought she was opening up to the delivery guy?

Watching the woman, Logan tried to breathe deeply for her. *Who did this to you?*

Interrupting a break-in didn't sound right. A thief wouldn't stick around to deliver this kind of personal attack. They'd just run away.

VANISHING DAY

No, this must have been personal. Or some crazy person. Logan tried to see out the window, but the curtains were shut.

She wondered how Ben was doing with Shannon, as she strained to hear the sounds of a siren.

After an excruciating wait, an ambulance turned up Killer Hill from PCH and Logan ran to the door to wave them down. Ben didn't know the address exactly, so she didn't want them wasting time driving up and down the street looking for the right house, or going to her place first. Lori might not have that much time. They parked in Lori's driveway and turned off the engine. A thirty-something-year-old woman and a large, bald man jogged up onto the porch, bags and backpacks in hand.

"Cops here yet?" the woman asked.

"No, the woman is in here," Logan said, hurrying them into the living room.

Hesitating only a second, the woman, Babs according to her name tag, nodded to her partner, Joe, then followed Logan into the house.

"Jeez!" Joe said.

For an EMT to react like that, with all he had probably seen in the course of his job, confirmed to Logan how bad Lori's injuries were.

Babs, already kneeling beside the victim, unpacked her bag, set her jaw, and asked when the woman was found and if they knew how long she had been unconscious. When Logan couldn't tell her much more than the time Shannon ran to her house and Ben came over and found Lori, both EMTs went to work.

Their well-orchestrated movements put Logan in a trance. She was staring at the IV they'd inserted when Babs sat back on her heels and brought Logan back into reality by repeating a question.

"They said there was a little girl here, too. Is that correct? Where is she?" she asked, "Does she need to be seen?"

"Yes," she said, dragging her eyes away from Lori. "Shannon, her daughter. She's next door with Ben. She doesn't seem to be injured, at least not physically. She ran to my house when this happened. As far as I can tell, she's not hurt, just very scared."

A rolling gurney magically appeared. Joe must have gone outside to get it. On three, they lifted Lori gently onto it and began rolling it as gently, but quickly, as possible toward the front door.

"We need to get mom here to the hospital," Babs said to Logan, hustling out the door, "If you know of any family, you may want to call them."

"Okay," Logan said, not feeling for one minute that anything about tonight's events were okay.

Lori never mentioned any family. Helpless, Logan watched as they loaded Lori into the ambulance, flipped on lights and sirens. Babs was talking on the radio, presumably to the hospital, while her partner monitored Lori in the back.

"The police are on their way—Children's Protective Services, too," Babs yelled out of the window as she backed out of the driveway.

The last Logan saw of the ambulance, it careened onto PCH at the light, racing toward Hoag hospital, almost twenty minutes north of Jasper.

20

Poor kid. Shannon probably just saw her mother viciously attacked, and now complete strangers from Children's Protective Services were coming to pick her up and put her in some kind of foster home. Logan didn't know how these things worked but doubted any of the upcoming options were good ones for Shannon. Shannon ran to her for help. The thought of handing her over to strangers went against every maternal instinct Logan had.

And what if her mom didn't get well? What if she died from her injuries, which, from the extent of them, seemed completely possible. What would happen to Shannon then?

When Amy had been a baby, Logan insisted and Jack finally agreed to set it up so if anything happened to them, Logan's Dad would raise Amy. The two were always close. Jack's very social parents put up a fuss for appearances, but quickly gave in. Jack's mom looked particularly relieved. She wasn't exactly the grandma type, always insisting Amy call her Monica.

The police weren't here yet.

She didn't think Lori would mind her going through her things if it was to find something to help Shannon. She went

VALERIE DAVISSON

back inside and shut the front door. It looked like the violence was limited to the living room, so she wouldn't be disturbing any forensic evidence by looking through a few drawers. Someone already dumped the contents of Lori's backpack onto the floor, or maybe everything fell out during the fight or attack, whatever it was. Still, she'd bet on the former. All the zippered pockets had been thoroughly emptied. There wasn't much there. A small zippered coin purse with seventeen dollars and change. A Burt's Bees tinted lip balm, this week's work schedule, pens, pencils, and the receipt from today's pet store shopping trip.

Ten minutes later, after looking through the few drawers and closets in the house, Logan had found nothing. Absolutely nothing. No drivers license, no passport, no banking records, no phone numbers, except for work. No baby books, or calendars. No computer, even.

She would check Facebook on her computer when she got home, but from what she'd seen here, she doubted she'd find anything.

It was like Lori and Shannon Wright didn't exist.

What was it the doctor's creed said? 'First, do no harm.' Well, until she could figure out what was going on, protecting Shannon was her first priority. No one was going to harm a hair on that child's head. It only took Logan a second to make up her mind.

First, she went into the kitchen and filled an empty grocery sack she found with a few others, stuffed in a drawer. Next, she raided the cupboards and refrigerator for some kid food for Shannon. Her search didn't yield much. Cheerios, mac and cheese and some applesauce.

She grabbed another bag and headed into Shannon's bedroom down the hall. She selected a few outfits, shoes, socks and a little toothbrush from the bathroom. At least she'd have some of her own things, even if the rest of her plan didn't work out.

Leaving everything else as it was for the police, she let herself out the way she came in, through the back door, dialing Rick as she went.

By the time Ben whipped up some macaroni and cheese, things were falling into place. Logan finished her phone call with Rick, made a call to Bonnie, and while she was encouraging Shannon to take "just one more bite" of dinner, wondered how she would explain where her mother was the next time the little girl asked. She'd have to tell her something eventually. She didn't lie to children, but this was a truth no three-year-old could handle.

Rick came through like a champ. She could always count on her little brother. Having a cop in the family came in handy more than once. Being in the Jasper, CA police department for over ten years, Rick knew everyone. He and Charlie, his German Shepherd K-9 partner, were well liked and often called out to a variety of crime scenes. Including those requiring the involvement of Children's Protective Services. Which is why she called him tonight.

21

Last month, Charlie helped locate a meth dealer's drug stash in a wailing, undernourished four-month-old infant's badly soiled diaper. Nothing got past Charlie's nose. After removing the drug package from the mess, Rick cleaned up the infant and, by the time the social worker, a Mrs. Croft, from Children's Protective Services arrived, had him cuddled in the crook of his arm, sucking down a bottle of sugar water.

Rick would have given him some formula, but there was no food, baby or otherwise, in the house, just a crusty bowl of sugar on the counter. Croft was pleased with the young man's empathy and pragmatic problem solving. Of course, the bottle wasn't sterilized, but the baby was severely dehydrated, so Rick's actions were the lesser of two evils, and the right action to take. Without immediate intervention, this child wouldn't have lasted the night.

She was also grateful because Rick's actions saved her department some very bad press. They'd received several child neglect calls for this address, but due to budget cuts—again— Croft hadn't been able to send anyone out yet. If the press got wind of that, her job would be toast. It wouldn't matter that it wasn't fair, or that she regularly put in fourteen-hour days.

She'd worked long enough in public service to know fair had nothing to do with it.

Rick wasn't one to brag, so Logan heard the story of Rick's baby rescue from Paula, his fiancée, and a dispatcher with the department. She said Mrs. Croft still hadn't stopped singing his praises downtown.

That's what gave her the idea to ask him to intervene on Shannon's behalf. Part of her intensely wanted to comfort and care for Shannon herself, but pragmatically, she knew Bonnie was better equipped. Not only did she and Mike have all the physical things a three-year-old little girl needed: spare bed, extra clothing her size, and a playroom full of toys she would enjoy, she had what Logan could not give her, a home full of caring people, including Haley, who could continue babysitting her, giving her some sense of continuity.

Logan didn't even have an extra bed, let alone a big, boisterous house full of kids and a Mom and Dad. Besides, she had to work every day. Bonnie did, too, but she had Haley and Mike to take up the slack.

It was a long shot Children's Services would approve the arrangement, but the only one she had. She didn't even take the time to call Bonnie first. She knew when a small child was in need, Bonnie and Mike would be on board. And she was right.

Bonnie's headlights swept across the front of the house. Croft's Toyota pulled up at the same time. Several sets of footsteps crunched up the driveway, creating an asymmetrical soundscape.

Bonnie knocked once, then entered without waiting, diaper bag slung over her shoulder. Haley was right behind her, lugging an infant carrier/car seat. Mrs. Croft entered last. Logan made introductions from the rocking chair, nodding for everyone to sit. Thirty minutes later, after a relatively short interview, during which Bonnie and Haley gave all the right answers, and Mrs. Croft observed the interaction of the child with Bonnie and her daughter, she gave her tentative approval. She seemed pleased that Bonnie, a teacher, and her husband, Mike, a fireman, had five children of their own, one of whom babysat the little girl already—Haley, the one she just met.

Haley could continue to watch Shannon when her parents were at work, causing the least amount of disruption to her routine, which was one of the most important factors to consider in placement.

Besides, she was low on families who would take an infant. With all the bad press, hardly anyone who should be, wanted to be foster parents. The ones who did were often in it only for the money, or worse.

Mrs. Croft inwardly sighed at the difficult nature of her job.

Later, if she could convince Bonnie and Mike to be a formal part of the program, they'd have to do all the paperwork and take the classes. She hoped they'd consider it. She'd work on that. For now, Shannon was entrusted to their care for the night.

Mrs. Croft said she'd come by tomorrow to inspect Bonnie and Mike's home and provide further instructions. If all went well, the temporary arrangement would be extended for another week. After that, they'd just have to wait and see how long it would take the mother to recover from her injuries.

"What if she doesn't make it?" Haley asked.

Everyone else had been thinking this, but they were afraid to say it out loud.

Mrs. Croft smiled patiently at Haley's worried expression. "We'll cross that bridge when we come to it, young lady," she said.

22

Logan loaded the diaper bag she brought with the clothes and kid food she grabbed for Shannon earlier that night.

Haley took it from her and slung it over her shoulder.

"Not much there," Logan said, "but she'll probably want some of her own things."

Kissing Shannon on her damp forehead, she handed her over to Bonnie.

She walked them to Bonnie's SUV.

"Call you tomorrow," Bonnie said, starting the engine after Haley gave her the thumbs up that Shannon was secured in her car seat.

As soon as Haley was buckled in, she backed out of the driveway and returned Logan's wave.

"She'll be fine," Bonnie said out her window as they drove away.

Waiting to be interviewed took another two hours at least. The responding officers collected Ben and Logan's initial statements, then asked them to wait. Two detectives were on their way and wanted to ask their own questions.

"Just one. Yeah," Logan heard Bradley, the officer in charge, say into his shoulder mike, "no sign of a robbery, yet."

Bradley directed the younger officer to begin wrapping yellow crime scene tape around Lori's property and everything from Logan's studio garage and the street in front of her house, where the guy had jumped into his Jeep. There was no knowing if the man had been in her studio or not, but they asked for the keys anyway.

Twenty minutes later, a blue van pulled up, disgorging two men, who, after pulling on plastic gloves, began to examine the taped off areas systematically, in what looked like ever-widening, concentric circles. The two men worked in grids, collecting and labeling small bits into plastic bags, placing small cones precisely here and there, then moved on to the next invisible treasure.

Still waiting to be released from 'house arrest', Logan made coffee. Ben broke out the brownies. She felt guilty for being hungry but ate three before she realized it. She'd started on her second large mug of coffee—she'd never sleep tonight— when the detectives arrived at the front door. Since her knee was really starting to hurt, Ben got up to let them in. Logan wanted to bury herself in the couch cushions when she saw who it was.

Detective Andrews.

If she could avoid ever having to talk with him again, it would be all right with her. Last year, she'd accidentally sprayed the man full in the face while fending off a would-be kidnapper holding her and a famous local sculptor, Solange Sauvage, hostage. If operant training worked, next time Detective Andrews came upon a damsel in distress, he would think twice about rushing in to save her without checking first to see if she was armed. That would definitely put a crimp in his arresting style.

"Ms. McKenna," Detective Andrews said, nodding curtly.

"Detective Andrews," she replied, wiping the smile off her face just in time. "This is my neighbor, Ben."

Ben stood, offering his hand. The men shook. Detective Andrews remained standing.

"I got here just after Shannon ran over from her house," Ben said, nodding at the preschooler in his lap.

"You the one called 911?"

"Yes," Ben said, "I had to come back for my cell phone. I left it on the counter when I went looking for Shannon's mom. I called from here."

"Okay. Officer Bradley will walk you back to your home, Ben. My partner, Detective Diaz, will meet you there and ask you some questions, get your statement," he said. "We will probably need to talk with both of you down at the station again and have you sign your formal statements."

He looked at both of them, "The officers will be talking with your neighbors. Anyone on vacation or out of town on this street?"

"I don't know everyone," Logan said, "but as far as I know, other than the house that's for sale across the street, everyone's home. And the house on the other side of Lori's is a business. They're only here during the day."

Andrews made some notes, then asked, "Either of you planning on going out of town?"

"I am," Logan said. "But not until next week. I have a work trip."

"You may need to reschedule," he said, without waiting for her to object.

Knowing she wouldn't get any, Logan didn't ask for clarification. Detective Andrews took her through the events of the day, starting from the time she and Lori went to the pet store to the time Logan heard the man running from the direction of Lori's house. To the best of her ability, she described what she saw when he jumped in his car, screeched through a u-turn and gunned it down the street.

"It happened so quick. TZ 2," Logan said. That's all I could see of the plate."

Once he had the timeline down to his satisfaction, Andrews moved on to a battery of more general questions. When did Lori and her daughter Shannon move in? Did she have the little girl with her when she moved in, or did she arrive later? When was the first time she spoke with her? Did she have any visitors? Where did she work? Did she ever mention any family or friends, anyone at all from before she lived in Jasper? Was there a boyfriend? A girlfriend? Did she have an accent? Anything out of the ordinary ever happen?

"Other than someone almost beating her to death?" Logan asked.

Detective Andrews kept on without skipping a beat, infuriatingly calm and steady.

Her knee was killing her. She'd answered all his questions several times already. By the clock on the microwave Ben had given her, it was one thirty in the morning. Enough was enough!

But the questions kept coming. What kind of parent was the woman? Attentive? Hovering? Neglectful? Keeping her temper, barely, Logan answered everything as completely as she could. If it would help find whoever did this to Lori, she'd keep answering questions all night.

Finally, Detective Andrews clicked his pen shut and pocketed his note pad. Logan, her knee stiff from sitting so long, still walked him to the door. He said either he or his partner would be in touch, and if she went out of town to leave her contact information with one of them.

VANISHING DAY

Engaging the deadbolt, Logan carried the coffee mugs into the kitchen, washing them out in the sink. She wondered if Ben was done being interviewed by Detective Diaz. It felt good to be doing something, even if it was only a few dishes. Cleaning was her go-to stress reliever.

As the warm water on her hands soothed her, she thought about how little her cursory search of Lori's house had produced. Lori, or whoever she was, had gone to an awful lot of trouble to erase any link to her past. What was she hiding from and who had found her?

Wiping down the counter, she saw the bag of puppy supplies. What was she supposed to do with these, now? She didn't even know when Shannon's birthday was.

23

Tibetan Bells chimed Logan awake. Weekdays, she liked to be showered, dressed, fed, phone available and at her computer in her studio office by 7:30 a.m. Luckily, she only had a ten-yard commute. She did a big cat stretch, yawned and wondered how things had gone with Shannon at Bonnie and Mike's last night. She'd give her a call after breakfast.

Intending to follow the aroma of toast and coffee wafting up the stairs, she threw off the covers and swung her legs out of bed. Halfway to standing, hot knives stabbed through her right knee, causing her to suck in a breath and flop right back down.

Not good.

Pulling up her cotton pajama bottoms, she inspected the damage. Her knee, swollen to the size of a basketball—well, maybe a small grapefruit—was warm to the touch and tender as hell. Tentatively, she lifted her thigh off the bed and attempted to straighten, then, bend her leg. Not much range of motion. She needed some ice. She needed her dad's first aid recipe for every sports injury: RICE. Rest, Ice, Compression, and Elevation had been drummed into her as the cure for everything bigger than a hangnail since she was a fetus. Ice was downstairs. She had an ace bandage somewhere.

Hopping to the landing, Logan lowered herself to a sitting position, then, placing her hands palms down next to her butt, lifted up with the strength of her arms and slowly descended, one stair at a time, until she reached the bottom.

Ben was flipping fried eggs. He did it so easily with one hand and never broke a yolk. He didn't even use a non-stick pan, but a cast-iron skillet he always brought from home. Well, he used to bring his from home. He got tired of lugging it back and forth and got her one of her own. Cruesette Cherry Red. Pretty. Not that she ever used it. Everything she tried to cook in it stuck.

"Hey there, handsome, when you get a minute, can you get me some ice?" she smiled apologetically, feeling bad for breaking his rhythm.

"I did a number on my knee," she explained, " I think there's a bag of frozen vegetables in the freezer."

Slipping the eggs onto a plate, Ben came over to take a look.

"Wow," he said, reaching down to help her over to the couch.

"Yep," she said.

Retrieving a bag of frozen peas, wrapping them in a dish-towel, Ben placed the ersatz ice pack on top of her knee.

"I think I've got an ace bandage under the sink; it'd be in that white, first aid kit," Logan said.

"Don't move. Hold that on. I'll get it," he said.

Logan had no plans to move.

The first aid kit yielded two ace bandages, one of which had Velcro ends, which made it much more convenient to use and reuse. She always managed to lose at least one of the metal hook/ clips on the old-school kind. Unless you needed a tourniquet, the bandage was then just about useless without the metal fasteners. She tried tucking them in, but they never stayed.

Ben took the ice pack off for a minute and expertly wrapped her in tight, but not too tight, figure eights, from upper thigh to mid-calf, then re-positioned the ice pack to cover as much knee real estate as possible. Finally, he tucked some pillows under her knee to make her more comfortable.

"Stay put, I'll bring breakfast," he said. "You need to elevate that after you eat."

Ben returned to the kitchen, found her favorite mermaid mug and poured her coffee. Placing coffee and a plate of eggs, Canadian bacon, and toast within reach on the coffee table, he went back for his own food and joined her on the couch. She must have slept in long enough for Ben to make a trip back to his place. She knew she had none of these supplies, except the coffee, in her kitchen.

He looked at his phone, "Do you want me to take you to urgent care?"

"No, you've got work. A day of this," she said, indicating her lolling about on the couch, "should do it."

"Are you sure? What if you've cracked it or something?"

24

"Tomorrow, I promise. If it's not better. Thanks, hon," she said, and meant it.

Logan treasured her independence, but one injury or illness was enough to make any woman realize that no matter how well prepared and independent we are, shit happens. We are all a split-second away from needing help. She truly was grateful for Ben in her life.

"Anything I can get for you before I leave?" he said.

"Yes, thanks. Can you bring me my phone and my computer? I can work mostly from here today."

After switching out the bag of frozen vegetables and making sure she had everything she needed within reach, including a warm-up on her coffee, Ben pulled on his work boots and told her to call him if she needed anything.

As long as she kept her knee bent at a 45-degree angle, propped up on pillows and iced every hour for about twenty minutes, her knee didn't really hurt that bad. But the first time she had to go to the bathroom, she discovered putting any weight on it was a very bad idea. Crawling over to the front closet, she dug around and located the hiking poles she and Ben used on some trails up at Wrightwood earlier that summer. Pulling one out, she tried various positions. It didn't take the weight completely off that leg like a crutch could, but it worked well enough for her to get to the bathroom and kitchen as needed. Her hardwood floors may never be the same, but oh well. . . .

After making the first initial flurry of phone calls and answering essential emails, Logan dozed from boredom, read a book on her phone, and generally got absolutely no work done. The sound of Ben's arrival that afternoon was a welcome one. It was not even three o'clock yet.

"Taylor said he'd finish up for me," he said as he let himself in. "Let's go see what you did, there's an urgent care just off PCH and Pelican. You got your insurance card?"

"I haven't even showered yet!" Logan objected.

Or brushed my teeth. Or shaved . . .

"You never stink," Ben said, smiling, shoveling her computer and cell phone into her bag.

Curious to know how bad it was, too, but not wanting to admit it, instead she allowed herself to be loaded into the truck and driven to the clinic.

Two hours later, an Indian or Pakistani doctor not much older than Amy greeted her and clipped an X-ray of her knee onto the light board. No accent. Must have been born or raised here.

"Right there between the femur and your tibia, see it?" he said, pointing with his pen to a faint squiggle between two long bones. "That's your meniscus."

That didn't sound good.

"Lucky for you, it looks like you haven't torn it. Or if you did, it's so small it's not showing up," he said, tapping his pen on the light board thoughtfully.

Logan just wanted the bottom line.

"Will it repair itself, or will I need surgery?"

"No, you shouldn't need surgery. We used to do that, but now, just do what you've been doing. RICE is still the best advice."

"In about six to eight weeks it should heal completely," he said.

"But I need to be in Oregon next week," Logan said.

The doctor shook his head and rolled his chair back, placing his pen back in his lab coat pocket. Logan could see several small blotches of ink where other pens already leaked.

"It's up to you," he said. "You should be able to walk on it in about a week or so, but if you put too much pressure on it before it is completely healed, it could tear through completely, and that would require surgery . . . and a lot more down time for rehab."

"Isn't there something I can do? Wear some kind of brace?" she asked.

In the end, after haggling back and forth, Logan left the clinic with a pair of crutches, a prescription for pain meds the doctor insisted she take, and a referral to a medical supplies store to pick up a hinged knee brace. That and a pinch of luck ought to do it, she hoped.

Not one to be unnecessarily brave, she filled the prescription, but hoped she wouldn't have to use it. They'd given her Vicodin after the accident. Never having been hurt like that before, she took them as directed, one every six hours. But as soon as she could stand the pain, she flushed the remaining tablets down the toilet. Even then it was a week before she had a decent bowel movement, and another week before her sleep cycle got back to normal.

Picking out a knee brace at the medical supply store proved

to be semi-fun. The owner recommended one with flexible webbing that held it in place securely. She had a choice of hot pink, gray, blue, or basic black. Definitely hot pink. Naturally, her insurance only covered a clunky, heavy one, consisting of a soft, neoprene sleeve that gave almost no support. The only thing recommending it was the price. It was the cheapest. She happily paid the difference for the Cadillac version with the webbing. Anything to avoid surgery and more down time. It's not like she had to save money to go dancing.

"Sexy," Ben said, watching from behind as Logan threaded her way through the parking lot on crutches, her knee ensconced in the new brace. He handily danced out of reach from the swipe she made with her crutch.

"Every woman in Jasper's going to want one," he said.

When they got to his truck, and he went to open the door, Logan punched him in the arm. She knew she shouldn't take it out on him, but being slowed down like this just from tripping over a stupid tree root she should have seen, pissed her off.

She was not in the mood. Wisely, Ben did not engage.

25

Lauren said she had "everything", but what exactly did that mean? And where did she hide it? Was she bluffing?

Garrett didn't think so. Lauren had stayed home for so long, he almost forgot she had an accounting degree. Hell, he met her in his friend's office. She was the manager of the department.

"You're stealing one of my best employees," his friend complained, only half kidding.

What was she doing snooping around? He controlled all their finances, so had a fully furnished home office. He even occasionally worked from home. Had she gotten into his computer, his files? How much did she know? The thought of his own wife betraying him; he just couldn't wrap his head around it.

Why? Why did she want to leave all the time? And why would she go to such lengths to ensure a permanent escape? He thought she was worthy of his love, his caring for her, taking care of her, but she wasn't. She didn't value his love. She threw it away. She didn't deserve his love. She didn't deserve to have a life with him. But first, he needed whatever it was she had.

Not once did it occur to him to wonder if his wife had any life left to live, after the beating he gave her. It was as if someone else delivered the attack . . . repeatedly punching, kicking, and then, lifting her like a rag doll and throwing her body against the wall. He tried to think. He wasn't missing any physical documents.

He would have noticed that. He had a copy machine at home, but paper copies would be too bulky to lug around, especially dragging a three-year-old with you. They could be in a computer file, but he hadn't seen a computer anywhere in the Jasper house, and she denied having one.

She could have sent a file with attachments to her mother, but he monitored all her mother's emails, so would have caught that if she tried. She had no other relatives, and no close friends anymore. She used to be on a softball team, but he put an end to that. The other women on the team were a bad influence. Only one was married. The rest were single or divorced. All they did was party and sleep around. He'd finally convinced her sports were unladylike, and a complete waste of time. Now that she was a wife and mother, she needed to give up distractions—get serious—she had more important obligations. No . . . she hadn't given documents or sent a computer file to anyone.

Neal? He knew his driver was soft on Lauren, but if he thought Lauren was even aware of those feelings, he would have gotten rid of Neal long ago. It was about time anyway. Neal's probation was up in October. After that, he'd have no incentive to do Garrett's bidding. Yes, he'd have to do something about Neal.

It had to be something small and portable. Probably a flash drive. Could be anywhere in the house. Probably taped under a shelf or in a plastic baggie in the toilet bowl. That's what they always did in the movies. He'd take Neal back down for one last job. With two of them looking, it shouldn't take long for them to find it. But it needed to happen soon. Lauren probably went to the hospital. She shouldn't have made him hit her so hard. But she was fine. She'd probably be kept overnight for observation and then sent home. And if by some fluke she died, her landlord would be there to clean the place out for the next renter, before he could find the flash drive.

What a mess. He still had access to the plane for another few days. Stan wasn't due back from Panama until Sunday. Garrett didn't think anyone had seen the Jeep last night, but to be on the safe side, he'd take one of the sedans. He hated regular cars, but a man had to do what a man had to do. Best to keep to his regular routine as much as possible. Several regular clients needed to be placated. He could leave right after lunch tomorrow.

26

Detective Diaz plopped into his chair and swiveled to face his partner. Short and stocky, his forehead was perpetually sweaty. Thick, black hair stuck out of his head like a chia pet. In another era he may have been described as "swarthy."

"Good wreck on PCH, just south of town, and three new break-ins. Sergeant's not going to give us anybody tonight," Diaz informed him.

"Shit," Andrews replied, leaning back in his chair.

Andrews' desk was in the opposite corner of the detective bureau. A small department, there were five detectives, all working out of the second floor. Andrews was Crimes Against Persons, Saunders was Property Crimes, and Latrell handled Financial. Diaz was officially Juvenile Crimes, but his caseload was light, so he'd been partnering with Andrews lately.

Even though each detective had an official assignment, in reality, they all helped each other with their cases as needed. Singh was the new hire, General Crimes, a kind of catchall designation where new detectives got their feet wet working with and being trained by older, more experienced detectives. In the time they occupied the position, they learned how to execute a search warrant, conduct an investigation, even research case law. It took about a year to bring them up to speed. The learning curve was steep and not everyone lasted.

It's not that he expected to get a dedicated guard on the Jane Doe's room for the night, but Andrews was hoping to squeeze out a few hours for her. Whoever just beat her to within an inch of her life, might come back to finish the job. Now, with the PCH wreck, all the uniforms would be spoken for.

Andrews stretched his long fingers, then let out a huff. "What about the reserves?" he asked, looking up.

"Don't know," Diaz answered. He considered it for a minute. "Yeah, I can give that a try."

Everyone wanted the police to protect them, but nobody wanted to pay for it. In recent years, the detectives had taken to utilizing the services of the few reserve officers still willing to work for nothing.

Diaz was already flipping through a well-thumbed Rolodex on top of the filing cabinet for a number.

Everyone had family and friends' numbers in their cell phones, but some lists, like reserve officers that were only accessed occasionally, hadn't made the transfer. Everything was done old school when they were in the office.

He found the number and located a reserve officer who could be at Hoag in twenty minutes. Andrews felt a lot better when he knew Gussler was on his way. Good guy. Gussler, a corporate pilot and father of six, had a lot of downtime on his job and held his own with the young bucks. Made it through the rigorous police academy training at age thirty-nine and was first in his class. A reserve officer for the last four years, he was trusted with a unit and a gun, even if there wasn't a regular uniform to accompany him. Good man.

Andrews already had over thirty cases. Above average, even for this time of year. If they couldn't get any traction on this one in a day or two, the Lieutenant would have them move it to the bottom of the pile. Unofficially. Unofficially or otherwise, Andrews never let a case go. None of them did. And, given the tenuous hold on life this assault victim had, they'd be working it hard, like a homicide, in case it turned into one.

Everything about this case screamed domestic violence, but since the victim had no ID, they couldn't interview family and friends to get a lead to follow. They'd have to start with what they had, which wasn't much. Coworkers and neighbors here in Jasper would all be interviewed thoroughly, but they'd only known her a few months.

No witnesses so far, either. Except for the one neighbor, the McKenna woman, everyone else was asleep or out of town at the time of the attack. At least she got a partial plate and fleeting glimpse of the guy as he ran. He had to hand it to her. She did better than most people could with a three-year-old hanging on her. Took balls to run after a fleeing suspect, one who just beat your neighbor to a bloody pulp. He would have to interview her again. Maybe she'd remember something else.

Right . . . you keep telling yourself that, Keith.

His mind filled with images of Logan's long legs sprinting down the beach that night. Time to go home.

They'd canvassed the neighborhood. Interviewed everyone. Nothing else they could do tonight. They'd tackle it fresh in the morning. Run down variations on the plate. Check surrounding business's CCTV footage.

Someone meeting the McKenna woman's description of the fleeing suspect just might show up on their cameras. And who knew? If they got lucky, they'd get a shot of him driving a car with a match for the partial plate. And if they got really lucky, the Jane Doe he left for dead, who was fighting for her life at Hoag, would be conscious in the morning, ready and able to tell them who beat her, and where to find him.

Had to be someone she knew. Boyfriend or husband.

27

Only eight in the morning and already Andrews felt the sun on the back of his neck as he made his way slowly back down Killer Hill. He did another walk through the house and wanted to canvass the street again in daylight. Diaz was called out this morning on a cyber-bullying incident at the middle school, so he was on his own. So far, nothing new. Two neighbors had home security cameras, but they were aimed at their front doors, trying to catch package thieves that had plagued the neighborhood since Christmas, not the street.

Only two houses could have heard anything, the McKenna home and the neighbors just across from her and two lots down. Directly across from the victim's home was an empty lot, and the owner of the next house was out of town. Had been for couple of months. Snowbirds. Had a place in Idaho during the summer. Came south for the winter. Weren't back yet.

Must be nice.

Andrews looked at his watch. The owner of the gas station was meeting him in ten minutes to give him access to their video feed. Normally, he would have had it last night, but the sole employee manning the register said she wasn't authorized, and even if she was, she didn't have the key or code or whatever you needed to get into it. Above her pay grade, she'd said. She exhibited no curiosity as to why the police were asking to see the video. Good posture. Former military. Called her manager.

The manager said only the owner had the pass code, and she was out of town on a fishing trip. She called the owner, who said the fish weren't biting anyway and to meet her at the station anytime after 8:00 a.m.

๐ ๐ ๐ ๐ ๐

FRIDAY, SEPTEMBER 9, 2016

Andrews was back at the gas station. The owner had car trouble and couldn't get back yesterday. She was waiting for him now.

Two bells dinged when Detective Andrews pushed open the heavy, glass door into the mini-mart. The smell of hazelnut coffee and hot dogs already turning on the warming rollers greeted him, along with a nod from the girl behind the register, who let him know he was expected.

A squat, middle-aged woman came barreling down the center aisle, stuck out her hand. The owner. Looked former military herself.

"Andrews?" she asked.

"Yes, ma'am," he said.

"Marge," she said, turning to lead him back to her office, "I've got everything back here."

After spending the first few minutes apologizing for not having a more modern system . . . meaning to upgrade, but everything costs so much and profit margins being what they were . . . she hoped he understood. He told her not to worry, the police appreciated her help.

Following her single-file between two tall, metal, shelving units stuffed with cleaning supplies and restaurant-sized cans of nacho cheese sauce and stacks of paper towels, they reached a small, cleared square of polished concrete floor. Marge sat behind a scarred, wooden desk and offered Andrews a metal and plastic, taped-up chair opposite. He wasn't tired, but he sat. You couldn't rush people. Another gem his training officer imparted.

"When Bill and I had the station out in Hemet, we used to just monitor the pumps," she said, "Gas-and-dash yahoos cost us a bundle. But after he died, I moved here—always wanted to live near the beach. I figured out just as much action happens inside, so now I just wire everything, particularly the cash register area," she said. "Chrissie didn't report any robbery attempts or anything major yesterday. Just a couple of kids shoplifting."

She shook her head, "Lots more of that out here, too."

"How far back do you want?" she asked, getting back to business.

"Everything from yesterday through last night, all cameras, if you have it," he said, handing her his card. "Just send the files to me at this email. If they're too large, we can use Dropbox."

"No problem. Should go through. If you need more, let me know and I'll see you get it," she said, getting up from her chair to shake his hand.

Before he left, Andrews added, "I'm going to need names and addresses of anyone working yesterday, delivery people or anyone who may have seen anything. All my numbers are on there." He pointed at his card she held in her hand. "Once I have a chance to go through these, I can narrow it down to time and place, if anything shows up."

"I wish you the best," Marge said, shaking her head. "That poor woman. What's the world coming to . . . people just attacking other people for no reason? What's the matter with this country?"

Her eyes clouded over, "You know, I fought for this country," she said, looking at Andrews, "but I hardly recognize it anymore."

Shaking it off, she extended her hand again.

"You tell me if you find anything," she said. "I really hope you catch the guy."

"We will," Andrews said, hoping that was true.

28

Logan hated being dependent on anyone. She'd been feeling so strong and good and healthy. She craved a good beach run, which she knew she wouldn't be able to enjoy for a long time.

Sulking and apologizing to Ben for being a witch with a capital B took up most of last night. By morning, Logan grudgingly accepted her temporary limitations, and after a few cups of Ben's high-octane coffee, made a plan to deal with them. It wasn't cancer, just a hugely inconvenient setback. She was surprised how wrenching her knee sharply brought back the same feelings of helplessness and pain she endured after her car accident. It had taken her over a year to recover from her injuries and she still had occasional back and neck trouble.

Pushing aside her fears, Logan logged onto Amazon. She found and ordered two large ice wraps with thick, Velcro straps for overnight delivery. The shipping cost more than the merchandise, but she didn't care. The bags of frozen vegetables kept slipping off. And they didn't go all the way around her knee. These ought to do the trick.

Lime green and royal blue. One wrap could be freezing while the other was doing RICE duty. Crutches at the ready.

Computer and phone within reach. She asked Ben to bring her a few files from her studio. If she absolutely needed anything else from her office, she could get there on crutches, then lift herself with her arms one stair step at a time, backward on her butt. Hopefully, her knee would calm down soon and that wouldn't be necessary. The studio had more stairs than the ones up to her bedroom, so it would take forever, but at least she'd be able to work her triceps. Hmmmm . . .

Stir crazy by noon, there wasn't much more Logan could do. One call she kept putting off making was to Rita, director of the New School. She should let her know about her knee. She wasn't cleared to travel yet, but hopefully she would be by next week. One way or the other, she was getting on that plane. Until then, she'd just have to be the perfect patient.

On the bright side, Sally was bringing In-N-Out for lunch, before she picked up Quinn at Bonnie's.

Rick stopped off after his shift to give Logan the update on Lori's condition. Everyone knew him down at the hospital. One of the ER docs gave him her status.

Multiple contusions, smashed jaw, dislocated shoulder, couple of cracked ribs. She'll be sipping food through a straw for a while. Lost a lot of blood, but no gunshot or stab wounds. Stitched up her scalp. Might lose her sight in one eye. Too early to tell. Whoever did this to her did it with his hands. And feet. Up close and personal.

"He said it's a good thing you and Ben interrupted her attacker.

If not, she'd probably be dead," Rick said.

"Jeez," Logan said, "do they think she's going to be okay? Will she recover?"

"He said he'd know more in twenty-four hours," Rick said, "If she doesn't stabilize, they may need surgery. She could have internal bleeding."

"Can she have visitors? Is she awake?"

"Not yet," Rick said, "They're still trying to locate family. Did she ever mention any family to you?"

"No, she was pretty tight-lipped about anything personal," Logan said. "I don't even know where they came from. What are they going to do about Shannon? Can she stay with Bonnie and Mike?"

"Haven't heard," Rick said.

Charlie, Rick's German Shepherd K9 partner, knowing she was off duty at Logan's house, licked her hand, begging for a treat she knew Logan always kept on hand, hot dogs cut up into one inch slices.

"You'll have to settle for a scratch behind the ears, girl," Logan said, rubbing her forehead on Charlie's, giving her a love. "I'm fresh out and couldn't get up to get you one if I had any."

Charlie's tail wagged furiously, anyway, and she licked Logan's face. Then she lowered herself gracefully down, laying on Logan's foot. Love was almost as good as hot dogs.

After Rick left, Logan called Bonnie. Good news on that front, anyway. Mrs. Croft came by and, after a thorough inspection, approved Shannon's temporary placement with Bonnie and Mike for the next two weeks, or until Lori could come home.

If she comes home.

"How is Shannon doing without her mom? Has she asked for her?" Logan said, "It's got to be tough on her. Has she said anything? Do you think she saw what happened?"

"No, she hasn't said anything. She did ask for her mom this morning, but I just told her mommy was working, and she seemed to accept that. At least for now. Bedtime will be another story," Bonnie said. "Haley's keeping her busy playing with Quinn."

"Sally's going to stop off here to bring me lunch first, but she should be there on time to pick him up," Logan said.

"That's right, you're grounded. How's the knee?" Bonnie asked. "Ben told me you managed to tear your meniscus."

In the middle of Logan's medical report, she heard a knock on the front door.

"Meals on Wheels is here, Bonnie. Gotta go!" she said. "Come in!" she called to the door.

Sally let herself in.

The aroma of crispy fries and seared meat permeated the house, making Logan salivate like Purgatory waiting eagerly to be tossed a Polish sausage off the grill. Suddenly starving, she was glad she ordered a triple. Sally plopped the bags on the coffee table. Handing Logan her meal first, with plenty of napkins, she grabbed her own and sat down in the rocking chair. Neither spoke until they'd taken the first few bites. Hot juices and secret sauce ran down Logan's chin.

Heaven!

Eating an In-N-Out burger was a messy business, but somebody had to do it.

29

When there were no Code Blues, the ICU was a peaceful place. At least Rhonda thought so. She'd worked there for the last seven years and loved it. Machines whirred, screens beeped and blipped reassuringly. No doctor's rounds, no new orders to fill. No meal delivery. Some patients even slept, which was good for everyone. Doctors tried to catch a few ZZZs in their respective call rooms in between pages. There were only two on the night shift. Nice to have them nearby, but not underfoot.

At the end of her circular path around the unit, Rhonda stopped at Room 217. Some nights she had two patients, but tonight she just had one, an assault victim they brought up two nights ago from the ER. She long ago learned to detach herself from the wrecks that lay before her on the bed, but this one was bad. This young woman she checked on every fifteen minutes until she stabilized. Today she dropped it down to every half hour. She still wasn't out of the woods.

Domestic violence cases, which this almost certainly was, were always harder to deal with than accident victims. How could one person inflict this much damage on another human being? And why?

At least she had the best tools at hand to care for her. It was one of the reasons Rhonda liked working the ICU. From the nurse's station in the center, she could see every room. They all had glass walls. In ten steps she could be at her patient's bedside and know instantly, by checking the monitors, how she or he was doing. ICU patients were usually heavily intubated, which freaked out family visitors, but all those tubes were actually viewed as a blessing when you understood what they were for.

A big tube sticking out of your mom's neck looked scary, but a regular IV line couldn't deliver enough fluids. You needed a bigger line. No one liked seeing a tube going into someone's nose, but an NG could deliver vital nutrients—proteins and carbohydrates—that the patient couldn't get any other way.

Every tube, going in or out, gave vital information to Rhonda and helped her know the second her patient needed her. When they first came in, she set the alarms on each device to signal when bags needed to be changed, or vital medicine administered. No guesswork or fly-by-the-seat-of-your-pants ER heroics. ER was just "treat and street." Any patient they couldn't discharge usually made his or her way to her. They got the hot messes, the sickest of the sick. Precision, organization, and critical thinking skills helped her patients survive.

Entering her patient's room, in a glance, she took in the information provided to her from the various monitors, after which she did a thorough visual assessment. Up, down, back and front, she checked it all. Made sure all lines were secure and her patient was comfortable as possible. Turned and clean. She even smelled the air. Satisfied, she went back to the nurse's station and grabbed a handful of gummy bears. Every nurse's station was the same—lots of goodies everywhere. She'd gained twenty-five pounds since she started working there.

When the ER nurse brought her up last night, he said her

new patient was officially still a Jane Doe. Her neighbor, a woman named Logan McKenna, said her name was Lori Wright, but the police didn't find any ID. The only other information in the EMT's notes was the fact that the victim had a young daughter, preschool age, presumably with Children's Services by now.

Rhonda hoped they found some family soon. She hated to think of the little girl funneled into foster care. She had a two-year-old in here last year who was a product of that system.

Each room in the ICU had one or two chairs stationed outside for visitors. Earlier this morning, the chair outside Lori's room encased the ample derrière of an Officer Gussler, a reserve police officer pulled in to do guard duty. But by noon, he'd been reassigned.

The chair was not unoccupied, however. Currently, it housed a Mrs. Santa Claus clone, complete with white hair, placidly knitting. She wore a dove gray sweater over a long-sleeved white, cotton blouse, jeans, and black, orthopedic tennis shoes. Passing within inches of her on the way out, Rhonda did not ask the woman what she was doing there or if she was family. She obviously saw her, but, ignoring the knitter, implicitly allowed her to stay.

The rhythmic clacking of the needles harmonized with the blips and beeps, creating a reassuring soundtrack for everyone on the hall, patients and nurses. The pool of calm surrounding Mrs. Claus may or may not have reached the young woman in the room behind her, who had yet to regain consciousness, but she certainly hoped so. Either way, she was here till morning. Staying up all night wasn't that hard. She hadn't needed much sleep since she turned seventy. She'd catnap with her Maine Coon, Fenway, when she got home.

A few minutes later, the woman looked up from her knitting

and stretched her neck and rolled her shoulders a few times. Rhonda nodded from her station and returned the smile. For the last few years, Sophia (she never gave a last name) showed up whenever they had a domestic violence case. DVs were always potentially dangerous. These guys didn't give up.

But no one got past Sophia. It was rumored she could do more than knit socks with those needles. Grabbing another handful of gummy bears, Rhonda went back to her computer. She almost hoped the guy would try. As an extra benefit, Sophia always donated her completed knitting projects to the neonatal unit. Tonight's baby booties were robin's egg blue with yellow trim around the top.

Her first year in the ICU, Rhonda's preceptor, Helen, unofficially filled her in about Sophia and friends. They were part of a highly secretive organization called the House of Ruth. Good at flying under the radar, they were Candy Stripers, orderlies, admitting clerks. Rhonda had no idea how many worked or volunteered at Hoag, but she suspected quite a few. They were all over the hospital, but most could be found in and around the ER. Which made sense, given their mission.

Helen explained that all these women—and a few men— were part of an underground railroad of sorts for abused women that stretched across the country and even helped sex slaves from as far away as Taiwan, Russia, and Mexico to find safe homes and make new lives for themselves.

One key to their success was that no one working with House of Ruth knew more than they needed to about the rest of the organization. The beneficiaries of their help rarely knew more than one contact, and only first names were ever used. If an abused wife went back to her husband and divulged the names of the people who helped her, it wouldn't matter, anyway, because they all used assumed names and met in public places.

VANISHING DAY

In her younger days, Rhonda would have told the police what she knew about the House of Ruth volunteers. But with a few years under her belt, she understood there was almost nothing the police could do to protect domestic violence victims. And the law? Men ignored or broke through restraining orders all the time.

The House of Ruth provided a very necessary service.

The volunteers probably wouldn't know Lori's real name or origin, anyway. They would only know the last location, not the first. According to Helen, they never housed an abused wife in the same town or state she was from.

But somehow, her abuser had found her. If he found her once, he'd be back. Her best chance was to lose herself in the underground railroad again. Maybe this time she'd stay lost.

Rhonda had every intention of keeping her patient safe so she'd recover and have that opportunity.

The doctors didn't have a clue; they never did.

○ ○ ○ ○ ○

Unaware of her guardian angels outside, beneath the layer of blips and bleeps, eyes closed, Lori floated, suspended in a sea of molasses. Ribbons of memories wound slowly through her mind. Her mom. Some of the cooks at Juan's. They were funny. Her new friend, Logan.

Drifting . . . familiar smells . . . She sat on the edge of a thin mattress, waiting for something. She was back in the emergency room in Seattle. She'd been here before. On the other side of a thin, blue curtain someone moaned.

Then, suddenly, searing pain! A doctor popped her arm back into place, then after a quick examination, had the nurse clean and apply butterfly bands to her cheek to hold the broken skin together. Once the doctor finished his work and left, the

ER nurse handed her clothes back to her and tucked a piece of paper into her palm. Leaning forward, she whispered into her ear.

"Call them, these people will help," she said, straightening up, looking directly into Lauren's eyes. She was still Lauren then.

Lori remembered looking away, pretending not to hear.

"I've seen your chart," the nurse said, waiting a beat to see if her words hit their target. "This is your third visit in two months. . . .

Lori hadn't realized she'd been here that often.

"It won't stop, you know," the nurse said as she turned to leave so she could get dressed. "Call them. They'll help."

Lori looked at the paper. No name, just a phone number. Keeping the card was not an option. Garrett went through all her things on a regular basis. How would she explain having a card with no name, just a phone number on it?

He'd think it was another man. That's what started it last week. She made the mistake of thanking the produce manager when he showed her where the avocados were. Garrett acted as if she was arranging a clandestine rendezvous.

Staring at the piece of paper, she repeated the sequence of numbers over and over in her mind as she pulled on her pants and top. She'd always been good with numbers.

The nurse was right. It hadn't gotten better. This time he went after Shannon. If she hadn't intervened to take the blame for the noise Shannon made when Garrett was on the phone, Lori knew he would have wrenched his daughter's arm out of its socket instead of hers, without realizing what he'd done until he was through venting.

She could take it, but she'd be damned if she'd ever let him lay a hand on Shannon.

30

Telling Patricia what restaurant he'd be at, and not to expect him back this afternoon, Garrett called Neal from the Audi. Neal answered on the first ring.

"Meet me at SeaTac in a couple of hours," Garrett said without explanation, "I should be there by 2:30 p.m."

"Should I pack?" Neal asked.

"No, short trip," Garrett said, "We'll be back before your bedtime."

Early-to-bed, early-to-rise. All part of Neal's post-prison, new-leaf routine. He even drank that kombucha shit. Still smoked though.

Leopards can't change their spots.

Garrett did not believe in rehabilitation.

o o o o o

When they got to Carlsbad, CA, Garrett tied down the Cessna and made sure it had enough gas to get back. The place was deserted. He grabbed the keys to Steve's other vehicle, an older-model Mercedes, and tossed them to Neal. The color was a god-awful green, but it ran well and, above all, it was quiet. He preferred the Jeep, but didn't want to risk anyone recognizing it from his last nocturnal visit.

When Garrett told Neal they were going to Lori's house to get back something she stole, he flinched slightly, but kept his speed steady, his eyes on the road, and said nothing. He was sure Neal didn't buy his lame story for a minute, but Neal wasn't paid to express his opinion.

No need to get a motel this time. He wasn't planning on them staying long. Find the flash drive and leave. He had Neal stop at a liquor store for food. Liquor stores had lots of people come and go. No one would remember one guy coming in for some beach grub. Cellophane-wrapped submarine sandwiches, bag of chips for him, apple for Neal. Gatorade. No beer.

Sunset still several hours away, they parked at the beach and ate in the car. Wadding up his trash, Garrett passed it up to Neal, then lay down in the back seat, pulling the baseball cap down to shade his eyes.

"Wake me when the sun sets," he said.

Neal, expressionless, remained in the driver's seat and watched the late afternoon surfers. They seemed so free.

An hour later, Garrett woke. Sunset was still hours away. They took in a movie and rotated through a few parking lots. Neal knew some tricks from his former life. Hiding in plain sight. No one would remember them.

○ ○ ○ ○ ○

11:45 p.m.

As Neal rolled quietly past Lori's house for the third time, Garrett, finally satisfied, instructed him to park across the street in front of the empty lot, facing toward PCH. The nosy neighbor's house was dark. There was police tape around the front porch, but no cops guarding the place. Didn't look like anyone was home.

Lori must be in the hospital, and they probably had Shannon in some kind of foster home. Frustration burned from his gut to his throat at the trouble Lauren caused, but he stayed focused. Once he had the flash drive, he'd be back in control. No sense wasting time on trying to get at her in the hospital, where he presumed she was. She hadn't been very cooperative last time he tried to reason with her, no reason she'd start now.

The door locks thunked open loudly, but there was no one near enough to hear. Following Neal's lead, Garrett ran low and quiet up to the porch. They dropped down silently behind the railings, so as not to create a silhouette should another car drive by. The front door was locked tight, but Neal made short work of it. They were inside in seconds. If he had any objections to searching Lori's home for a flash drive or anything like it, he didn't say.

For a job like this, Garrett deferred to Neal's experience. They agreed to twenty minutes tops before it became too dangerous to stay. Starting in the back of the house, Garrett took Lori's room; Neal, Shannon's and the bathroom. The bathroom was a particular favorite hiding place for people, Neal said. They assumed no one would look there, so it was the first place to try.

Garrett checked his watch. The IWC Pilot was a gift to himself not long after taking Mr. Yoshimoto on as a client. The luminous silver hands showed it had only been ten minutes, but it felt much longer. They hadn't found a thing. The kitchen was next. It was almost a tie with the bathroom, Neal said.

As each drawer or cupboard yielded nothing but junk— cheap silverware and plastic dishes—he grew increasingly furious with Lauren.

Where is it?!

Finally, Neal tapped his own watch. It was time to go. They'd searched every room and found nothing. Garrett even checked for hidden compartments in the walls and along the baseboards, and Neal checked the garage, including Lori's junker. While he was there, Garrett had him remove the tracker. No sense arousing suspicion. He wanted the police to think Lori's attack was just a burglary gone wrong. The mess they made tonight would go a long way toward supporting that theory that there were thieves in the neighborhood. Or maybe some random stranger did that to her.

The world was full of crazies.

Neal yanked his head toward the front door. It was time to go. They'd already exceeded their twenty minutes. But until he had that flash drive, Garrett knew he would always be looking over his shoulder. He wasn't going home without it.

Lori said it wasn't in the house. He figured she was lying, but unless they missed it, she'd been telling the truth. If it wasn't here, it must be at someone else's house—and the only person Neal had seen her with was the neighbor. The woman his daughter ran to for safety—from him. As if he would ever do anything to hurt his little girl.

Women always stuck together against men.

Instead of leaving out the front, Garrett urgently pointed toward the back door and waved Neal to follow. From the look on his face, Neal obviously thought this was a bad idea, but did as his boss requested.

Before they were ten yards away from the house, a light came on in the neighbor's house. Quickly, Garrett ducked behind the small, detached garage that squatted between the two houses, gratefully blocking him from the neighbor's view should she look outside. The two men held their breath for what felt like forever, but no one came out, and the light was soon turned off.

VANISHING DAY

When all was quiet again, Garrett and Neal crouch-ran to the car, doubling back, avoiding the gravel this time. Soft grass all the way. Garrett was grateful for Neal's get-away expertise. He'd parked downhill so he wouldn't have to start the car and make a screeching u-turn like he had to do the other night. That made enough noise to wake a banshee.

Neal put the Mercedes in neutral and let it roll. He didn't engage the engine until they reached the intersection at the bottom of the steep hill. While Neal drove south on a surprisingly busy PCH toward Carlsbad, Garrett's mind started doing its hyper, hamster-wheel thing.

31

Neal hadn't said two words on the drive back to the airport. As he pulled into the FBO and parked the Mercedes, Garrett said, "Promised I'd get you home before dawn, right, Sleeping Beauty?"

Cinderella, you moron, not Sleeping Beauty, and she had to get home before midnight, not dawn.

Barely keeping his cool, Neal shut the car door with a bit more force than necessary.

"How about one for the road?" Garrett said.

Nothing fazed the man. Neal watched the back of Garrett's head as he strode into one of the offices and sat behind a massive oak desk. There were pictures of someone's wife and kids set at an angle on one corner, and several plants on the shelf behind him tucked in with technical manuals. His wife probably got him the plants.

Why couldn't Garrett be happy with Lori? Then he wouldn't be caught in the middle of all this.

"Knob Hill," Garrett said, lifting a bottle out of the bottom, right drawer. "Steve showed me where they keep the good stuff."

Rummaging in the break room, he found a couple of mugs in the dish drainer near the sink. With a flourish, he brought them back and poured them both double shots.

"Here's to faithless wives and stolen property!" Garrett said.

Neal rarely drank these days, but he halfheartedly raised his mug and downed the bourbon in one gulp. The faster they got in the air the better. He had an appointment with his parole officer in the morning. He just had to hold it together until then. How he hated this man. What in the world had Lauren seen in him?

Maybe he'd let the cops know what Garrett had been up to once his parole was officially fulfilled. Sure, Garrett probably assumed he still had him by the balls, but Neal wore gloves on their little excursion. Garrett didn't. Still, it would be his word against Garrett's. And even with fingerprints, who would the cops believe? The wealthy hedge fund, pillar of the community, manager, or the ex-con? No, he'd just keep his mouth shut and move as far away from Seattle as possible as soon as he got clear. They were wheels up in ten. Mainly a commuter airport, the tower was down for the night. Not much traffic at 1:30 a.m.

Soon, they were flying over Orange County. Neal breathed deeply and relaxed into his seat. It looked so beautiful from up here. The peaceful ocean somewhere down below in the dark. Off on the right, a carpet of lights lay glittering. Up here, you could believe in humanity. No human filth. No scrambling for a living. No jail. The only part of this job Neal enjoyed was when Garrett took him up in the Cessna. Such a feeling of freedom, of soaring above it all. It was so peaceful up here.

His arms and legs felt heavy. So heavy. He couldn't lift his arm if he wanted to. And he didn't want to.

Looking to his left, Garrett was smiling. "Feeling good, buddy?" he said.

Why was Garrett lowering the landing gear? It wasn't time to land yet! Even Neal knew that! Giggles bubbled up from somewhere inside. This was so hilarious! He felt dizzy, like he was watching himself and Garrett from the ceiling of the plane. Did you call it a ceiling on a plane . . . or was it a cockpit inverse platform thingamajiggy? He couldn't help himself. He broke out in giggles again. That was just too funny!

"That's right, big guy . . . you're feelin' fine now, aren't you?" Garrett said.

Neal tried to focus. None of this made any sense. Was he dreaming or was he awake?

The next thirty seconds rolled by in slow motion.

First, Garrett calmly turned halfway toward Neal and unlatched his seat belt, carefully freeing his arms—just like a mom getting her toddler out of the car seat to go into the grocery store. Then he reached all the way across Neal's chest and unlocked the door.

Neal's mind couldn't keep up. What was he doing?

No longer held up by the safety harness, Neal started sliding down the seat, unable to make his arms and legs work. Garrett flipped a switch labeled autopilot. One of the gauges read 78 knots and was dropping. The landing gear was still down.

Turning completely sideways in his seat, Garrett grinned, braced his back against his door; then lifted his feet up like he was getting ready to do some leg presses.

"Sorry you won't be getting a piece of Lauren tail; I know you wanted some!" he said cheerfully, "Say hello to the sharks!"

Then, while Neal struggled to sit up, Garrett's legs shot past his face, and kicked open the door.

Cold air rushed in briefly before the door slapped back again.

He didn't think it shut, though.

What?

Getting into position again, this time Neal felt Garrett's right foot planted firmly against the left side of his body, while his left foot pushed against the door.

What was he doing?

As if from a very great distance, he heard Garrett inhale deeply and exhale with a grunt, shoving him against the door. For a second, the door held, then with one last, rib-cracking kick, the door opened just enough for Garrett to push him all the way out. He heard the door bang shut.

This couldn't be happening!

He bounced off something metal. The wing? Lashed by hundred-mile-an-hour winds, freezing air snatched and kept his breath. In a few seconds, his plummeting body reached terminal velocity, 186 feet per second. Fortunately, he passed out long before his body broke apart on the salted steel of the open ocean.

◊ ◊ ◊ ◊ ◊

Garrett was pleased. He hadn't been sure how much Ketamine to use.

He usually kept some K on hand for nights when Lauren was less than cooperative. She never felt frisky anymore, but at least it loosened her up. Made it more fun for both of them.

Estimating by weight, to be on the safe side, he tripled the dose for Neal. Had to make sure he was good and out of it. No other way was Neal going to let Garrett throw him out of an airplane three thousand feet up.

Snapping back, but not closing completely, even the two-inch gap between the door and the body of the plane let in the roar of rushing wind.

Hands shaking, Garrett crawled far enough over to grab the door handle but wasn't strong enough to close and lock it. He could bring it close, but not all the way in.

Screw it!

Frustrated, he backed into his seat. Loud, but not a huge deal. He'd just have to put up with the noise until he got back. Back over land in a few, from there it was a straight shot to Seattle. He'd be home in time for breakfast. Take a quick shower and be in the office by 9:00. No one would even know he'd gone.

He pushed the throttle to increase power, then attempted to raise the landing gear. Screeching, grinding metal greeted his first try. At the same time, the Cessna steeply yawed to the right. Immediately, he stepped on the right rudder to correct the yaw and lowered the landing gear.

Not good.

He tried again but got the same thing. Neal's body must not have cleared it—it must have hit it on the way down. He could fly with the landing gear down. That wasn't the problem. Trying to land on partial gear could be. That was a feat he never wanted to attempt. And explaining the damaged gear to Steve. If Neal hit it hard enough to break it or bend it, there could be blood on it, or bits of skin or hair. Steve was still in Costa Rica, though. No one would be at the hangar. He could clean it. Maybe it was only bent, and he could straighten it out.

But there was a bigger problem. With the extra drag, he was going to burn up a lot more fuel. He'd never make it to Seattle. He'd have to land in Medford. And Medford's tower was full time. Manned 24/7. There'd be a record of his flight and no chance for him to take care of the landing gear without being seen.

He didn't know why he was worrying. No one saw him at Lauren's, he wasn't driving his own car, and Neal's body would never be found. No one was going to put it all together and come looking for him. Besides, if he needed one, his lovely assistant would be more than happy to give him an alibi if he asked. He might pay her a visit anyway.

Pushing a button on the yoke, he disconnected the autopilot and pointed the Cessna north.

32

More redolent of warm bodies, hot asphalt, suntan oil, and sandy beaches than the crisp scents of fall leaves and wood-burning fireplaces back East, September in Southern California was one of the hottest months of the year. Summer gave one last push before allowing the mercury to drop a few degrees for what passed for winter in Jasper.

Logan didn't mind the heat, but appreciated Jasper's coastal breezes. Even a few miles inland, you felt the difference. The heat was palpable. To escape the stifling temps, Bonnie was bringing her girls out, including her new charge, for an impromptu BBQ later in the day. Logan hoped being here wouldn't upset Shannon, but Mrs. Croft said as long as they didn't take her back to her mom's house, it might even do her some good. Baby steps. The little girl obviously viewed Logan's home as a safe haven. And she loved Ben and Purgatory.

Since it wasn't the whole crowd, they were keeping the menu simple. Well, simple for Ben. Simple in Ben's world meant homemade German potato salad, grilled brats, three different kinds of mustard, four different varieties of craft beer, and a chocolate layer cake with real whipped cream. Logan supplied the coleslaw and some of Jean's crispy rolls from Tava'e's. Jean was Tava'e's French husband. No one had ever seen him. He stayed in the kitchen, baking away. Ben would split and grill the rolls on the BBQ. Bonnie was bringing root beer float makings for the kids.

Logan couldn't put her finger on it, but something was bugging Ben. For one thing, he didn't stay over the last two nights. Said he was tired. Since when was Ben ever tired? But he showed up as promised this morning to help her assemble some strawberry pots. Bonnie swore she could grow strawberries year round if she bought Seascape and Albion varieties vs. the June harvest type. Since Logan trusted her friend's gardening acumen more than her own, she was making one pot for Bonnie, one for Amy, and keeping one for her and Ben. Maybe whatever was bothering Ben had nothing to do with her. Could he be having trouble with one of his jobs?

She had some starter plants and the clay pots lined up and ready to go. If she kept her knee bent at a 45-degree angle, propped up on a folding chair, wrapped in her new ice pack—God Bless Amazon's overnight shipping—she could reach everything.

Looking as if bitten into, then pulled out by a chipmunk's two front teeth, at intermittent locations around the outside, each pot sported little pouches anchoring mini-archways, from which the vines would eventually emerge, heavy with sweet, fragrant fruit. Ben was contributing the compost and potting soil. He lugged everything over about an hour ago.

They'd worked companionably side-by-side. Still, he hadn't said two words since he got here. She was about to ask him if something was wrong, when Taylor showed up. He stopped by on his way back from a 9/11 memorial event down at the beach, to ask Ben if he needed him on Monday.

Once the two men started talking shop, Logan might as well

have been invisible. This must be how Ben felt when anyone from Fractals came over, or she, Ned and Sally reminisced about their old gigs or new arrangements for the Otter Festival.

Fair enough. She didn't take it personally. Brushing the loose soil off the last pot, she grabbed a broom and swept the gardening detritus into a pile against the house, then went inside.

Logan didn't realize she'd been sweating, until the inside air cooled her forehead and arms. It felt great! She stopped at the sink to splash her face. Reaching blind for the flour sack dish towel she always kept by the sink, she overshot the drying rack, grabbing instead the handle of a shopping bag. She opened one eye.

Oh yeah, the puppy toys for Shannon's birthday. She'd have to hide that bag in the closet before Bonnie got here with the little girl. She still hadn't figured out what to do with the stuff if . . . no, Lori was going to pull through. She had to.

Face dried and dish towel tossed in the laundry, Logan looked at the clock. Almost lunch time. She looked outside. Taylor now had a beer. Long legs stretched out in front of him, he wasn't going anywhere anytime soon.

Might as well make lunch. She cobbled together some slices of Black Forest ham, a few carrots and celery sticks (Ben was trying to diet), and a couple of scrubbed radishes. At the last minute, she stole a small scoop of German potato salad from tonight's BBQ makings. A man has to keep up his strength.

Ben kept the outdoor fridge supplied with adult beverages, but she made iced tea with lemon just in case. It just wasn't summer without iced tea. She and her dad drank gallons of it when she was growing up.

Her generosity paid off. Even though she didn't get any alone time with Ben, she could tell he appreciated the snack, and she managed to find out how things were going with Taylor and

Iona. Apparently very well. That's why Taylor was asking Ben about Monday. He and Iona were going camping for a few days. If the man felt an ounce of awkwardness at seeing an older—much older—woman, he didn't let on.

33

After Taylor left, Ben filled the trash bags while Logan swept the patio and straightened up. When there was no more cleaning up to do, Ben got himself another beer, pulled out a chair, adjusted the umbrella to shade the table and sat down, asking Logan to take the seat across from him. Logan poured the last of the iced tea into her tall glass and sat as instructed.

Something was definitely up.

With the tension in the air, Logan wasn't sure she wanted to hear whatever it was Ben had to say, but she couldn't wait for him to say it.

"I . . ." Ben paused, then tried again, "I'm sorry about last night . . ."—It had been two nights, but who was counting?—". . . but I just needed some time to think through some things."

He searched the clouds, then looked back at Logan.

"I didn't expect to feel this way . . . to have these feelings," he said.

God. Had he found someone else? Was he breaking up with her? That would be awkward, living right next door. And why? Things had been going great. She knew he loved her. In every bone she knew it. And she loved him. What was this about? Why did men have to rock the boat??!!

Just hear him out, Logan.

"When . . . No," he stopped himself, "I think I always felt this, wanted this—I just didn't think I could have it," he said.

He wasn't making any sense.

"Let me try again," he said, "When Julie and I were engaged, she said she just wanted to wait a while to have children. I know now that was just an excuse, but I guess I thought she'd change her mind. The biological clock and all that. I figured every woman had one, but Julie didn't stand in that line. The truth is, I made Julie into something she wasn't. She wasn't the maternal type. Not like you are with Amy.

Anyway, she just kept moving getting married and having a family down the road, 'after graduate school, after I make partner' and then, of course, you know the rest. It all blew up. I don't think she wanted kids ever."

Logan held her breath.

Please don't say what I think you're going to say.

"I love my nephews. I get a ton of kid time with them," Ben said, "I thought that was enough."

So far, Ben had been talking to the table, and then to a spot over Logan's left shoulder. Now, he looked deeply into Logan's green eyes with his soft, chambray blue ones.

"I didn't think I'd ever love anyone again, either, but then you came along and I guess that kind of knocked things around inside. The bottom line is, I know now. I want my own children, Logan," he said.

Filled with intense, conflicting emotions, Logan gathered both his hands into hers, surrounding him with warmth, but didn't speak. She didn't trust herself to speak. What could she say? She knew exactly what Ben wanted. She already had that. She had Amy and wouldn't trade that experience for the world. Of course, Ben deserved to have that, too. If that's what he really wanted, she wouldn't stand in his way. She steeled herself for what was coming next.

"And I want to have them with you," he said simply.

Logan was dumbfounded. She had assumed he meant with someone else. A younger woman. Of course, she was physically still capable of bearing children, but just barely. She was in her early forties—well, closer to mid-forties. Not exactly prime childbearing years.

On the other hand, the thought of having a child with a good, loving man like Ben would be amazing. Why hadn't she met him twenty years ago? Jack was a fun dad, but not much help when it came to diapers and homework. In hindsight, Logan realized she pretty much raised Amy on her own. Jack was a child himself.

"I know it seems crazy," Ben admitted, "Why now? I've been asking myself the same question. I can't answer that exactly, except to say that when I saw Shannon on your lap the other night, in the rocking chair, comforting her, and then Shannon hung onto my neck and wouldn't let go, it just triggered something," he said, opening and stretching his hands, then letting them fall back onto the table.

"You don't have to answer now, of course," Ben said, leaning back in his chair, apparently relieved to have gotten that off his chest, "I just wanted you to know."

Wow.

Well, at least she didn't have to wonder what was on Ben's mind anymore.

34

"Yes?" Garrett said, leaning forward to speak into the intercom. "Mr. Leo Rudaski for you on line one," his assistant's voice came through sounding tinny.

Right. Garrett expected this call, but he'd been busy all morning combing through files. Busy trying to figure out how to lessen the damage Lauren might do to him when she got out of the hospital. There was no telling when she betrayed him and how much dirt she had. She could have been spying on him and snooping for the last few years, or only right before she left. He wasn't sure how far back to go. God knows what she had.

Right now, he wished he'd never heard Mr. Yoshimoto's name. Before he'd taken him on as a client, there was nothing for her to report.

Pressing the button for line 1, Garrett put on his business-is-good, all-is-well voice.

"Mr. Rudaski, what can I do for you? Garrett said, "Did you receive the letter? I had my assistant mail it out last week. Neal is an excellent employee."

"Yes, I got it. All his paperwork is in order, but that's not why I'm calling," he said, "Mr. Everly did not show up for his final appointment with me today."

"Really? Wow. I'm surprised to hear that. This was his final meeting, right? I gave him the day off specifically to meet with you and turn in his paperwork to the judge. He said something about proof of compliance and then he was done with all that."

"Well, his appointment with me was at 9:00 a.m., and I haven't seen him yet. Any idea where he might be? I'd like to get this file closed and off my desk," Rudaski said.

"Not a clue," Garrett lied.

He started to embellish, but thought better of it. Short lies were easier to remember.

Rudaski huffed in frustration. "Okay. Let me know if you hear from him. Doesn't make sense, this last appointment is not one they usually miss . . . anything unusual happen with him? Break up with a girlfriend? Trouble at work? Anything that might explain a no-show on his release day?"

Garrett repressed a giggle.

"No, everything's been fine as far as I know," he said.

If you don't count free-falling from a Cessna over the Pacific Ocean!

o o o o o

"Okay. If you do see him or hear from him, have him call me. Tell him if I don't hear from him by five o'clock tonight, I'll have to put out a warrant for his arrest."

"Will do, of course," Garrett said, keeping the verbal equivalent of a straight face, "I'm sure he'll turn up. Neal has always been a very reliable employee."

Rudaski gave his number again before saying goodbye.

Garrett sat back and smiled. Dead drivers tell no tales. And they certainly don't call their parole officers.

Patricia buzzed in on the intercom again, "Mr. Yoshimoto on line three for you, Mr. Delaney. I didn't think you'd want to be interrupted, so he's been on hold a few minutes."

Garrett did a slow burn. You did not keep Yoshimoto on hold—ever. He told her that. He snapped up the receiver.

"Mr. Yoshimoto," he said, trying to keep his voice calm, rushing to apologize before his client could complain, "I am so sorry you were made to wait."

Silence.

"That should not have happened," he added. More silence.

This was not good.

"I will speak to my assistant," Garrett said, "It will not happen again."

Without accepting his apology, Yoshimoto apparently handed the receiver to an underling, because a voice unknown to Garrett came on the line, saying simply, "Mr. Yoshimoto has not yet received this week's reports."

Garrett's intestines clenched. The report was only two hours late. But he had never been late before.

"Yes, I was just going to call you. I was unavoidably called out of the office on business last week. Because Mr. Yoshimoto is my most valued client, I handle all of his business personally, so it could not be given to anyone else to put together. Please express my apologies and tell him he will have the reports by the end of the day. I will place it in the hands of our best courier service myself, at the highest priority."

"That will not be necessary. I will be there at 4:00 p.m.," he said.

Garrett was left with nothing but dial tone and eight hours work to fit into three. After testily reminding his assistant that

Mr. Yoshimoto was never to be kept waiting, and to inform him immediately when his representative arrived, Garrett had her hold all calls and got to work.

Once he dug into the accounts, what seemed a grinding chore proved useful. While compiling an accounting of this week's transactions and account balances, with an update on various real estate investments, he took note of the continuing unbelievable rise in the Monero wallet. The path seemed clear. He couldn't erase bank records from Yoshimoto's original deposits. There was always a paper trail. But from here on out, all of Mr. Yoshimoto's money was going into crypto. Untraceable.

This could still work.

Now, all he had to do was recover the flash drive or laptop containing the documents Lauren stole from him. Destroy those, and he'd be free and clear. If they didn't know the names of the banks, the SEC couldn't find the old accounts. He wasn't a complete idiot. He'd been careful to do all Yoshimoto's business on his personal computer. Garrett didn't know how to wipe data from it, but he could hire someone who did.

Yoshimoto would never have to know his information was compromised. He'd keep giving Garrett money, and he, Garrett, would wash it so white it would become invisible. Everybody would be happy. No reason to give up the goose. He could use a few more golden eggs.

Yoshimoto's emissary, a short, ugly man in a dark suit, with dandruff on his shoulders and a cowlick sticking straight up out of the crown of his head, arrived at 3:57 p.m. He did not return Garrett's confident smile or respond to his comments on the beautiful day. He entered the room, reached out his hand for the report, and let himself out without saying a word.

35

They hadn't talked much since Ben dropped the kid bomb on Sunday. For one thing, Ben woke up Monday morning with an impacted wisdom tooth. Took two days to get in to see the oral surgeon, but he was there now. The normal wait time for this particular surgeon was two months, not two days, but Ben had done the landscaping for his new office and they'd become friends.

Logan was home babysitting Purgatory. The dog was downstairs and she was up in the bedroom packing for her trip. She didn't want to leave with Ben having surgery, but he reassured her he'd be fine. His sister already arranged to fill his prescriptions and stay over if needed, and Bonnie already stocked his fridge with plenty of soft foods to eat for the first few days. As he exited the car this morning, Ben reminded her he was a big boy and had been taking care of himself for years before she came along. Still, she would have stayed if she didn't have this trip.

Working on-site at the New School several times a year was part of her new contract with Rita. Not something she could reschedule easily. She had a 7:30 a.m. flight out of John Wayne. She'd arrive in Portland mid-morning, hopefully grab some *Pho* at Than's downtown, visit with her briefly, then book it out to meet Huey in his lab by 2:00 p.m. That didn't leave her any extra time in Portland, but Friday was a conference day—a rare, student-free day for Huey. He wasn't a homeroom teacher, so didn't have to hold any parent-teacher conferences unless specifically required for a particular student. Logan was planning on digging into a variety of projects with him, mapping out their year. This was just a short trip. He was due down her way for a week in November.

At least the drive was beautiful. Once you got through Beaverton and Tigard, it was an hour's open drive through rolling, green hills and the occasional red barn. Five minutes after the turnoff, the narrow road quickly wound its way through towering green corridors, touched occasionally by Whisper Creek, which playfully ran alongside and sometimes under the road as it crossed several bridges, one of them constructed of rounded, mossy stones. Logan always looked forward to that part of the drive.

And it would give her some time and space to think about Ben's unexpected revelation. Hopefully, his whole 'I-want-a-family-of-my-own' surge of emotion would die down while she was gone.

Ben needed to think about what having a child at this point in his life would mean. The reality of diapers, no sleep, college tuition, and the 18-plus-forever time commitment. Being a parent didn't have a graduation date. You were in it for life. She didn't think Ben had any idea what being a parent entailed. But then, neither did she when she got pregnant twenty-four years ago. And she wouldn't trade Amy for anything.

Knowing this wasn't a problem she could solve right now, Logan focused on her packing. Satisfied she had everything she needed for her trip, she zipped up her carry-on and pressed the Velcro handles together over the top. Part of a three-piece set she'd had for years, the roller bag was made of a tough, hot pink canvas and came with a diminutive, stuffed gorilla hanging off the ID pouch. Made baggage-claim a breeze if she ever needed to check it. You could spot that thing from three miles off. She wore the bulky items like her boots and carried her jacket. Everything else fit in the bag. She believed in traveling light.

Logan hadn't taken any vacation time since launching Fractals, so when she made her reservations earlier in the summer, she tacked on a week of personal time on the end of her work at the New School. Rose, a weaver she met a couple of years ago at the Otter Festival, a friend of Thomas and Lisa's, had invited her to stop by her shop on the coast. Ben insisted she stick to her original plans and not rush home, but Logan said she'd call in a couple of days and see how he was doing. She'd decide then.

Her original plan was to find an AirBnB or cheap hotel in Lincoln City, OR where Rose lived. Rose apologized for not being able to put her up at her place, but she was in the midst of a remodel and her large, 1940s Cape Cod was torn up.

When Rita heard of her plans, she insisted Logan stay at a home she kept out in a small, coastal community called Little Whale Cove, about ten miles south of Lincoln City, OR.

"Nothing fancy, but it's a five-minute walk to the beach and the house backs onto acres of old-growth forest. Miles of paths. Just the thing for a get-away," Rita said, "You'll love it. It's smack dab between Lincoln City and Newport. Absolutely nothing to do but look at green trees and whale watch."

Sounded perfect to Logan. Placing her bag by the bathroom door so she wouldn't forget to tuck in her toothbrush in the morning, Logan started down the stairs to check on Purgatory. He was potty trained, but probably needed to go for a walk soon.

When she reached the living room, she stopped dead in her tracks. Pleased as punch, Purgatory lay there, grinning up at her with a goofy, doggie smile, thumping his tail on the ground. He was quite happy where he was, toys strewn around his proud, Sphinx self, along with the now empty gift bag Lori had filled for Shannon's upcoming puppy.

36

Logan groaned. The gift bag never quite made it into the hall closet as originally planned.

Realizing it wasn't the dog's fault, but hers for leaving temptation within reach, Logan sighed and went over to begin collecting the items, salvaging what she could. No sense yelling at Purgatory. Whatever he had destroyed could be replaced. The counter was eye level for him. He just couldn't resist the smell of dog treats wafting from the gift bag perched invitingly there.

After scooping up the items on the floor back into the bag, most of which were as yet unmolested, she gave the "Drop It" command Ben taught her and, with one last lick to get at the treats still inside, Purgatory opened his mouth and released the toy he'd been chewing into her hand.

She carried the drool-covered rubber toy to the sink to rinse it off. She'd get Lori a new one. Purgatory obviously liked this one. Before she could flip on the faucet, she looked inside the hole drilled in the middle of the toy to make sure all the treats were out.

What?

A small, silver flash drive had been taped inside.

Grateful she hadn't run water through it yet, she carefully lifted the tape, and removed it, turning it over in her hand, as if it would reveal its secrets. Nothing written on the label.

Curiouser and curiouser . . .

Checking it for dampness or any damage from Purgatory's foraging tongue, she took it over to her laptop and inserted it into the USB port. The thought occurred to her as she did this that it might contain something that would damage her MacBook Air, but she'd just backed it up last night in preparation for her trip. Besides, if anything got messed up, she could always have Huey fix it. The man was a genius.

When the icon appeared on her desktop, Logan double clicked it and waited for it to open.

Nothing.

Why would Lori bother to tape a flash-drive into a dog toy, cover it up with treats and hide it in a bag? Obviously, something important was on it. Could Lori have made a mistake? Could there be another flash drive that had something she wanted to hide on it and she grabbed a blank one by mistake? This only deepened the mystery of Lori's true identity and what she was doing in Jasper. Did the flash drive contain her secrets or someone else's? And if so, why was it blank? It made no sense.

And why hadn't Lori just asked Logan to keep it for her? She took a big risk hiding it in the toy. It could have gotten lost or thrown out . . . or eaten by a certain neighbor's dog!

Logan looked down at Purgatory who was sitting politely, waiting to be rewarded for giving up his prize. She got him some cheese from the fridge. He ate it in one gulp, so she rummaged in the gift bag and got him something called a bully stick that looked like a rawhide cigar.

"There," she said as Purgatory trotted over to the door and

plopped down, happily chewing his new stick, "That might take you a second and a half to demolish."

She turned her attention back to her computer.

Staring at the empty window wasn't going to make files magically appear. Selecting the icon, she ejected the drive from her computer, then physically removed it. If she didn't eject it first, her computer yelled at her. Temperamental beast. One of the only features she didn't like about Apple. She dropped the small drive into the inside, zippered compartment of her computer bag/purse. She'd have Huey check it out when she got to the New School. Maybe he could see if anything was on it she couldn't access. Probably nothing, but worth a try.

Maybe that's why Lori was attacked. Maybe they were looking for this drive. If they wanted it that bad, they'd be back. She hoped they wouldn't realize she had it. Lori was in no condition to protect herself, and other than her supply of pepper spray, neither was Logan.

If Huey found anything, maybe it would lead the police to Lori's attacker before he came back. Logan considered how to get it back to her. It had been a week since the attack and she still wasn't allowed visitors. And Logan couldn't just leave it on Lori's kitchen counter. Lori obviously felt it needed to be hidden away from her home or she would have left it there herself.

She felt sorry for the young woman, but was Lori what she appeared to be? Maybe the drive had something on it that would point to something bad she had done.

Oh, hell.

Frustrated, Logan got up and snagged Detective Andrews' card from the mail holder on the counter. She was just going to leave a message for him, telling him what she found and that she would drop the flash drive off for him at the front desk, but the operator put her through right away.

"Andrews here," the Detective answered.

Logan hung up. She couldn't help it, the words got stuck in her throat. Detective Andrews already thought she was an idiot. She wasn't about to hand him a blank flash drive and tell him it might be important. He'd laugh her out of his office.

Lori trusted her. The least she could do was hold onto it until she could return it in person. Even if Huey pulled something incriminating to Lori off of it—it wasn't her job to be judge and jury.

It depends on what's on there, if anything.

She could always take it down to Detective Andrews and let him deal with it, but for now, she'd hold off. There was obviously no rush. Lori was still in the ICU. It's not like she'd be asking for it anytime soon.

37

Well, I'll be damned.

It was the McKenna woman. He'd had the front desk trace the call and it was definitely her cell. Logan McKenna. It was almost a week since he interviewed her and gave her his card. Why call now? And if she had something to tell him, why hang up? Was she involved in all this somehow? What was it about her that she was always close to trouble? Making a note of the time of her call in the file, he went back to the timeline.

It was seven days since the woman on Killer Hill was attacked, and the investigation was stalled. The only new entry in the file was the break in. Monday he sent a couple uniforms to take down the crime scene tape, and they called it in. Someone had trashed the place, but good. Maybe kids saw no one was home and broke in looking for things to sell for drug money. Could be a party but looked more like a search. Could have been his perp, but if so, what was he looking for?

Again, no one saw or heard anything.

Feeling cooped up inside, without a lead to follow, Andrews' mood darkened. Not that he was giving up, but maybe he needed a fresh perspective. Diaz was out sick today. Might as well give the newbie some practice.

He gave Singh, the new General Crimes Detective trainee, the file to read through. About an hour later, Singh came back over. Andrews had him pull up a chair on the other side of his desk, then went into teaching mode.

"So, what do we know?"

Singh, whose name meant lion in Sanskrit, had a face more like a small, chocolate kitten with big eyes. Leaning forward in his chair, he spread the file open on Andrews' desk and sat up straight. His first few weeks he worked with Latrell in Financial Crimes. This was his first Crimes Against Persons case. It was where he wanted to be, although he was sure his mother would prefer he continue working with numbers and computers. He hoped to be a Homicide Detective someday. Maybe in LA.

He'd read the file five times.

"Not much. Officially, she's a Jane Doe. Known as Lori Wright, but no ID was found and no one knows where she's from. Landlord said she paid cash, didn't have any trouble. If they know anything, her coworkers aren't sharing. Mostly undocumented workers, don't want any attention from ICE."

Andrews nodded. Most of the hotels and restaurants in town employed illegals on the bottom rung of the ladder. Only Juan's paid them a fair wage. Jasper wasn't a sanctuary city, but they left them alone as long as they didn't cause any trouble. It wasn't their job to do ICE's work for them.

Singh went on, "Female, Caucasian, small build, medium brown hair. Currently in ICU at Hoag. Still alive. Multiple injuries consistent with physical attack. No gunshot wounds. No bullets or casings found at the scene. Fingerprints, but no matches except neighbor, mother and child, and neighbor's neighbor, a Ben Halvard. He found her and called it in."

Looking Singh in the eye, Andrews asked, "Assault or homicide? How are we investigating this one?"

Crimes Against Persons handled both, so Singh hesitated.

"Homicide," Andrews filled in, "If she doesn't make it, it turns into a homicide. If you start out treating it that way, we've got a head start on the investigation. Those first few hours are critical. If we waited until it was official, we'd lose traction."

Andrews had seen the woman. The bastard really did a number on her. He hoped it didn't turn into a homicide, but he'd be ready if it did. He nodded toward the file, giving the junior detective back the floor.

Singh filled in more details, "Organic material, skin and blood found under several of her fingernails. All collected and stored properly. When . . ."

When, not if.

The boy was confident.

". . . we have a suspect, DNA could be matched. One unknown, male assailant, tall, thin, broad shouldered, dark hair. According to neighbor, who saw him get into the vehicle, driving a dark, possibly black, Jeep. Partial plates TZ2 . . . , light background, blue or black lettering. Probably California."

"Anything else?"

"Nothing more about the victim, but her young daughter may have witnessed the attack. Ran to a neighbor's house. Currently in temporary foster care. Neighbor," he glanced down at the open file, "Logan McKenna, female, forty-six, says mother self-reported child's age as three, birthday coming up soon, so nearer to four, but no verifying documentation found on premises for either child or mother. The child wasn't in school or preschool, so no records there."

He looked to Andrews for approval.

"And . . . ?"

"Well, we don't even know if our Jane Doe is the child's mother. She says she is, but could be a kidnapping," he added.

"Good," Andrews said, "Never assume. 'To assume makes an ass out of you and me.'"

That was one of his favorite quotes.

He rolled his chair a few inches away from his desk and looked at Singh, ticking off points on his fingers.

"Okay. We've got no family, no ID. Canvassed the neighborhood. No witnesses. No one saw anything except the one neighbor. Where would you start?" he asked.

"The little girl? There was nothing in the file about it, but with an experienced interviewer, I've read cases where the right interviewer was able to get good information out of a child witness-one as young as four. Even if it couldn't be used in court, it may provide a lead."

"You're right, we're on the list for that. The child psychologist on deck is backed up with court. Takes a while. What else?" Andrews asked.

"The partial plate. I'd see if any of the neighbors have a security cam."

"Good, but we checked. Nothing useful there," Andrews said, "None of them point in the direction of the house."

When Singh had no more to add, Andrews gave him his last bit of wisdom for the day. He normally didn't waste his time, but Singh was bright. He'd make a good detective someday.

"Criminals do what we do, Singh. Think about it. Before going to work, which in their case means committing a crime, they stop for gas. You need to have plenty of gas for the getaway, maybe get some cash from an ATM machine, go to the bathroom, buy some snacks. You prepare. So, the logical place to start looking for video is at any gas station in a five-mile radius of the crime."

Just then, his desk phone rang. Andrews answered and asked whoever was on the line to hold.

"Unfortunately, I took a look at these already. Video quality is okay, but no match for the partial. If he'd been there, we would have seen something."

Singh needed to know it wasn't easy. Took legwork. They'd keep chipping, something would shake loose. Andrews went back to his call, signaling lesson over to Singh, who returned to his desk.

"Where?" Andrews rose from his chair and scooped up his keys in one movement.

"Be there in ten." Finally, something to do. "Rookie, you're up!"

Might as well see how strong his stomach was.

38

Andrews pulled in behind the ambulance, then reached into the glove compartment for the digital camera and handed it to Singh. They got out of the car and started toward a gap between two houses that led to the beach. Andrews took the lead.

Slinging the camera strap over his shoulder, Singh kept up. He looked nervous. They picked their way down an uneven foot path next to a low, cement wall, which curved into a sea wall in the front of the house on the right. The path was unmarked. Unofficial beach access between two mid-century, glass-fronted homes.

A man Andrews knew was stooped over the body. Tyler Jacobs, the coroner. Jasper wasn't big enough to have a medical examiner. A uniformed patrol officer, probably first to arrive on the scene, stood a few feet downwind. From the house on the left, a neighbor, presumably the one who called it in, rushed frantically down the steps of his deck, where he had been asked to wait.

"I just saw him! He was just laying there! I just got home and went out onto the deck to check the waves. I looked down. I saw him. Right there! Was there a boating accident? I've been at work all day. I haven't heard anything. Do you know who he is?"

Andrews expertly deflected the man's insistent advances and asked him to wait inside, promising they'd be back in a few minutes to take his statement. The man did as he was told, but not happily. The detectives continued onto the small, crescent beach. The sand was harder here. And wetter. He wished he'd changed shoes.

"Hey Ty, what have we got?" Andrews asked.

A pale, blue-streaked, bloated, sodden body, garnished in dark green seaweed, lay face down in the sand at their feet. Black pants. Black, long-sleeved turtleneck sweater.

Funny wardrobe for as warm as it had been the last few days. "Male, Caucasian, about six foot, two . . ."

"How long?"

"Best guess: one or two days in, no gunshot or obvious stab wounds. Nothing visible, other than what you'd expect from being banged into rocks out there. Fish bites took their fair share. Can't tell anything much till I get him back on the table," the coroner answered.

Andrews reached down and removed a sodden, dark brown lump sticking out of the DB's back pocket.

"Let's see who our mystery player is," he said, handing the cheap, leather wallet to Andrews with gloved fingers, who was pulling on his own pair.

The uniformed patrol officer started a log of everyone entering and leaving the scene. Singh continued to observe and pulled out a small notebook to take notes.

"Everly, Neal . . . Seattle WA . . . thirty-four," Andrews read aloud after extracting a driver's license from the slot. He looked through the rest of it. "No credit cards or insurance cards. No personal pictures.

Thirty-four dollars in folding money," he read to Singh, who dutifully recorded the contents as Andrews read them off.

After bagging the wallet, Andrews looked down at the man, then at the surrounding area. Not a large beach. More of a cove. Pacific current ran south, which meant this guy went into the water north of here. Two days? Santa Barbara? Or could have died right here and just got snagged on something, held down for a while, then rose to the surface when it bloated, then washed in. Hard to tell.

After taking pictures, he and Singh did a thorough search, including digging through a pile of bulbous, smelly seaweed, but found nothing else related to their DB. Just sand crabs and screaming gulls, wanting a snack. Finally, as satisfied as he was going to get for now, he released the body to the coroner, who had his people load him up.

Probably just a tourist got drunk and fell off a boat. Nothing to connect what looked like an accidental death with any of his ongoing cases. Still . . . two violent assaults in one week in a small town . . . one definitely not accidental.

When they got back into their vehicle, he turned to Singh, who was still taking notes, "Run this guy through NCIC and see if anything pops. I'll sit on Jacobs and see if he can get any prints. Make sure the ID matches our vic."

He smiled at his own joke and rolled down the window. He couldn't make a connection yet, but his gut told him there was a connection. That familiar feeling of adrenaline starting to trickle into his veins. Things were moving. He pressed on the gas.

When they got back to the station, Diaz was there. Rocky from the flu, but feeling better. Andrews brought him up to speed while Singh went to his desk to make the phone calls and submit the name to the database. If Diaz felt territorial about Singh working their case, he didn't show it.

Within minutes, Singh was back over, printout in hand.

"Got a match on NCIC. If it's the same Neal Everly, he did three of a five-year sentence in Monroe. It's up near Seattle, WA. Out on parole."

"Who's his . . ." Diaz started to ask.

"Leo Rudowski," Singh read from, then handed Andrews, a piece of paper, "number's on there."

"Thanks, Singh," Andrews said.

Diaz's eyebrows shot up to his hairline.

"Don't worry, you were gone, he did a few things," Andrews said. If Diaz had issues with giving the rookie some practice, he needed to get over it.

"What makes you think they're connected?" Diaz said.

Andrews shrugged. "Don't know if they are. Either way, we're working both cases."

While Diaz called the coroner about the fingerprints, Andrews called the PO, who sounded surprised and more than that, sad, when he heard Neal was dead.

"That explains why he didn't show," Rudowski said, "Do you know what he was doing down there? What happened?"

"No, I was hoping you could shed some light on that," Andrews said.

"Doesn't make sense. He was done. Had his final check-in with me on Monday, would have been free as a bird after taking the paperwork to the judge. No way he would have missed that or risked going out of state two days before he was free and clear. He was one of the good ones. Kept his nose clean, stayed out of trouble," he said, "thought he was going to make it."

"What can you tell me about him?" Andrews asked.

The PO then summarized Everly's short, unfortunate life

from the notes in his file, and the little his PO knew of him from their initial conversation.

"Grew up in South Park, moved to Othello. Not much of an improvement. Crime rate's half again as high as the rest of Seattle. Single mom. Five kids. No abuse I know of, just not enough money or attention to go around. Still, only two out of the five kids have criminal records."

"What did he do?" Andrews asked, "for a living I mean— when he got out."

He knew all parolees must find gainful employment and keep it. There was a pause on the line as Rudowski looked up Garrett's last name and number.

"Drove for a family out in Lakeside. Delaney, Garrett. Want his number?"

"Yeah, address and numbers should do it for now," Andrews said.

Rudowski rattled off landline, cell and office numbers, said he'd copy whatever Andrews wanted from his file and send it over as soon as he could.

"What kind of driving did he do for Delaney? Take him back and forth to work, appointments, airport?" Andrews asked.

"No, just home stuff. He had him driving his family around— school, shopping, like that. Said it was a dangerous world out there," he said.

Just before Rudowski hung up, Andrews asked, "What kind of car did Neal have?"

"Didn't own one, had an old motorcycle to get around. I've got the license number in here somewhere. If you give me a minute, I'll find it."

"Okay . . . What'd he drive for Delaney?"

"Volvo."

Would have been nice if it'd been a black Jeep.

39

Logan didn't mention the flash drive to Ben when she picked him up. Even if she had, he probably wouldn't have remembered anything. He was still pretty woozy. So cute—all six feet of him wobbly on his feet. Logan smiled.

A male nurse helped Ben from the wheelchair into the car. Hospital policy. He told Logan inside that the operation had gone well, no complications. The patient just needed to take it easy, drink only liquids first, then eat only soft foods. After loading Ben into the front seat, making sure he was strapped in, he handed Logan a bag with multiple pieces of paper, encased in a large baggie.

". . . noodles, gelatin, applesauce, cottage cheese, pudding . . . absolutely no hot liquids and do NOT let him drink with a straw. You don't want him pulling out a blood clot and getting dry socket," he warned.

Logan wondered if she should cancel her flight and stay with him.

The nurse eyed her crutches tucked behind the front seats and raised his eyebrows at her, but said nothing. Instead, he commented on the car.

"Nice ride," he said, admiring Lola's curves, then, "Don't worry. Just follow the instructions. It's all in there. Call if you have any questions," he said, hurrying back inside to help the next patient. There were two people waiting.

Since it was a short trip, Logan took her car to pick up Ben. Six days of RICE and her knee was much better, so they were only along for backup. She left Purgatory at her house, not wanting to risk him pulling out stitches by launching all 145 pounds of Welcome Home in joyful abandon onto his master. Good decision. When they arrived home, Ben had to sit in a chair and let Purgatory lick his face for at least a full minute before he calmed down enough to be trusted to keep all four paws on the floor.

Logan stayed with him until 10:00 p.m. when his sister arrived, then drove Lola around the block, parked and dragged herself inside. What a day. She fed Dimebox and gave him a scratch behind the ears, enjoying the firm press of his body against her arm. He was grateful Mom was home. Dimebox usually cleared out whenever Purgatory was around.

But he was self-sufficient and Logan didn't worry about him out and about. Good thing cats were low maintenance. Bonnie said she'd feed and water "the monster" while she was out of town until Ben recovered sufficiently to take over.

○ ○ ○ ○ ○

9:30 a.m.

Portland Airport Enterprise didn't have the compact car she reserved.

Of course not.

Even though Rita generously footed her travel bill, Logan still shopped around and found a great deal on an economy car. She swore car rental companies did this just to make an extra buck. Suck you in with a deal and tack on the upgrade charge once you got there. Was that even legal? Legal or not, they knew travelers didn't have time to stand there and haggle; they'd just pay the difference, grab the keys, and get on with getting where they needed to go.

"I know it's not what you asked for, ma'am," he said, "but I've got a Hyundai Tucson, black. If you don't mind upgrading to a mini SUV, free of charge of course, it's ready to go."

Good things do happen to good people! Yeah!

She put all thoughts of suing Enterprise on hold. Signing the papers and collecting the keys before the guy could change his mind, Logan hoisted her computer bag onto her shoulder, pulled up the handle on her rolling bag, and headed for C5, only a few yards away, and one sharp right, from the customer service area. He was right. The parking area was empty except for the shiny Tucson.

Embarrassed she didn't know how to open the tailgate to put in her rolling bag, Logan had to turn around and go back inside to get help. She waited a few minutes for the last woman in line to be helped before the service rep was free to come out and show her the ropes. Lola was old school. Logan had so far been able to avoid learning the new stuff.

After clicking open the rear door, the young man loaded her bag in the back, and waited for her to get settled into the driver's seat and adjust the mirrors.

"Just keep your foot on the brake and press in the start button," he said, his tone of voice aiming for nonchalant, trying valiantly not to make her feel too stupid.

"Where does the key need to be?" she asked. Her dad always said it was better to look foolish for an instant and come away a wiser woman than look cool and remain ignorant.

"Oh, just anywhere nearby. You can keep it in your purse, drop it into the drink holder; you can even put it in your pocket. Just know that if you walk by the back door with the key in your pocket, the lift will automatically start going up. It's a great feature if your hands are full."

"What if I don't want it to go up?"

"Just press this section of the key," he showed her where.

He went on to demonstrate the hands-free calling feature, backup camera, and cruise control.

"Okay," Logan said. She never used cruise control. The backup camera was cool, but she was feeling grumpy and defeated by the rest of the new technology. She felt ninety. What was wrong with keys? Lola worked fine with a key. Key. Ignition. Put the key into the ignition and the car starts!

This was probably how her grandmother felt when they started making cars with electric windows instead of ones that rolled up and down with little, manual cranks. Realizing she was being curmudgeonly, she thanked the young man and practiced turning her car off and on before putting it in gear and heading downtown. It was only 10:30 a.m., but she was starved. Destination? Than's Pho.

Nothing a huge, hot bowl of beef noodle soup couldn't fix.

Traffic was light, so she decided to try the hands-free calling feature to check in with Ben. She glanced down at her phone to make sure Bluetooth was on. It automatically paired with the Tucson.

"Call Ben," she said, speaking slowly and at higher volume, like people do to the hard of hearing, or foreigners.

"Calling Ben," a pleasant, female voice lilted in response. Ben answered on the second ring.

"Hi, Beautiful! You make it in okay?"

He sounded much more coherent than he did last night when she tucked him into bed and kissed him goodnight on the forehead. They talked for a few minutes, then he said his sister was calling him for lunch. If he was upset about her not immediately embracing his desire to have a baby, he didn't let it show.

Good.

Logan wasn't ready to talk about that yet.

40

"**M**r. Delaney?"

"Yes?"

Andrews identified himself as the Crimes Against Persons Detective from Jasper, CA.

Garrett started to sweat. Jasper.

What was a Crimes Against Persons Detective? How much did the police know and why were they calling? He'd have to be very careful how he answered this guy's questions.

Even though the Detective couldn't see him, Garrett sat up straighter, then leaned back in his chair, the picture of relaxation and a man who had nothing to hide.

"Mr. Delaney, I am calling to check on the whereabouts of one of your employees, Mr. Neal Everly," Andrews stated. "Has he reported for work today or have you heard from him?"

Of course, Neal's PO would have him down as the employer. But that didn't explain how a Detective in Jasper even knew Neal Everly existed. Unless . . . Garrett's stomach did a flip. He thought he might lose his lunch.

There was only one explanation.

Neal's body must have washed up. He didn't see how that

was possible, but it must have or this Detective wouldn't be calling.

"No, he hasn't reported for work today," he said, "in fact, all week. I've been very concerned. He didn't show up Monday morning. I haven't seen or heard from him since last Friday."

"What about your family or other employees. Has anyone had any contact with Mr. Everly since you last saw him on Friday? Did anyone see him after you did? Have you or your family received any emails, phone calls, or personal visits?" Andrews asked.

"No, as I said, we have heard nothing from him," Garrett said, a defensive tone creeping into his voice. He decided to ad lib.

"He did mention something about wanting to visit family. We don't have any of his personal information. His parole officer would, I presume. It would have to be local family, of course, I don't know if you were aware, but Mr. Everly was on parole. They don't let them go out of state without previous permission. I don't know, maybe he had that. Have you checked with his parole officer?"

Andrews continued without acknowledging or answering Garrett's questions. "What was the exact nature of Mr. Everly's employment with you?"

"I did him a favor, really," Garrett said, sounding really put out now. "I try to give back to the community whenever I can. That'll teach me, right?"

"What did you hire him to do?" Andrews asked again, getting annoyed with this guy.

"He was just a driver," Garrett said.

"What kind of driving, Mr. Delaney?"

"I hired him to drive my family to and from appointments, school, errands, etc.," Garrett said.

"He was your chauffeur? Did he live on the premises?"

"No, nothing that formal. He lived on his own. Reported for work at the house by 7:30 a.m., then made himself available as needed during the day. Clocked out at 5:00 p.m."

"Has your wife heard from him?"

"No, of course not. He simply did the driving. He would have no reason to contact my wife. All contact was through me," Garrett added.

"Why would you hire a criminal to drive your family around, Mr. Delaney?" Andrews asked. "Doesn't seem the normal job candidate pool to pull from."

He wanted to rattle this guy's cage. Delaney was hiding something, Andrews just didn't know what.

"To be honest, I hired him before I knew he was on parole. I was at a social gathering, talking about how hard it was to find someone reliable who'd work on call for an hourly rate, and a business acquaintance told me about his driver. He was having to let him go because he was relocating. He gave him a glowing reference.

Later, when I found out Neal had a prison record, I called his parole officer and was assured Neal—Mr. Everly—was completely non-violent and had fulfilled all of his correctional obligations. Until this week, when he didn't show up for work, I would have given him a stellar review myself," he said.

This guy was almost too easy to needle.

Andrews continued in a crisp monotone, "Regardless, I'll need to speak with your wife, get the full names of your children and their schools. You never know, sometimes drivers get friendlier with the wife and kids than with their employer. I assume he was with them many hours every day."

Andrews let the innuendo dangle.

Delaney seethed, but kept a lid on it. How dare this asshole imply Lauren and Neal were 'friendly'!

"My wife is out of town right now, Detective, family camping trip. I'm supposed to join them this weekend. I'll have her contact you Monday," Garrett said. "But I doubt she has any pertinent information for you. Lauren's focused on taking care of the home and our daughter. I handle all the finances."

"Okay Mr. Delaney, I'll be in touch," he said.

Andrews wasn't buying any of this, but he didn't want to push this guy yet.

He'd get on a plane right now if the wife and daughter turned out to be Lori and Shannon. But there was a slim to zero chance of that. He couldn't be that lucky. If Delaney was Lori's husband and she ran away from him, she would almost certainly have changed her name, so there was a chance.

If it was them, then Delaney must have tracked them down somehow. This guy fit at least one trait of the typical spousal abuser: controlling male chauvinist, but Andrews knew he would need a lot more than loose connections, guesses and coincidences before he could take it to a judge and get a warrant.

On the other hand, the driver looked good for it. Ex-con, couldn't place him at the scene, but he was in town, not Delaney. He had the criminal record. Delaney could have sent the driver down to get his wife and daughter, but that didn't explain the beating, and it didn't fit the profile. Spousal abusers reached high rage in person. What reason would the driver have to put his employer's wife in the hospital?

No, it wasn't that simple. There was more going on here. He wasn't even sure the two cases were related. It would be a huge coincidence, but it's possible Neal Everly's death had nothing to do with his Jane Doe winding up in ICU at Hoag.

He itched to grill Delaney, but first, he needed to do his homework. Build a case. From the ground up.

As soon as they had enough, Andrews could coordinate with Seattle PD. Canvass the guy's neighborhood, workplace, get a search warrant for the driver's residence.

Until then, there was a lot they could do here. Diaz was back. They divvied up the legwork. Diaz would do the computer searches: Find out the full names of the wife and daughter, along with her maiden name. Get in touch with any relatives. Get their pictures, the number and type of vehicles this guy owned. Name of the school the child attended, any incidents, call outs to the home, etc. The woman going by the name of Lori Wright couldn't be matched to any pictures due to her facial injuries. They could do a preliminary search with approximate age, build, and coloring—but nothing definitive. The little girl's pictures should match, though. Even if she dyed her hair, they'd be able to tell if it was her.

Andrews reached for the phone. He needed to speak with Everly's parole officer again, see if he had a history of violence or abuse. Just because Delaney said he was clean, didn't mean he was. He also needed to run Delaney's name through every database they had and look into his hedge fund company. Andrews knew his limitations when it came to money beyond keeping his checking account from going in the red. The stock market, investing, that new thing, crypto-currency, they were equally foreign to him. He rationalized his ignorance. If he had any money to invest, he would learn about it, but that had never been much of a problem.

He'd see if Lutrell in Financial Crimes could walk him through the basics . . . enough to know what he should look for.

Andrews felt the first trickle of adrenaline in his veins. He didn't know which piece of evidence would unlock the puzzle, but he knew it was in there, buried amidst mountains of useless information.

And they were going to find it.

41

Logan found parking on Alder and crossed at the light to the food court. These two downtown blocks offered some of the best eating in Portland. Food truck heaven. Thai, Korean, Japanese, German, Korean, Chinese, Middle Eastern, gelato, donuts, coffee . . . the heavenly aromas were a daily offering to the culinary gods. If Martha Stewart had an altar, this would be her incense.

Logan headed for a small white truck, brand spanking new, tucked in between the Korean fusion truck on the corner and a kabob place on the other side. Huey had filled Logan in. After the insurance company finally paid up, Thanh was able to replace the old Airstream with a newer, larger truck, hire some help, and expand her menu. Still primarily a *Pho* truck, she now offered Vietnamese sandwiches, *banh mi*, and a wider variety of coffee drinks, including a thick, Syrian brew supplied by the proprietor of the kabob truck next door, a shy, handsome young man named Tamim. The fire that destroyed her original truck had started a fire that destroyed most of his as well. While cleaning up and refitting both sites, the two had been spending quite a bit of time together.

Lunch was just ramping up and Thanh finished taking an order at the front window, then passed it back to her new helpers. When she turned back, she caught sight of Logan walking up.

"Hey! Huey said you might come by," she said. "Don't tell me, beef *Pho* large, very hot—beef raw and on the side—right?"

Thanh had taught her how to order. By adding the thinly sliced beef medallions directly into the scalding broth, they cooked instantly and tasted much fresher than if they were added in first and then served.

"Yes! I'm starved. It smells so good, Thanh," Logan answered, her mouth watering. She grabbed a chair at one of the cafe tables and sat down. Even though there were double what there used to be, Logan knew from experience seating was scarce. Most had no space between their serving space and the curb. Thanh was in a great spot.

Another customer stepped forward, and then a group of four. Thanh took their orders quickly and efficiently, then motioned for someone to cover the window while she brought Logan's food out. "I added some *banh mi* for us," she said, joining Logan at her table, grabbing half a crusty baguette sandwich for herself. "We just started carrying these. I brought out a sampler. You'll have to tell me which ones you like."

Logan dug in. She didn't have to be asked twice, and had no trouble polishing off two of the sandwich samples in addition to her pho.

Thanh absolutely glowed with good health and happiness. Logan couldn't believe this was the same woman. When Huey introduced Logan to his sister, Thanh was deathly sick with Hepatitis C and in desperate need of a liver transplant. Days later, she lost her mother-in-law and only source of livelihood in the violent explosion of her food truck. As soon as he found out he was a good match, Huey came to the rescue and the operation was a success. Thanh spent the next two years mourning the death of her former mother-in-law, regaining her strength and health, and re-creating her business. Amazing woman.

Lunch rush in full swing now, Thanh needed to go back inside, but made Logan promise to stop by on her return trip and spend more time—maybe grab dinner out or find some live music. Paula's old roommate, Rheanna, dispatcher by day, singer by night, was always performing somewhere in town.

12:30 p.m.

Time to hit the road. Back in the car, Logan pointed the Tucson west and kept her fingers crossed. Portland traffic wasn't as bad as LA, or even Seattle, but sometimes it got close. Lunch hour and 5:00 p.m. rush were getting almost indistinguishable.

Accepting the diminished pace, Logan lowered her shoulders from around her ears, and gave Bonnie a call. How had she ever lived without Bluetooth calling? Bonnie's voice came through loud and clear from the speakers. She was in the teacher's lounge but stepped outside so she could hear. It was always loud in there.

Trapped in their classrooms all day, knowing they had only forty minutes to enjoy some adult conversation, not counting going to the bathroom, teachers talked up a storm to fit everything in before the bell rang. Then they all queued up at either the copy machine or the restroom to try to squeeze in one more item of personal business before their kids got restless in line or the principal noticed they were late.

"Hi, where are you?" Bonnie asked.

"Just outside Portland. Stopped by Thanh's for lunch," Logan said.

"How's she doing?" Bonnie asked.

"Great!" Logan said.

Knowing she only had a few more minutes, Bonnie got right to the point.

"Well, nothing much new happening here. Lori is still in the ICU. Shannon's fine, adjusting well—for now anyway. We all adore her and Haley is hooked. I don't think kids process time the way we do; she asks for her mom at night, but she's okay during the day," she said. "And how about you? Have you thought anymore about what Ben said?"

Bonnie had been the first person Logan called when Ben sprang his news on her.

"No, not really. I haven't had time. Maybe after I finish up with Huey and get to Rita's house out on the coast I'll be able to think it through," Logan said. "I don't know a soul out there and Rita swears there's nothing but ocean, beach and trees."

"That would drive me crazy, but it sounds perfect for you," Bonnie said.

Logan laughed. Bonnie wasn't happy unless she was surrounded by noise, juggling a gazillion projects in the air, while simultaneously bandaging a child's knee and talking on the phone. There was absolutely no white space on Bonnie's calendar.

Logan heard a familiar, insistent clanging in the background. She was so glad she didn't have to live her life by the bell anymore. She'd lasted only one year as a classroom teacher.

"Okay, gotta run," Bonnie said, "but I've got some information on that score for you. Just some things for you to think about. I'll fill you in later!"

And with that she was gone.

Logan wondered what ground Bonnie wanted to cover they hadn't already covered in their marathon phone call Monday night. Guess she'd find out later. For now, she was looking forward to getting to the New School and spending the rest of the afternoon ensconced in the computer lab with Huey. When she talked math and music, the rest of the world faded away. They'd work for a few hours. Dinner was promptly at 6:00. Students ate breakfast and lunch on campus in the large dining hall, but would all have been picked up by 4:00 or 5:00 p.m.

Logan looked forward to catching up with everyone. Glenda, an experienced herbalist, was Logan's old school nurse from Jasper. She was Logan's original contact at the New School, introduced her to Rita as well as Carla, the office manager who made killer oatmeal cookies the size of a dinner plate; G.I. Joe, homeless Vietnam vet turned master gardener; Nick, their talented chef; Brittany, the botanist and woodworker who jump-started the organic garden and designed the clever, movable chicken runs. Logan really loved the people Rita had attracted to her dream project.

Some people were missing, but not all were missed. Logan was sad to hear the Southern Gentleman, as they'd nicknamed Greg, a popular English teacher at the school, had moved on to greener pastures. Carla's lazy, surly, now ex-husband, left last year. Carla finally drop-kicked him to the curb.

Good riddance!

Taking the second turnoff after Red Barn Antiques and Fruit Stand, Logan soon found herself smoothly climbing up the gently winding road. She reached up and opened the sunroof, letting in the sibilant babble of Whisper Creek, and the heavily oxygenated and moisture-laden air. Up here in the Pacific Northwest, although the day was bright and sunny, the air was cool and it had rained earlier this morning, washing everything clean and green.

As always, when relaxed, Logan's thoughts turned to food.

She wondered what delicious repast Nick was whipping up for dinner tonight. Since today was a non-student day, he didn't have to make lunch for the kiddos. Maybe he would have more time to indulge his creative chef side.

With a will of its own, Logan's right foot responded to her subconscious request and pressed just a little harder on the accelerator. The Tucson didn't handle as well as Lola on the curves, but it had surprising power and, with the sunroof open, almost felt like a top-down ride.

42

Logan worked with Huey in the lab until 4:00 p.m. He had to leave then to attend a student's parent-teacher conference. This particular student was on an Independent Study Program. The talented young actor couldn't keep regular school hours due to filming obligations, which were often in LA or up in Canada.

With the use of some elegant, interactive technology, Huey helped his teacher and parents design a program that so far had worked well. He attended class when he was in town, so he continued to get plenty of socialization with his peers and completed other assignments remotely when he traveled. Initially, his parents were worried about him being college-ready, but so far, he was ahead of, not behind, the rest of the students his age. Huey said he seemed to be a balanced, well-adjusted kid, in spite of his unusual life.

Logan forgot to mention the flash drive to Huey before he left. It was still in her computer bag. Now she would have to wait until Sunday night to give it to him, when he returned from Portland.

For as long as she'd known him, Huey drove up every weekend to help Thanh out at the truck. Even though she didn't need him as often now as she used to, it was a tradition both were loathe to break. Huey got a three-day weekend out of it this time, because Rita and the board always scheduled a day off after every quarterly parent-teacher conference day. The New School had gone to an alternate schedule, spreading the school year out somewhere between a year-round and a traditional calendar. This helped with learning retention, but still gave kids two solid months off in the summer.

With no work to do and a couple hours to kill before dinner, Logan decided to take a short hike through the forest. There was a trail head not far from the small, Japanese foot bridge that arched over Whisper Creek. From the edge of campus, past the classrooms, garden, and art building, a well-worn, pine needle-strewn path led to the various faculty cottages, one of which was Glenda's, who Logan stayed with whenever she came up. She stopped off there first and got a sweater. Definitely cooler here than Jasper, particularly among the trees, where sunlight only shafted down between the branches sporadically.

When she stepped back out, a slight drizzle had started, so she added a rain shell to her ensemble and continued on. At the last minute, she stuffed the knee brace into her backpack. She didn't think she'd need it, her knee was almost 100%, but just in case.

"I'm washable . . . and dryable!" Logan said to no one in particular.

Don't quit your day job, Logan.

Brittany and Nick had taken Logan on this trail last summer. The minute she entered the trees, her mind quieted. The entire trail made a seven-mile loop up to a mini-waterfall and back, but today, Logan was only doing half of it. Just enough to stretch her legs before dinner. About a half-mile in, her knee reminded her she probably wasn't going to make it more than a mile before she needed to stop and rest. She slowed her pace and carefully placed each foot straight down on the path, avoiding twisting it on either side. Just a little farther . . .

Thanks to Brittany's flora and fauna tour guide bits, Logan knew she was in the midst of a Douglas Fir forest, one of twelve types of forests in Oregon. Douglas Firs were the state tree for a reason. Adaptable to many climates, the large conifers could be found up and down the state. Over half of the state was covered in forests, and 80% of conifers in those forests were Douglas Fir. They were not only the undisputed champions of the building industry for their stability and strength, but they were loved by tree huggers as an important habitat for nesting birds and other wildlife. Even dead and dying trees were valuable. Called snags, left upright to decay naturally, Brittany said they provided habitat for over a thousand species of wildlife nationally.

Logan just knew they were beautiful. Particularly now, in the fall, the turning leaves of the oaks and maples put on a good show. Not all had turned, but around almost every bend in the path, Logan could see rounded bursts of red, yellow, and orange, creating a counterpoint to the rich, deep greens of pine and fir. So different from the dusty scrub oak that dotted the yellow and brown hills of Southern California. Of course, that was her home and So Cal had the ocean. The Pacific was quite a consolation prize. In Logan's mind it wasn't a contest. She appreciated both.

Logan closed her eyes and listened. Ignoring her throbbing knee, she hoped to hear some owls, and strained to hear their easily recognizable calls, but it was still several hours until sunset. Probably have to wait until after dinner. She often heard them at one spot on the way back to Glenda's cabin. Ubiquitous stellar jays and crows took up the audio slack with their raucous chorus, almost drowning out Whisper Creek. She even heard a woodpecker deeper in, but didn't see him.

For a while, she simply lost herself in the surround sound of the forest—the thrum of hummingbird wings, the occasional hoarse bark of a gray squirrel—all cushioned by the soft, rustling branches as the wind pushed through the trees and playfully ruffled the low-lying shrubs. A thick, sunny patch of wild blackberries tumbled along the bank of Whisper Creek.

Logan wondered if bears liked berries. Hopefully not. Cartoon bears liked them. Hopefully not real ones. Not wanting to give into the fear of Ursus Americanus, Logan made herself walk a few minutes farther, then found a comfortable hillock of reasonably dry moss, sat down and rubbed her knee, straightening it to make sure it still worked, then dug her water bottle out of her jacket pocket. Even on a short hike, Logan knew to bring water and a high-calorie snack.

She pulled open the top with her teeth and took a long pull, then reached in for the half-eaten Payday bar she knew was in there somewhere. She had carefully folded over the end of the wrapper so it wouldn't gather pocket lint. All good. She tore off a big bite. The peanuts were salty, the caramel, sweet and chewy, the water, still cold. Hit the spot.

Logan was glad she thought to bring the knee brace. She'd pull it on for the return trip. The creek was louder here. Wet twigs and leaves created a kind of temporary dam along the spine of a fallen branch. For a while, Logan sat mesmerized by the swirls and eddies. One or two leaves, not yet water logged, floated downstream.

Thoughts she had pushed to the back of her mind while working forced their way to the surface. She wondered how Lori was. What was going to happen to Shannon if her mom didn't make it? Was there anything on that flash drive that would help Lori? It felt like a land mine.

Her thoughts continued to drift. What was she going to do about Ben?

A child. What would it be like to have a child now? Sitting right here, next to her. Showing him the leaves, the water, the sky. Maybe he would play an instrument. She suddenly realized she thought of this probably-never-going-to-exist-child as a boy.

She'd loved showing Amy the world—running in the park, teaching her how to dive into the waves, and what to do if you got caught in a rip tide. 'Don't fight it, let it carry you out, then swim parallel to the shore until you can swim back in.' But there was so much more she would do now. She'd be more relaxed. And not so busy. She and Jack worked long hours when they started their computer training business. Sometimes all she managed with Amy was a bedtime story and a tuck in before lights out. Not a lot of long, rambling nature walks in the afternoon. Of course, Fractals took time, too, but in its third year, with Rita's financial support, was running pretty smoothly. And Logan knew how to manage her time better in her forties than she did in her twenties.

And Ben. Ben would be a great father. She'd seen him with his nephews. Kids and dogs loved Ben. He was fun, but he wasn't just a buddy to them. He set boundaries. He made his nephews do chores and made sure their homework was finished before letting them run down to the beach. And he had the patience of Job with her. Logan knew she wasn't an easy woman to be in a relationship with sometimes. Yes, Ben passed all the tests.

But did she? Even if the spirit was willing, the flesh was weak. She may feel thirty-five, but her physical body had logged closer to forty-five years. Was it selfish to try to have a baby at her age? What were the chances there would be complications for the fetus?

Her sciatica gave her left, big toe a stab, reminding her it was time to get moving. Logan wished all her body parts would cooperate at the same time. She thought of all the years she carelessly threw her body around in swimming and sports, with never a thought that someday she'd have to be careful with it. Youth is indeed wasted on the young.

That was the other concern. The car accident had left Logan with neck and back injuries. With exercise and some caution, she could almost function normally now, but what would a pregnancy do to her? Would she be able to carry a baby full term without winding up in a wheelchair? Her doctor had warned her not to take up skiing or golfing, any activities that would put a strain on her back. There was always a danger of rupturing a lumbar disc. Logan wondered what she would have to say about her patient possibly procreating?

No sense having a baby if you couldn't take care of him or her as they grew up. She could check with doctors, but Logan already knew no doctor was going to give her a 100% green light.

Whatever she decided, there would be no guarantees.

Feeling chilled, Logan shelved her worries for now and looked at the sky. Her knee had stiffened up considerably. A hike, even a short, easy one, was probably not the best choice of activities post knee-injury. The sun was still out, but the temperature was dropping. She stood up, rubbed her arms, and shook out her leg to get her knee to pop and the blood circulating before putting on her brace for the return trip. She probably shouldn't have pushed it, but she rationalized the hike with the mantra her doctor had given her, 'Healing takes place in the presence of motion,' and headed back to the cabin to get ready for dinner.

43

Dinner, as always, was perfect. Nick liked to stretch his wings on the weekends, when his meal didn't have to fit into the narrower dietary preferences of kids or a lunch hour. He could also add wine. Pork roast, caramelized onions, scalloped carrots, spinach salad, piles of French bread, and several bottles of white to sample: a fruity Pinot Gris, two toasty Chardonnays, and a crisp, fresh Viognier. For dessert, Nick served his fall specialty, Baked Apples. GI Joe, who now helped in the kitchen as well as the garden, made the hand-churned vanilla bean ice cream. Even after stuffing herself with dinner, Logan polished off the entire walnut and raisin stuffed Rome apple topped with a generous scoop of ice cream. The comforting aroma of cinnamon and perfect balance of hot and cold in each bite almost made her swoon.

When Nick informed her there were only five ingredients, Logan asked for the recipe. Even a non-cook like her could handle five ingredients. She'd have to buy the ice cream, but it would be close enough. Ben would be impressed. Bonnie would faint.

It was past 9:00 p.m. before anyone made a move to leave.

The last week caught up with Logan all at once. She could barely keep her eyes open. Glenda needed to talk with Rita about getting some time off for a book talk and workshop she was giving in Chicago. Her new *Herb Bible* continued to be a real hit. Since almost no one lived on farms anymore, or even had large yards, her newest edition included pictures and instructions for vertical and indoor herb gardens, which were becoming all the rage. It didn't hurt that a popular TV show often showcased creative, indoor, herb-planted displays in their remodeling reveals.

After thanking Nick again for the great meal, Logan let herself out the back door, stepping carefully down each step to the ground. The small stoop leading to the garden was one item that hadn't been upgraded yet. Wi-Fi had been, though, so Logan pulled out her phone to call Bonnie. She'd save her call to Ben for later. She loved to hear his warm, gruff voice just before dropping off to sleep.

"Hi," Bonnie answered.

"Am I calling at a good time?" Logan asked. "Figured I'd wait until the kids were all in bed."

"Yep, they're all fed, watered, brushed, and bathed," Bonnie said, "Haley's in there reading a bedtime story to Shannon."

Logan didn't ask about Mike; she knew this was one of his station days. A fireman, he worked a typical twenty-four on, forty-eight off schedule.

"How's she doing?" Logan asked.

"Shannon?" Bonnie asked.

"Yeah, how's she holding up? Has she asked anymore about her mom?"

"Just at night. That's why Haley gives her so much attention then. She seems to be satisfied with the vague answers we're giving her, although I'm not sure how long that will last."

"Any more news on that end? Has Lori come out of it yet? Has anyone seen or talked with her?" Logan asked, thinking of the flash drive in her computer bag.

"They won't tell me anything because I'm not family, but I was talking to Paula this morning. She stopped by to look at some fabric samples I pulled for her couch. She's redecorating the living room at Rick's . . ."

"Yes, I know. It's nice of you to help her with that," Logan interrupted, trying to get her friend back on track. "What did she say about Lori? Has she seen her?"

"No, but she overheard your Detective Andrews talking on his cell in the parking lot, and it sounds like she's conscious, anyway. Don't know what shape she's in. Oh! I forgot to tell you, I bumped into Iona the other day."

It was almost impossible to keep Bonnie on point.

". . . You won't believe it—I hardly recognized her!" Bonnie continued.

"What do you mean?" Logan asked, curious now.

"I don't even know where to start, Logan. No more penciled in eyebrows—she did some kind of soft, feathered thing. Her eyebrows are naturally blonde or white, not sure, but she didn't do that whole harsh, dark brown, upside-down frown thing she usually does. And her hair! The beehive is gone! She got it cut short! Don't know if her hair is naturally curly, but she has a kind of layered cut that really brings out her eyes. Wardrobe's pretty much the same, but her lipstick doesn't scream at you anymore."

"Wow! Did you take pictures?" Logan asked.

"I was too stunned," Bonnie replied, "But I did compliment her. I mean, you couldn't just ignore it—I had to say something!"

Bonnie took a breath.

"She said she had a makeover at the mall," Bonnie said, "'Time for a new look,'" she said!"

"Double wow," Logan said. She had a hard time picturing Iona Slatterly walking into a luxury department store. They must have shit their pants when she walked up to the counter.

"Her wardrobe's about the same—same skin-tight jeans and western, long-sleeve blouses, even in the summer," Bonnie said, "but, I gotta say, she looked ten years younger and pretty. She said Taylor was teaching her to play guitar."

"Good for her. I guess an old dog can learn new tricks, Logan said.

"Good for her!" she repeated, feeling ancient.

If Iona could change her life . . . But a makeover wasn't as drastic a change as having a baby. Big difference.

They talked another few minutes, then Logan finally got the conversation turned back to Lori, but Bonnie didn't have much to add. Paula hadn't talked with Lori, just knew she had gained consciousness and might be moved out of the ICU soon.

When she reached Glenda's cabin, Logan disconnected the call and let herself in. A warm, grassy aroma greeted her. Glenda's custom blend of herbs she called "Bedtime Tea" sat steeping in two large mugs.

"Thought you might be coming in soon," she said, "These will be ready in a minute."

Glenda was big on giving herbs time to sit in the hot water long enough for the full flavors and medicinal benefits to be extracted from them.

Glenda had finished her business with Rita and made it back to the cabin before her, while Logan was talking with Bonnie on the phone.

They visited for a while, enjoying the tea with a dollop of

New School honey Glenda always kept at the ready, then Logan said good night and took a hot shower before pulling on her pajama bottoms and a long-sleeved t-shirt.

Glenda kept extra blankets and quilts at the foot of the bed for her. Logan liked to sleep with the windows open, even when the temperature dropped. Fresh air was essential.

Once she was snuggled in, she pulled her favorite quilt, an abstract, log cabin design, up under her chin and looked down at the slender sections that made up each block. Glenda made it for her Mom when she had lung cancer. Using only black, white, and cream fabrics, both solid and print, the design chronicled her mother's journey from pain of a rough childhood, to peace as an adult. It also expressed the easing of her mother's physical pain to 'celestial rest' as Glenda put it. The bottom left corner was all black fabrics, slowly transitioning to all white fabrics in the final quilt block in the upper right corner. Every time she looked at it, Logan saw something new.

Ben was expecting her call. Just the sound of his voice made Logan feel loved. After they hung up, Logan's eyelids grew heavy and she started to drift into sleep, but every time she reached the edge, thoughts of Lori, Shannon, and the flash drive popped into her mind and pulled her back. She thought of all the possibilities: incriminating photographs, kiddie porn, the location of secret truffle hunting spots? State secrets??

What was on that thing?

44

Friday was spent in one of Logan's least favorite activities: paperwork. Fractals came with a bundle of it. Rita was generous, but a real stickler for supporting documentation. She understood, and Logan was learning, that most donors weren't like the generous, trusting Mrs. Hauser. They didn't just fund your grant, then wave goodbye and assume all would be well. They wanted to know where every dime of their money went and if it was being used not only honestly, but as efficiently as possible, for the intended good. And did it work? What were the results?

You had to know your donor. Corporate donors often gave not out of the generosity of their hearts, but for good publicity and a tax write-off. They wanted to see splashy projects that got on the news. Rita screened her donors and didn't accept money from some of the greedier ones, who were looking for good press to cover bad deeds. She wanted nothing to do with them, no matter how much money they dangled.

Most of Fractals' donors were hard-working individuals, families, and small businesses who wanted to give back or simply use their money to support organizations they felt made the world a better place. Logan didn't mind explaining herself and her program to these donors.

No matter the motive, all donors needed detailed proof of where the money they gave went, and how that money was used. Each grant had its own specific requirements. Rita had Carla set up a Gantt chart for Logan to keep it all straight. It listed each donor, the grant amount, and all tasks to be completed, with accompanying costs, which tasks were dependent on other tasks being completed first, and due dates for projects and reports. All color coded. It was a work of art. Carla, a fast learner, was becoming an invaluable member of Rita's team.

Today, Carla was showing Rita and Logan how to pull subsets of information from the raw data for the written reports. It was a slog, but they got through it. When Carla left to finish her own work, Rita stood up and stretched, then gave Logan directions to Little Whale Cove, where she would be staying for the vacation part of her trip.

"Your GPS should work, but here's a map for you just in case," Rita said, opening the paper drawer on the printer, pulling out a blank sheet, then popping the drawer shut.

"It's about twenty minutes south of Lincoln City. After you leave your friend's place, just turn south. Watch out for the speed changes as you enter Depoe Bay. It's twenty-five miles per hour in town and they enforce it. Don't blink, or you'll miss it. Park across from the shops on the ocean side, next to the sea wall and get some whale watching in. This time of year, you should see some up close.

There's a whale watching center you can stop in at the end of town near the bridge. There's usually someone there who can tell you more if you're interested. Kind of a hexagon, the white building on the right. Everything's within walking distance. Gracie's Sea Hag is a good stop for lunch or dinner. She makes a killer Cioppino. Well, Gracie's not there anymore, but her kids keep the quality and service up."

"Is your place in Depoe Bay?" Logan asked.

"Technically, yes. The address says Depoe Bay, but we're about a half-mile out of town. Keep going over the bridge and look for a low, blue, wooden sign on your right that says Little Whale Cove. You turn in front of it. Takes you right in."

Rita reached into her pocket and handed Logan a clicker and a set of keys.

"It's gated, so use this. If for any reason it doesn't work, check with the community manager at the gatehouse. I let her know you're coming. She'll let you in. Name's Diane," Rita said. "Big key is for the house, 75 Cedar Way, the little one is for the mail. We're A17."

Logan pocketed both clicker and keys, thanking Rita again for the use of her house next week.

"My pleasure, Logan. We don't get to use it as much as we'd like. Sits empty half the time," Rita said. "Take advantage of the trails—they've got over twelve miles of them throughout the forest and along the bluff. We pay for all of them, so you might as well use them.

Oh," she said, going back to her desk to retrieve a white, rectangular piece of hard plastic, handing it to Logan, "Here's the keycard for the clubhouse. There's a pool and jacuzzi in there.

"There are basics in the freezer and out in the garage are canned goods, but you'll want to stop at Thriftway on your way into Depoe Bay for fresh groceries. For big shopping, we go into Newport or Lincoln City. Just throw away what you don't use and take it to the trash. There are recycling directions on a piece of paper on the fridge. Our trash bins are across from the clubhouse."

Logan's brain was approaching overload.

"Don't worry, wrote it all down here on the map," Rita smiled, handing it to her.

Logan spent the rest of the weekend polishing her reports, triple checking the figures. Satisfied with her results, she took a well-deserved nap. Actually, she never slept, just read a few more chapters on her Kindle, then took a short wake-up shower, arriving at the dining hall just as everyone was gathering. She was getting to know the faculty better, enjoying a discussion of the link between Visual Arts and Music with the woman in charge of the art department, when Huey came in. She removed the jacket she'd thrown over the seat on her right so he could sit down.

When the art director got up to get one of the craft beers peeking out of a small tub of ice, Logan took the opportunity to fish in her pocket for the flash drive she put there earlier.

"Before I forget," she said as she handed it to Huey. He took it and said, "What's this?"

She gave him as much information as she could, which wasn't much.

"I didn't see anything when I looked, but could there be something on it?"

"The short answer is yes," Huey said, "but depending on what they used, it may take some time. I'll try the usual, low-level approaches, but if they don't work—if someone really wanted to hide something on here and knew what they were doing—I'll have to get some help. I know someone with the programs I'd need— and the expertise. Is it okay if I share this with him if I can't find anything?"

Logan hesitated.

"Can you trust them? I don't want to get Lori into any trouble," Logan said.

"Well, let's hope I can get into it. If not, I think we're safe with this guy. People who know how to get into things they shouldn't are not the type to report anyone else's questionable activities," he smiled.

Huey slipped the flash drive into his shirt pocket as the art director sat down to resume her conversation with Logan. GI Joe clanged a triangle he'd hung by the kitchen window and everyone trooped up to fill their bowls, cowboy style. In addition to becoming a master gardener, Joe also started keeping bees. His honey butter was a hit on the cornbread.

Just when she thought she couldn't eat another bite, Joe fired up the BBQ and grilled fresh peaches for dessert, topped with the rest of his vanilla bean ice cream.

45

By 9:00 a.m. Logan was on the road to Lincoln City. Both she and the Tucson were full. Breakfast for Logan was leftover grilled peaches on waffles, topped with whipped cream, with plenty of high-octane coffee. The Tucson had to settle for regular gas. Made Logan glad she wasn't a car.

Traffic was light. Most people were heading the other direction, back to Portland, after enjoying a weekend on the coast. About five miles out, she took a sharp left to merge onto Highway 18, which took her through open country. She stopped for a bathroom break at Spirit Mountain Casino in Grande Ronde. The place was huge. Nothing else around. People must drive here specifically to gamble. It amazed Logan that anyone would want to sit in front of a slot machine in a stuffy room, throwing away money.

Just before Highway 18 merged onto the 101, the trees got closer together, until she was passing through a lush tunnel of green she later learned was called the Van Duzer corridor. It was gorgeous, but she wouldn't want to get stuck driving it on a foggy night or in a storm.

She was meeting Rose at her shop around 10:30. Stretching seven miles along Highway 101, Lincoln City, like most cities along the coast, had no town center to speak of. It was more of an extended wide spot in the road, created as businesses and homes sprouted up on either side of the highway. Premium real estate was on the ocean side. There was a cluster of tourist shops and restaurants between North 21st and 14th Street that looked like a downtown, but the shops were only one building deep, all facing the road.

Still, as she drove slowly south on 101, Logan liked what she saw. An old Art Deco theater called The Bijou, several antique stores, an upscale newer store called Prehistoric, fronted by a mechanical T-Rex. She almost missed it, but spotted Rose's place, Coastal Threads, two doors south of the Bijou, on her left, next to a store sporting pirate hats and t-shirts advertising last summer's kite festival.

Fifteen minutes after ten, the Tucson's GPS informed her she'd arrived at her destination. She pulled into an available parking spot and went to feed the meter, but was surprised to see there weren't any. Awesome. Crossing the street at the light, she stopped to admire the wooden loom, mid-project, Rose had in her window. A large, wooden bowl overflowing with skeins of thick, natural yarns sat at the foot of the loom, next to a plaque that read, "Those who weave in summer are warm in winter."

People must have taken the sign at face value, because Coastal Threads had more customers than either of the neighboring shops, other than Prehistoric across the street. T-Rex was a big draw. A brother and sister squealed with delighted fright as they scurried past the monster into the store, parents in tow.

Logan stepped aside for two women with full bags of yarn and various knitting or weaving implements as they exited past her onto the sidewalk. Silver bells chimed melodically when Logan pushed open the door and let herself in. Recessed lighting highlighted one wall of shelves, displaying natural fibers and yarns arranged by color family. Hanging Tiffany lamps created a soft interior glow over stacked display tables scattered here and there with artful arrangements of hats, scarves, sweaters and baby clothes. Abstract weavings hung along the wall behind the long checkout counter on the right.

Tucked into the back, right-hand corner was a well-lit table and work area where some women worked on individual projects, several of them Christmas stockings. This seemed odd, but then again, Logan realized you must have to start early if you made your gifts and wanted them all done by the holidays. A tall, skinny woman hoisted a bulging tote bag on her shoulder and pushed in her chair. The rest were gathering their things, following suit.

Behind the counter, Rose, an imposing forest goddess clad in a linen tunic and loose pants, luxuriously draped in sage-green and taupe scarves, looked up from helping a customer. Her hazel eyes sparkled when she saw who had entered. Sturdy and straight, crowned with cinnamon and silver curls, Rose always reminded Logan of a towering redwood.

"You made it! Open workshop is just ending," Rose said over her departing customer's head. "Let me finish up here. I'll kick these lagging ladies out," she winked back at the group in the work area, obviously old friends. "Then I'll lock up and we can go get some lunch."

Logan browsed while Rose finished cleaning up. It took her host longer than a few minutes, as she graciously stopped to help one woman untangle a mess she'd made of her project and get her back on the right track.

"You'll finish it in plenty of time, Ronnie!" she said as she clapped the woman on the back, thus pushing her toward the door. "Your daughter's going to love it!"

This whole world was foreign to Logan. She complimented Rose on the samples that filled the store.

"These are beautiful, Rose. Amy would faint dead away if I ever tried to do anything crafty like this," she said.

Rose bristled slightly, "We prefer the term Textile Arts. Hopefully we're a step above popsicle sticks and pot holders."

Properly chastised, Logan changed the subject, asking Rose about current projects. As soon as they were seated at the Grilled Eggplant, a vegetarian restaurant a few doors down, and their orders taken, Logan filled Rose in on the news of their mutual friends, Thomas and Lisa Delgado, who introduced them originally. Rose participated as one of the guest artists at the Otter Arts Festival every summer.

"How's Lisa? Still in remission?"

"Doing great last I saw. Amazing difference. She gives her aunt all the credit for her current remission," Logan said, taking a big bite of her Greek salad. Lisa's aunt was an herbalist and Native American healer specializing in cleansing ceremonies.

Rose took a bite of her *souvlaki*, which looked delicious. "I'll bet none of those treatments are covered by insurance, either."

She emphasized her point by stabbing her fork at Logan, "They never cover anything that actually works! Those insurance companies have it all wrapped up. Big Pharma keeps tight control over their profit margins."

She took a sip of cucumber iced tea, then said, "Are you registered to vote, Logan? You'd better be. No one can afford to sit this one out."

Not waiting for an answer, Rose continued, "You've got to feel the Bern!"

"I'd like to vote for a woman," Rose continued, "but Hillary's just more of the same. We need a public health option, a single-payer system. Bernie sings a one-note song, but I like his music!"

She laughed at her own joke.

"Hillary will probably win, but even so, she's already adjusting her platform to accommodate us. We lefties mean business! We won't settle for status quo anymore!"

"Who are you voting for?" Rose asked. Not a shy woman.

"I haven't decided yet," Logan replied, truthfully.

She sure as hell wasn't voting for The Donald. She couldn't believe the things he had been taped saying about women — was he just a side show? She was surprised he'd made it this far, but she wasn't crazy about the other two options, either. So far, the debates were a circus . . . everyone repeating the same canned position statements, no matter what questions were asked of them.

Why was there never a candidate she could get excited about? Where were the educated, intelligent, experienced and honest men or women who spoke from the heart and weren't bought and paid for by corporate lobbyists? Not one candidate truly represented her. It seemed by the time they worked their way up to become candidates, they were already part of the very system they needed to change.

When the waitress brought the dessert menu, Rose ordered a strawberry and ganache-topped, rich chocolate brownie, finished with a generous dollop of whipped cream. Since she had more driving to do anyway, and no schedule to keep for the next few days, Logan got a double espresso with some baklava.

Promising to visit both Bernie's and Hillary's websites . . . Rose was open minded and wanted to make sure Logan looked at both the liberal candidates; she didn't count Stein . . . Logan flagged the waitress down and tried to pay her part of the bill. Rose snatched it up and insisted it was her treat. Logan said she'd return the favor when she came back through town.

She was suddenly anxious to get to Rita's house and be alone. Rose was wonderful, as was everyone at the New School, but she was all caught up and wanted nothing more than her own company for a few days.

She had a lot to think about, what with Ben's surprise revelation. He hadn't given her any ultimatums or set a time limit, but nature had. Any eggs she had left were nearing their expiration date.

They walked back toward the shop and Logan clicked her car door open and got in, an old salt at keyless entries now.

"Don't forget to stop by on your way back to the airport," Rose said, bending down so Logan could see her through the driver's side window.

Without making any promises, Logan nodded and said she would if she could, then backed out and pulled onto Highway 101, waving goodbye in the rearview mirror.

46

Detective Andrews took off his jacket, hung it on the back of his chair, and sat down. Three more cases landed on his desk this morning. He just came back from grabbing lunch off the taco truck.

Diaz was all but dancing out of his chair. He hung up the call he was on.

"It's them!"

He flipped his screen around so Andrews could see what he was looking at.

"Say hello to our Jane Doe, Lauren Alicia Delaney and her three-year-old daughter, Shannon Katherine Delaney. Wife and daughter of one Mr. Garrett 'Dirtbag' Delaney."

He smiled smugly. "Just verified it with a sweet widow lady named Mrs. McCluskey, next door neighbor to the Delaney's. Oh, and not a big fan of the father."

Andrews looked hopeful. He wanted this guy.

"Don't get excited—nothing specific, just a feeling she has about him," Diaz explained.

"How'd she see the pictures? We haven't sent anything up to Seattle PD yet," Andrews asked.

VALERIE DAVISSON

"The old dearie is surprisingly computer literate. Has a Facebook page to keep in touch with her granddaughter. I just uploaded a couple photos the social worker sent over of the little girl, described our Jane Doe. Mrs. McCluskey opened them on her end." He tapped the screen with his pencil. "No hesitation at all. Says it's them. Says she hasn't seen either of them for months. That fits."

Another piece of the puzzle just fell neatly into place. It was coming together. They had Garrett's wife on the run, presumably from Garrett. Andrews was sure they'd find ER records now that they had a name. That would establish a pattern of behavior, if not motive, for this attack. The little girl seemed unharmed, they couldn't get him on that, but maybe he just hadn't gotten around to smacking her around yet.

He mentally ticked off the list. Wife was a runner. They had his driver washed up dead in the same town where she gets beat half to death. Strong coincidence. Lots of circumstantial evidence. No eye witnesses of the attack. Except the victim, of course, if she ever regained consciousness. Just Logan McKenna's brief glimpse of the guy hightailing it out of there. Hadn't found the car yet.

Not enough.

Since it would be a felony charge, if they could get an arrest warrant, they could force him to do a cheek swab. The DNA would clinch it. They still had the tissue from under the assault victim's fingernails under lock and key. If they could get a match—game over! In the meantime, they had enough for a search warrant. Andrews grinned and grabbed his jacket from the back of his chair, putting it on as he flew down the hall.

"See what you can find on the ER visits. Keep digging," he said over his shoulder. "And have Singh go over that CCTV footage again. We need to place that asshole there that night. We need that Jeep."

226

47

"**F**ractals, student speaking," a cheerful, teenage voice answered the phone.

A Google search for Logan McKenna quickly yielded quite a bit of information on Lauren's neighbor. One of the first listings was an article on the new Music/Math program, Fractals, the Tilcott school district had launched, with a Logan McKenna as the Director. Including contact information. Still, he needed to double check.

"Yes, Mr. McNamara here," Garrett said, "Lloyd McNamara. Is Logan McKenna available? Is she still the Director of a student program called Fractals?"

If they put him through, he could always hang up.

"Yes, Ms. McKenna runs things around here," the student said, obviously enamored of the woman. "She started the whole program. She's awesome, but she's not here right now. If you want to talk with her, she'll be back Monday. Want me to take a message?"

It sounded like the boy was scrabbling around for something to write with and on.

"No, I don't think that would work. We're on kind of a

deadline here. We really need to get in touch with her".

"Well, I don't think I'm supposed to give out that kind of information," he said.

Garrett tried another tack, "I understand your hesitation, and respect your loyalty . . . what was your name?"

"Brandon, Brandon Lancaster."

"Well, Brandon, this is the situation," Garrett said, clearing his throat for effect, going for the landed gentry tone — authoritative, but not condescending. Kids were easily impressed.

"We're considering giving Ms. McKenna a lot of money for Fractals. More than she asked for in her original grant request. It's between her program and another, very worthy one. The board is meeting now. If I can't get in touch with her in the next hour or so, to sign the adjustment, I'm afraid we're going to have to fund the other program instead of yours. Do you know where I can find her?"

He paused. 'Yours' was a nice touch. Made the boy feel it was his personal program that was on the line here, unless he could tell him where his mentor was.

"I promise not to share Ms. McKenna's whereabouts or contact information with anyone," he added, "of course."

"Of course," Brandon said, "I can't give you her cell phone number or anything like that, but I can tell you she's up at The New School in Oregon. Here, I'll get their number."

He repeated the number twice, then said, "Oh, well, She was there, but she might not be there now. She went on vacation to the coast—I wish I was there—I hear they have some awesome waves . . ."

Garrett cut him off. He didn't have time for this surfer boy's jabbering.

"Do you have an address for her there?" he asked.

"Well, not an address, but I know she's staying at Rita

Wolfe's house for a few days. Like I said, she said she'd be back here Monday at the latest, so she should still be there."

"Where is there, Brandon?"

It took all Garrett had to keep his cool. He was so close.

"Uh, she said it's a ways south of Lincoln City, about a half hour. Deep Pot Bay . . . something like that," he continued, wanting very much to be helpful and help get the grant. He wasn't sure how grants worked, but he knew without them, the program would fold.

With subdued glee, Garrett jotted down the address and disconnected the call, then pulled up Google Maps.

Deep . . . Dep . . . Ahhh! Depoe Bay, 12.2 miles south of Lincoln City. Right on the beach. There it was.

Next cyber stop was an online property records search for anything owned by Rita Wolfe. He used one of those fee-for-service search sites, but it was worth it. Within the hour, he sat looking at an address, a plat map, and the top of the roof of a little house hemmed in by a bunch of trees.

75 SW Cedar Way, Depoe Bay, OR.

From there, he got the land line number. Then he entered in his own address in Google Maps in Directions. Five and a half hours there, five and a half back. An hour to get the job done. It would only take a day. No one would know. He'd tell Patricia he was working from home tomorrow. He could take her calls on the road, say he was driving in town, visiting clients, taking a lunch break, doing errands.

Get ready, Ms. Logan McKenna. You've got company coming!

48

Highway 101 was the wild cousin of the Pacific Coast Highway back home. Both hugged the ocean, but PCH in Southern California was much tamer, broader. More used to people. Edged with palm trees, upscale shopping malls, clay rooftops, suburban homes, and adobe missions, sandy beaches dotted with sunbathers and volleyball courts stretched to where surfers rode the waves. Other than sand, nothing natural remained. Every square inch of Southern California was developed.

Highway 101, on the other hand—at least this stretch of it in central Oregon—was a narrow ribbon of road carved into dense, green forest, sprinkled with dramatic ocean vistas around every winding curve. The ocean here was fiercer, younger, and more ancient, all at once. Twisted, dark pines jutted from the outer lips of sheer cliffs. Sharp black, basalt cliffs, broken over time, sent huge chunks of rock tumbling into the crashing waves. Frame after beautifully imperfect frame, arranged by gods of forest and sea, pleased the eye and spirit.

Logan had never seen anything so beautiful. The word awesome was not hyperbole when used here. Lewis and Clark must have been awed into silence when they saw this for the first time. The highway crossed several rivers with Indian names. After skimming over a wide, flat one called the Siletz, a hand-painted sign caught her eye. It pointed east, away from the highway, up a narrow, gravel road, reading simply "Borden's Ceramic Studio."

She wanted to stop, but she didn't know when it got dark here and wanted to find Rita's house before it did. She wondered how they made a living. Not very many people would see the sign in time to drive up and find them. And it didn't say how far back in they were. Maybe they sold their work online. Maybe it was just someone's hobby, and they worked at a gas station in town. Where were the gas stations? There must have been one in town, but she hadn't seen it.

Logan checked her odometer. Good, she hadn't missed it. Just a few more miles to go. She'd been so busy looky-looing, she hadn't been paying attention. She got through Depoe Bay without a ticket. Rita was right, the speed limit changed at least three times, it was a strict 25 mph in town, and town was only three blocks long.

A half-mile later she started looking for a low, blue and white wooden sign, the only entrance to Little Whale Cove. Some fog rolled in and, although the mist was pretty, she was glad it wasn't too thick or nighttime yet. Rita said LWC community didn't believe in streetlights. If she needed to go out, she should use the flashlight in the kitchen junk drawer.

She saw the sign in plenty of time and turned right, digging in her purse for the gate clicker to get in. She found it, and the wooden arm lifted to admit her. The posted speed limit was 18 mph throughout Little Whale Cove. Funny—why didn't they just round up to twenty? Logan's inner rebel wouldn't let her go less than 19 mph.

Two lefts and a right onto Cedar Way. Rita's house was a single-story Northwest cottage, tucked into an older section of the development, at the end of a cul-de-sac. It had been in her family since the early '70s. Several large cedar trees towered above the roof line and spread graceful, lacy branches over the walk. She pulled into the cobblestone driveway and parked.

Everywhere she looked, Logan saw giant trees and mounds of green shrubs and ferns. No one had lawns, just natural landscaping, and it looked as if they didn't believe in cutting down trees. She also saw several empty lots that must have been too expensive to develop, or they would have been built on by now. She couldn't remember the exact number, but Rita said there were several miles of walking paths running through twelve acres of old-growth forest in here. According to the map Rita showed her, one of the paths started two doors down. She couldn't wait to explore tomorrow.

Tonight, she just wanted to eat, shower and crawl into bed.

She forgot to stop at the little market Rita told her about on the way in. Hopefully, there would be at least a can of beans and coffee to tide her over. She'd go into town for supplies tomorrow.

She checked the fridge when she got inside. No fresh food, but she found a box of frozen waffles and a couple of frozen dinners in the freezer, and plenty of staples like olive oil, spices, and a bunch of canned goods in some shelves in the garage. Small, but efficient, the house had been modernized, so Logan zapped a frozen lasagna dinner and had some applesauce for dessert. Even found some cinnamon in a drawer of spices to sprinkle on top. She dug in. She stored the rest of it in the fridge. She'd have it for breakfast with the waffles before she went to the store.

Dinner done, she went back to the garage, where she'd spotted a small stash of wine. Hoping she wasn't drinking some hundred-dollar bottle of Bordeaux, she took a chance, picked out a red, brought it in and opened it. Smelled good. She poured herself a glass, opened the slider in back, and walked out on the deck. Since no one else had porch lights on that she could see, she didn't turn hers on either. She could see well enough to pull a folding chair out. She sat down to unwind.

49

Logan thought Rita was exaggerating when she said her place backed onto a forest, but the trees were just a few feet away. If she got up and leaned over the railing of the deck just right, she could probably touch the nearest one.

Modest, but adequate, the deck had no stairs. A gas BBQ sat at one end, a small cafe table on the other. Kuan Yin graced the corner, pouring her endless supply of mercy onto graceful pots of white heather and blue lithadora in a variety of sizes, below her feet. Needle-strewn, mossy ground sloped down and away from the deck, providing just enough space to walk all the way around the house. In the distance, she heard the lyric lullaby of a stream. So different from California, or even the New School. Entirely different ecosystem, dripping in green. It hurt her neck just to look up to try to see the tops of all the trees, so she settled for looking straight out in front of her.

From here, according to a book called Flora and Fauna of Little Whale Cove she found on the coffee table and looked through during dinner, Logan could make out what she thought might be the lighter and smoother bark of cedars, next to the darker, rougher skin of shore pines. Lacy, western hemlocks peeked out here and there. An alder glowed ghostly white, a slim interloper among her thicker, forest siblings. Mounds of salal and ferns filled in the low-lying gaps, all anchored by a carpet of moss and twigs.

The drive was beautiful, but any long drive left her stiff after the accident. Logan placed her feet flat on the deck and rested her arms in her lap, then took a few minutes to run through a muscle relaxing exercise her physical therapist taught her. She scrunched her shoulders up to her ears, held them for the count of five, then let them drop all at once, releasing any tension held there. After repeating this for muscle groups in her head, back and arms, she sat still, listening to the forest. She closed her eyes and breathed. The air smelled fresh, alive, and full of oxygen.

As the night deepened, a surprising number of stars emerged overhead. Now that traffic had died down on the 101, she could hear the distant boom of the waves. Rita hadn't been kidding. The ocean must be really close here. Douglas squirrels chittered and chattered loudly, scolding her for intruding on their territory. Or maybe they were sharing acorn-pie recipes. The book said there were deer, raccoons, a few resident coyotes, and even an occasional brown bear in here. She wouldn't mind seeing a deer or even a raccoon, maybe even a coyote, but she hoped the bears kept to themselves.

After about twenty minutes, she finished the rest of her wine and realized it was cold outside. Not wanting to go to bed yet, she was about to get a jacket when her phone burred in her pocket. It was Huey. She pulled open the slider and stepped inside. The trees weren't going anywhere.

"Hi, Huey," Logan answered.

"Good, I was hoping I wasn't calling too late," Huey said, "I got something on that flash drive. You got a minute?"

"Yeah, of course," she said, walking into the living room, "what did you find?"

She curled up in one of the overstuffed chairs flanking the gas fireplace. Reaching down, she cranked the gas key up to high.

"I was able to get in without too much trouble," Huey said, "but I'm not sure what I found."

"What do you mean?" Logan asked, "What did you find?"

"Bank records, mostly. Also, a record of online transactions purchasing some crypto-currency called Monero."

"I've heard of Bitcoin, but not Monero. I don't really know what crypto-currency is, exactly," Logan said.

"Just think of it as banking without the bank. It's electronic money, in a way," Huey said.

"Huh . . . Is Lori on any of these accounts? Do you see her name anywhere? Her last name is Wright."

"No. Most of the records I've looked at so far list a Mr. Yoshimoto. There are also some other records—real estate, restaurants, stocks— involving a company called Delaney Investments. Either of those names ring a bell?"

"No, Lori never mentioned either of those names to me," Logan said.

"This woman is a friend of yours?" Huey asked. "How well do you know her?"

"New friend, and not very," Logan admitted. "She moved in next door. Seems nice. She told me her name was Lori Wright, but they didn't find any ID on her when they took her to the hospital, and there was none in the house. No birth certificate for her daughter, either. I assume she's in some kind of trouble."

"No driver's license?" Huey asked.

"Nope. Obviously she didn't trust anyone, including me, to tell them what this file is or why she was hiding it," Logan said. "Does anything on there look like something worth attacking someone for?"

"I don't know. My friend, Lucas Kai, is a finance guy, heavy into crypto. I hope you don't mind . . . I didn't tell him why I wanted to know . . . but I asked him if there was anything special about Monero. Oh, and another crypto-currency wallet, with a smaller balance, called Z-Cash. He said Monero is known for being the most anonymous. Money deposited and withdrawn from Monero is virtually untraceable."

"Wow," Logan said. "I bet the banks don't like it."

"Or the government. Hard to tax money you don't know exists," Huey said. "He also said it was used, or rumored to be, for money laundering. Any chance your friend was involved in anything like that?"

"I don't know," Logan answered.

"If this little flash drive got your friend attacked, you shouldn't hang onto it. Whoever came after her is going to come after you if they find out you have it," Huey said.

"I don't see how anyone would know I have it. I didn't even know I had it until Purgatory discovered it in that doggie toy," she said. "And we don't know it's even related. It could be completely innocent."

"Well, if it was me, I'd turn it over to the police. I can overnight it to you . . . you going to be there for a few days, right?" he asked.

"Yes, I'm here till Thursday," Logan said, "I've got a flight out of Portland Friday. And thanks, Huey. I owe you one."

"Just promise me you'll take it to the police when you get back."

"I promise, Huey," she said.

As soon as I open it up and take a tiny peek at those files.

50

How weird. The room was somewhat light, so it must be morning. Logan took one of her earplugs out, sat up in bed and listened. Nothing. Absolute quiet. No alarm, no traffic. Wow. It was like someone put the world on mute.

Because she slept with the windows open, even at home, Logan was in the habit of using earplugs to drown out noise. Here, there wasn't any. She took out the other earplug, got out of bed and went over to the window. Twisting open the blinds set off a flurry of wing beats as four or five black and orange birds flew up to perch in the safety of the nearest low-hanging cedar branches.

Logan watched for a few minutes, but they remained hidden, so she padded into the kitchen to start some coffee. She'd spied half a bag in the refrigerator last night, and a basic coffee maker on the counter next to the toaster. No cream, but she'd live.

Though the house was compact, it was obvious Rita put some money into the remodel. The kitchen counter tops were made from a gorgeous white granite that looked like marble, streaked with black, gray, and shades of jade green.

Coffee ready, she poured herself a cup, grabbed a kitchen towel, and went out onto the deck. After drying off one of the cafe chairs, she settled in. Propping one of her feet up on the middle railing of the deck, she thought back to her conversation with Huey last night and what the discoveries on the flash drive meant.

She remembered Lori made some comment about taxes once. Sounded like she knew something about managing money. Could these be her accounts? Whose money was being laundered, if anyone's was? Where did the money come from in the first place? Her illegal or corrupt activities, or was she laundering money for someone else, then taking a cut? And the biggest question of all: who attacked her and why? It may not have had anything to do with the financial records on the drive.

There were just too many possibilities. All of these documents could belong to someone else, someone else involved in criminal activities, and that someone wanted them back. Bad. Bad enough to violently attack Lori and force her to give them up.

Did Lori get these records for insurance for herself, or was she blackmailing this Mr. Yoshimoto or Delaney Investments?

No matter what Huey said, now that the files were unlocked, she was going to dig through that flash drive and see if she could make sense of it. Then she'd know what to do. Either give it to the police, or back to Lori. Huey said it would be there sometime after 2:00 p.m., so she'd just have to wait until then. Nothing she could do about it today.

That decision made, Logan decided to spend the morning exploring some of those forest paths, hoping she could find the one Rita said ran along the bluffs with spectacular views of the ocean. Maybe she'd even see a whale! She'd stop in town and have a little lunch, walk the shops, then go to the local market and be back in plenty of time for the package to get there by the 2:00 p.m. estimated arrival time.

Cool but sunny outside, Logan opted for lightweight North-face pants and a white t-shirt, a dab of sunscreen on the bridge of her nose, tinted lip balm, and Teva sandals. All the pants she brought were loose enough to fit over her knee brace. It had leveled off pain-wise, as long as she didn't overdo. She clicked on local news while finishing her second cup of coffee.

"Get out and enjoy this high-pressure holiday today, 'cause a low is sweeping in tonight. Get out your umbrellas, ladies and gents . . ."

Next, Logan checked email and messages on her phone. One from Bonnie saying Lori was doing much better, but it would still be a while before she was well enough to go home—maybe in another week. She couldn't talk yet, but the doctor said no permanent damage. The social worker told Bonnie and Mike they'd reunite mother and daughter as soon as possible. Bonnie said they were all going to miss their little charge. Everyone in the family had fallen in love with Shannon.

Rinsing her coffee cup out, leaving it upside down on a paper towel next to the sink, Logan put on some old Timberland hiking shoes she brought and let herself out the front door. Two doors down, she entered the forest.

Ten feet in, she was surrounded by nodding branches and mossy tree trunks. To make it easier for residents to enjoy the forest, the Little Whale Cove community built several miles of wooden boardwalks that wove in and around the trees, connected to regular asphalt paths in some of the newer areas. Rita said they enjoyed the forest paths even more than the ones along the ocean. Wanting to take a closer look at some large, pumpkin-colored mushrooms, curled at the edges, growing a few feet off the path, Logan took a step to her right. Before she could grab anything to hold onto, her foot shot out from under her. Luckily, she caught herself, but just barely. She did not want to break any more body parts!

Looking down, she saw the boardwalk was constructed of short lengths of two-by-six planks, about four feet wide, sometimes with side rails when it crossed back and forth over streams and gullies. A strip of sturdy, sandpaper-like material was tacked firmly into place down the center, to prevent slippage. As long as she stayed on that, she was fine. But on either side of the strip six inches of wooden planks were exposed, streaked in green and slicker than snot for anyone not paying attention.

Once she figured that out, she enjoyed the rest of her walk. Taking out her phone, she admired the mushrooms from afar, or stepped widely over the mossy edges directly onto the forest floor. Some looked like shiitake and others like little bouquets of oyster mushrooms, but she wasn't sure. Just before the path turned into asphalt, she spotted a perfectly smooth, round dome of bright red, like a lollipop, with evenly-spaced, bright-white polka dots all over it. It was so bright, it looked fake. She expected to see a garden gnome propped next to it.

Five minutes after setting off, following the map Rita gave her, she took a right past some houses. The path emerged from the quiet, subdued greens of the forest onto a bright, sunny path that ran parallel along the top of the bluff.

Forty feet below, the ocean roared and crashed against black, jagged rocks, then slid back into the vast expanse. White, puffy clouds punched out of a sky so bright blue it hurt her eyes. On the inside curve of the cove, centuries or millennia of battering waves had created a rock formation of rounded squares, resembling giant, blackened, pull-apart dinner rolls.

Absolutely spectacular.

A few feet from the drop-off, a lone bench bravely perched

on the edge of a forty-foot cliff, overlooking miles of turquoise and navy ocean. Looking around, Logan could see she had the place to herself. Again, she was amazed. In Southern California, there'd be a wide safety zone with a thick fence, a dozen people lined up taking pictures, and the path behind her would be filled with joggers, baby strollers, skate boarders, and bikers, shoulder to shoulder, all out enjoying the 365-days-a-year sun.

To top it off, a couple of barnacle-backed gray whales cruised south, not twenty feet from shore. When they dove again, one went straight down and hovered for a minute, showing off its tail.

Cool!

An hour later, after more whale watching and exploring, Logan headed home. Her knee was starting to bother her, and she still had to run to the store to pick up food for the next few days. Shouldn't take her too long, it was only a mile away on the other side of Depoe Bay, which was only half a mile north of Little Whale Cove. She'd be back in plenty of time for Huey's package delivery.

51

Downtown traffic was a mess. To be expected. Morning rush hour wasn't over yet—it never was. Seattle was getting to be one perpetual snarl no matter what time of day you tried to get anywhere.

Garrett took the exit ramp for First Avenue off the I-5 South. Half a mile later, he parked his car around the block. He could walk from there.

It was barely drizzling, but he put his raincoat on before getting out. Aiming the key fob at the car, he clicked the locks shut. Keeping his head down and his collar turned up, he hurried toward a plain, two-story, cement building. A blinking neon sign declared it to be Dollar Smart Storage. Skipping the front office, he went directly to the smaller, self-storage section, pulled out his key and opened G18, letting himself into a mostly empty three-by-five space. Filing cabinet, a few cardboard boxes, bike. What he needed was in a metal box in the bottom drawer of the filing cabinet. Unlocking both, he removed several stacks of Cash. Fifty thousand to be exact. Crisp and new. Wrapped tight in neat little packages. He left the gold.

Just then his phone rang. It was Patricia.

It was already 9:00 a.m. He needed to get on the road. But he didn't want to raise any red flags. He answered.

"Patricia. What's up?"

Garrett's voice was clipped, but not unfriendly. He still had plenty of time.

"I'm sorry to bother you, Mr. Delaney. I know you have appointments out of the office today and I wouldn't call unless it was important, but the police are here," she said.

"The police?"

"Yes, and they have a search warrant. At least that's what they said. It looked like a search warrant. I've never seen one before," she said. "I don't know what to do. They're searching your office. Everything, including my desk and all the files."

She whispered into the phone, "They want to know where you are. What do I tell them?"

His assistant sounded like she might lose it. He'd have to keep her calm. He felt anything but.

"Don't worry, Patricia. I'm sure this is all a misunderstanding. They must have the wrong address. Just tell them I'll be there as soon as I can. I'm at least an hour out, but I'm on my way. Tell them I'm on my way," he said, disconnecting the call before she could ask any more questions, or hand her phone to the nearest, nosy cop.

He was only thirty minutes away, at best, but he didn't want the police to know that. Why were they there? What police? Seattle police? Could someone have gotten wind of Mr. Yoshimoto's accounts? No way. He'd been very careful.

It must be that Detective from Jasper, Andrews, but what did he have that would be enough to get a search warrant? What did he know? How close was he? He knew Neal was his driver, but Garrett knew nothing put him in Jasper that night.

He'd covered everything. He hadn't been driving his own car. He hadn't booked any commercial flights.

This couldn't be happening.

Garrett made a decision. He re-opened the metal box. This time he took the passports and the gold coins. He looked around. There was nothing else in there except a racing bike from his college days, and some boxes of Lauren's grand-mother's china. He hated it and rarely let her use it. When they moved to the new place, he finally made her box it up. The old-fashioned rose pattern did not fit into the sleek, modern decor. It wound up here because he told Lauren he was taking it to the new house, but he stopped to rent this place on the way, and just dumped it. Made the transaction look more legit. Paid cash, so no one knew about it. When Lauren asked about the dishes, he said they were accidentally buried in the attic behind the keepsake boxes. Too far back to dig out now. He locked the door behind him. He doubted he would ever be back.

◎ ◎ ◎ ◎ ◎

A slight, Asian man exited the elevator into the hallway, directly across from Delaney Investments. Stopping just outside the doors, he leaned against a wall, pretending to check his phone.

Normally quiet, Delaney Investments was a very busy place today.

A female, uniformed police officer was taping up and labeling cardboard storage boxes. Two men in suits could be seen through the open door to Delaney's personal office, one going through his desk, the other his book shelf. A woman he recognized as the receptionist came out of the Women's Restroom down the hall, slipping her cell phone into her pocket. He turned away so she could not see him, but he needn't have worried. She wasn't even looking his way. She was focused on what was happening inside. Looking back into the office, the man saw why. One of the suited men had stepped behind her desk and was taking files out of drawers. Delaney was nowhere to be seen. The man turned silently back to the elevator and pushed L for Lobby.

Mr. Yoshimoto was not going to like this. Not at all.

52

Huey's package didn't arrive until after 5:00 p.m. Must have had a lot of deliveries. When the driver handed her the small, stiff rectangle, he looked tired.

"Sorry I'm a little late," he said, sounding like he genuinely was. "These addresses are impossible to find in here."

Not stopping to chat, he turned on his heel and jogged back to his truck left running at the curb.

"That's okay . . ." she said to his back. He didn't hear the rest of her sentence. They work those guys too hard.

She heard they had impossible delivery schedules and if they couldn't keep up, the company didn't care. There was a line out the door of people waiting to take their jobs.

What they need is a good union, she thought. Maybe they had one. Not her problem.

Logan shut the door and returned to the living room. Plopping down on the couch, she ripped open the Fed Ex envelope, removed the flash drive and plugged it into her laptop. She hoped it had something on it that would tell her why Lori was hiding out in Jasper—as it appeared she was—and why she was attacked. If she had put files on here as some kind of insurance, it would be ironic if the very files she collected in order to protect herself and her daughter, were the ones that almost got her killed.

When the icon materialized on her desktop, Logan double-clicked it. There were three blue folders labeled 2014, 2015 and 2016. Excited, she started with 2014. But after several hours of searching through the files, Logan was just as much in the dark as when she started. Not one file had Lori's name or Wright, or even anything close to that, on it. Just like Huey said, the only name that showed up with any regularity was Yoshimoto, along with several banks and investment companies. The one that showed up the most often was Delaney Investments.

Nothing. Frustrated, she closed the files and ejected the flash drive, then physically removed it from the USB port. Unsure where to put it, she put it on the coffee table, next to her phone. She wanted to try again later. Maybe she missed something.

It was way past the dinner hour, unless you were European. Logan's French foreign exchange student mom regularly served dinner between 8:00 and 8:30 p.m. She remembered how strange it was for the meal to go on for hours, everyone just talking and enjoying their meal, but that was then. For years, she'd been back on American time.

When Amy was little, Jack was either watching sports or playing them, so they often just ate in front of the TV. Since Jack died, and before she got together with Ben, who cooked sit-down-worthy meals, Logan could inhale a microwave meal over the kitchen sink in under five minutes, and regularly did.

During the time she'd been sitting at her computer, the temperature dropped into the fifties. Late summer nights rarely dipped below sixty back home. Logan felt the chill. A woman on a mission, she made her way down the hall into the back room where she'd put her carry-on.

Most of the rooms in the house were small, but in addition

to a generous sleeping area, double-sink bathroom and walk-in closet on the left as you entered, the master bedroom felt spacious.

On the right, there was a typical queen-size bed, two nightstands and a dresser, but in the left, back corner, was a small, reading alcove furnished with two wingback chairs, a good lamp, and a round, leather ottoman. A three-panel, bay window offered an unobstructed view of the naturally landscaped front yard. Several colors of rhododendron and hydrangea still bloomed, and river rock edged the bark-chip paths meandering through the cedars and western hemlocks, some hung with a variety of bird feeders.

Ben would love this place. He was always going on about the importance of native plants, and that's all the community allowed to be planted in here, according to Rita. Logan realized she hadn't called him yet. They usually talked every night. Ben was an early-to-bed, early-to-rise kind of guy, anyway, and she knew he was leaving super early for a job tomorrow morning and was going over to watch his nephews in the school play later. They were doing *the Little Mermaid.* Cooper was an octopus and Calvin got to be Sebastian. Logan made Ben promise to take lots of video.

She pulled her phone out of her back pocket, scrolled down to recent contacts, plopped back flat on the bed, and tapped his name on the screen. Ben answered on the first ring.

"Hey there, Beautiful," he said.

Just the sound of Ben's voice anchored her day. They talked about everything and nothing until the light outside the window began to fade and hunger pangs reminded her she hadn't eaten. Ben promised again to take lots of pictures.

Neither of them mentioned babies, and she knew they'd have to have that talk when she returned, but for now, she just allowed herself to love and be loved.

53

After disconnecting the call, Logan stood and stretched. An unfamiliar, deep pang took her by surprise. She really, really missed Ben, but there was nothing she could do about it now. She could have flown home after her work days at the New School, but she needed the time to think. And she hadn't taken any vacation time for herself in . . . well, she couldn't think of the last time, or any time, she'd taken a solo trip just for fun.

Parking those feelings for now, Logan walked around to the small roller-bag she left open on the other side of the bed. As long as she was here, she might as well enjoy the full Pacific Northwest experience. Rummaging around, she found a 3/4 zip, navy blue hoodie and some blue and green plaid, flannel pajama bottoms. Very north-westy. Peeling off her jeans, she threw them onto the back of one of the chairs for tomorrow.

Next, she stuffed her less-than-fresh t-shirt, along with the socks and underwear she wore that day, into an old pillowcase she brought just for that purpose. Her bra was the last item of clothing to be removed. "Ahhhh . . . !" She freed the girls and rubbed the skin around her rib cage where the band was always a little too tight, then pulled on the hoodie, which was warm and soft. She had a hard time getting bras that fit.

Logan glanced down at the bulging pillowcase. It held all her dirty clothes from her stay at the New School, too. Rita had a washing machine. Maybe she'd do a load of laundry before she left on Thursday. Or not. She tossed it onto the floor, next to the chair, then closed and zipped her suitcase, placing it next to the pillowcase. She planned on using both sides of the bed. When Ben wasn't around, she slept diagonally, enjoying the luxury of space.

As long as she was back here, Logan got things ready for bed. She put her Kindle and a pair of neon green earplugs on the nightstand. At home, Purgatory usually got them when Ben stayed over, but here, they were safe from canine consumption. She probably wouldn't need them, it was so quiet, but habits were hard to break. Finally, she pulled on her PJs and made sure one of the windows was cracked open. She couldn't sleep without fresh air. Much better.

Satisfied with her preparations, Logan grabbed her phone and padded barefoot back to the kitchen. She was about to go back and get some socks, when she spotted some Ugg sheepskin slippers on a bench near the front door. Hopefully, Rita wore a size 7 or 8.

They were a little big, and barely stayed on her feet, but worked well enough for around the house. She just needed to keep her tootsies warm. She wasn't going to be running marathons in them. Feet safely ensconced in the Uggs, she put her phone back by her computer and shuffled into the garage to raid the wine cellar.

Uncertain whether white or red went best with hot dogs and beans, Logan decided to stick with the red she already had open in the kitchen. When faced with menu decisions at the market this afternoon, she had opted for anything that didn't require cooking. Zapping a few things in the microwave was about as far as she was prepared to go.

VANISHING DAY

It was a small market, but catered to vacationing Portlanders, so had a pretty good deli selection, including blue cheese stuffed olives and tabouli. Logan took a little of each, including some coleslaw she was going to enjoy with the hot dogs and beans.

She opened the fridge. Several take-out containers now shared shelf space with a Sauvignon Blanc and a pint of real cream for her coffee. A cantaloupe sat next to some apples on the counter. They in turn nuzzled a still-aromatic bag of fresh caramel corn from a salt-water taffy shop in Depoe Bay. She was forced to pull over and buy some on her way home when the tempting siren smell reached through the car window as she drove by. Instigating a twenty-five-mile-an-hour zone past the tourist shops was pure genius on the part of local merchants.

Taking her bachelor meal out on the deck, Logan sat at the cafe table and took a deep drink of her wine. Excellent. Red was definitely the correct choice.

An hour later, bean bowl and wine glass washed, Logan was back out on the deck, snuggled under her jacket with the bag of caramel corn, settling in for some forest breathing.

7:15 p.m.

Up here, nightfall arrived fashionably late. And when it did, it snuck up on you. The sun played hide and seek behind the trees as it floated down to the horizon. Its light grew softer and softer, like a dimmer switch being slowly turned down. Bright patches of blue sky, visible here and there through the branches, faded to pale rose. Sunlit yellow leaves darkened into hunter greens, finally washing out into shades of gray.

The sun must have set, but it was in no rush to pull in its beams completely. As the forest hung onto the last vestiges of daylight, pine squirrels upped the volume, chattering and scolding, racing up and around the trunks of several trees, squabbling over territory until darkness muffled the scene. Somewhere, from deep within the forest, a solitary bird pierced the night with heartbreaking song.

Sitting in one chair, legs draped across the arm, feet propped up on the railing, Logan didn't need the relaxation exercise. She was already there. Eyelids heavy . . . warm under the jacket . . . cool night air on her face . . . so perfect . . .

A loud knock rudely brought her out of her reverie.

She must have drifted off. It was really dark now. She opened her eyes and blinked. Nothing. No lights from the houses she knew were on the other side of the forest. No street lights from the distant highway. Totally dark. The kind of dark that 'pitch black' didn't begin to describe. She couldn't even see the trees a few feet from the deck.

She liked it, but it was a little unsettling at the same time.

Squeezing her eyes and shaking her head, Logan rubbed her legs to get the blood moving, then rose to go inside. She stumbled her way into the kitchen, found the light switch and flipped it on. She glanced at the clock on the microwave on her way to answer the door.

Who'd be stopping by for a visit at eight-thirty at night?

54

No one, apparently. The porch was empty.

After trying several light switches by the door, one finally worked. An old-style carriage lamp came on at the corner of the garage, but only illuminated a few feet beyond the driveway. Carefully, she made her way across the porch and down the walkway. It had rained, releasing a sharp, woodsy smell from the bark chip in the front yard. She checked around the house as far as she could go without bumping into trees.

Maybe she imagined it. She had dozed off. Must have been a dream. If so, it was a pretty vivid dream. She'd never had one wake her up. After another couple of minutes of staring and listening for bears or raccoons, she went back inside.

Making sure the front door was locked and the garage light out . . . another rule they had here to keep it natural—no outside lights left on all night. She went back out on the deck and listened. Just the faint sound of the ocean and Highway 101 in the distance. Placing her hands in the small of her back, Logan arched into a good stretch. When she looked up, she gasped.

The sky above her was jam packed with stars. Bright ones

overlapped with faint ones, some groupings looked like constellations, but she couldn't remember what they were called. Maybe Orion. She tried to find the Big Dipper. That bright star must be Venus—not a star at all. She vaguely remembered planets didn't twinkle.

She stared until her neck started to cramp. Rubbing the muscles she could reach, satisfied there wasn't anything else she could check tonight, Logan picked up her wine glass and went inside, pulling the heavy, sliding glass door closed behind her. Dutifully, she placed the wooden dowel she removed earlier, snugly in the track as she found it.

Back in her room, she splashed her face at one of the sinks and swirled some water in her mouth in lieu of brushing her teeth. She was lights out, snuggled under the covers, and sinking into sleep in less than five minutes.

◊ ◊ ◊ ◊ ◊

Logan sat up, fully awake. Slightly disoriented, she fumbled for her phone to see the time. Not finding the phone, she patted the bed next to her pillow for her Kindle and flipped open the cover. The bright screen displayed the last page she read. Tapping the upper inch of the screen, she got the home page, which had all the settings and navigation features, including the time. Blinking her eyes into focus, she squinted.

Almost midnight.

Just as she was shutting the Kindle down, throwing herself back on the bed, throwing herself back on the bed, her blood froze. An amorphous, dark shape was forming at the window. Animal, vegetable, mineral? What looked very much like a man was climbing in the window. His back to her, crouched low, he reached in with his left foot, straightening slowly to his full height.

Tall, dark and the scariest thing she'd ever seen.

The man in the Jeep. Lori's attacker. It was him, she was sure of it, but how had he found her? She didn't have to guess what he was after.

Reacting purely on instinct, Logan threw off the covers and hit the floor running, Kindle tumbling to the floor. By the time she reached the living room, she could hear him thudding down the hallway after her. No reason to be quiet now.

Scooping up the flash drive and her phone off the coffee table on her way, she threw the deadbolt, swung open the front door, and launched herself off the porch into the darkness. Hopefully, he wouldn't take the time to find the light switch.

He did.

Logan turned back and saw the ferocious, determined look on her pursuer's face. Thundering down the wooden stairs, he was right behind her. Knowing she was in full sight where she was, Logan hesitated for only a split second, then turned left, stuffing the flash drive and phone into her pocket as she ran. She only knew one path that led into the forest. The boardwalk she took this morning, two houses down. It was easy to find, even in the dark, and not one the man would be familiar with, but she hadn't counted on how loud she would be. The wooden boards magnified every pounding step as she fled.

She had to get off this thing. It would lead him right to her. But there was nothing but untracked forest on either side. She'd break an ankle in the dark if she tried to run in there. He was gaining on her. Any second now she expected to be grabbed. She had no illusions she could fight off a grown man. She had to hide somewhere until hopefully he gave up, and she could go for help. There was a bridge up here somewhere, with a little stream running under it through tree roots and giant ferns. Her ears picked up the faint burbling sound up ahead. She'd just have to risk it.

Wishing she could see where she was jumping, Logan took a leap of faith off the path, toward the sound of water. At the last second, she remembered to try to land with most of her weight on her left leg.

It took less time to reach the ground than she expected. When she did, blinding pain took her breath away. Her right foot hit something on the way down, glancing off a tree root or downed nurse log, jamming her knee. Staying low, moving as quietly as she could, she crawled forward in the dark, ignoring the stabbing pain, toward the sound of rushing water. When she got to the bank of the stream, she made herself as small as she could, pulling herself under some kind of bush or fern. Sound carried in the forest. She could hear her attacker's footsteps slow, then stop.

Heart pounding, Logan tried to breathe as slowly and evenly as she could. Maybe she made it. But where was this guy? She would feel better if she could hear his footsteps running away, fading into the distance.

You're not that lucky, Logan.

She'd just have to wait it out. She couldn't run anyway. At least her clothing was dark. She wished she could rub mud on her face. And her feet. She could feel the air caressing her ankles, but was afraid to pull them in closer.

Willing her body to stillness, Logan focused on slowing her breath, keeping it shallow, counting . . .

Ten in . . . ten out. Ten in . . . ten out . . . ten . . .

It was quiet. Too quiet. Then she saw the last thing she wanted to see. A narrow beam of yellow light began methodically zigzagging down the hill, exposing everything in its path.

Reading her mind, the man's disembodied voice said, "Cell phone app. Great little feature. I know you're down there. Just give me the flash drive. That's all I want."

Every muscle in Logan's body was tense as steel.

The narrow light continued to work its way down the hill, closer and closer. In high-definition detail, Logan watched it as it illuminated moss-covered branches, mud, twigs and loose leaves.

"I saw you grab it off the table on your way out the door. That's it, isn't it? Lauren's little blackmail drive."

Logan held her breath. Her leg was starting to cramp. Charlie horse. Should have eaten a banana.

For some reason, this thought was hilarious. Giggles started to bubble up. She was one step away from hysteria.

Breathe in . . . breathe out . . .

"I don't know what lies Lauren's told you, but your new friend is a thief. And a liar. I'll bet she didn't tell you she had a husband. I'm Garrett, Lauren's husband, and whatever's on that drive is mine. The wife who was supposed to love and obey is the little bitch that tried to blackmail me with my own files. Those files represent business that bought her that big house and every scrap of clothing on her back. Oh, and she kidnapped my daughter, did she tell you that? I bet not. And she's done it more than once. I've been sick with worry."

Sick, yes. Worried? Logan doubted it.

He continued to list Lauren's crimes.

"Stole money to buy her runaway car. I'll bet she forgot to mention that little detail."

The pieces were beginning to fall into place. Lauren was obviously Lori. She risked a lot to escape her husband and keep Shannon safely away from him, which, as far as Logan could tell, was a very wise move.

Any doubts about Lori's secrecy and actions before, evaporated. Logan was firmly in Lori's camp now. She just had to live long enough to get this evidence back to her.

55

From her hiding place, Logan looked out between the leaves watching the relentless progress of the light beam as it made its way down the side of the ravine—only a few feet away now.

As quietly as possible, Logan felt blindly around her, looking for anything she could use as a weapon. No rocks . . . lots of soft, spongy moss . . . twigs . . . useless! She needed something heavy. When the light found her, she had no doubt he'd be on her in a second.

She didn't know if he had a gun, or a knife, but she knew she didn't have either. Mano-a-mano, he'd win. If she could find something to hit him with, she'd aim for his head and hope she could stop him long enough to use her own phone to call for help. If she screamed now, someone might hear her, but he'd get to her before anyone could come to the rescue.

No, she was on her own.

And it was already too late. She looked down. The yellow beam of light was dancing off her bare feet.

"Hello!" Garrett said.

Logan had never heard a more chilling word. Fear gripped her body. Plunging into the icy stream, her only thought was to get away. Garrett came plunging down the hill.

Desperately crawling away, Logan tried to climb out the other side. Her hands slipped in the mud and scraped across something rough, landing her hard on her elbow, drenching her pajamas. Fighting panic, she managed drag herself up and run. She pushed pain into another part of her mind. Her wet clothing snagged and caught, but somehow she didn't fall again.

She thought the stream ran down to Little Whale Cove. There were houses there. And rocks. She heard Garrett sliding down the last few feet of the bank, splashing into the water, cursing.

"Bitch!" he yelled, "You're going to pay for this!"

Logan raced blindly. Any second he was going to reach out and grab her.

Suddenly she was jerked off her feet. She struggled, but Garrett held on like death. He had a handful of hoodie and auburn hair. Like a wild animal caught, Logan twisted away, lunging forward in panic, until he lost his grip.

She kept running until she saw the cove up ahead.

Two hulking, granite boulders rose before her. The stream narrowed and rushed between them, then opened up a few yards away onto the small, crescent of rough beach called Little Whale Cove. Instead of soft sand, it was covered in small stones and broken shells, strewn with large, driftwood logs. It was low tide and smelled strongly of seaweed.

Logan looked up. Several houses perched atop the cliff. The ones with dramatic ocean views she had so admired this morning while walking on the path above that wound along the coast at the top of the bluffs. Scrabbling the last few feet,

Logan hobbled into the open, cupped her hands, and yelled up at the houses as loud as she could.

"Help! Call the police!"

Logan could only hope an insomniac lived in one of the houses and slept with the windows open like she did. She struggled to keep her balance just as Garrett emerged onto the beach. Her plan was to dive back into the forest—her only hope for survival was in the dark.

A weak moon shone ghostly white on the beach. Shredded, gauzy clouds hung over the trees in a dull, navy sky. She could see her attacker clearly now. And he could see her. Crouched and ready to spring, Logan looked like the devil herself. Sopping wet, bare toes gripping sharp rocks and shells, hair whipping into her face by the cold wind, she was spitting mad. Damned if she was going to let this guy kill her, which she knew he would do as soon as he got what he wanted. She looked directly into his eyes. Isn't that what wolves did? Establish dominance. She wasn't backing down.

If she could have made her feet move, she would have circled, looking for a good opening. Instead, Garrett sprinted forward and lurched into her. Logan went down scratching and screaming, like a wounded banshee. If the people in the houses on the cliff weren't awake already, they would be soon. Hope faltered when she remembered many of the residents here were part timers. Rita said most had already left for their winter homes in drier climates, like Arizona and Colorado. No one was going to hear her.

With grim determination, Logan grabbed a handful of beach debris. Smiling when she realized what her hand landed on, she rotated it around with her fingers and let the smaller pebbles fall through. Gripping the large, jagged mussel shell, she sliced it down Garrett's face. It was his turn to scream.

Next, she went for his throat, but missed. Heavier and stronger, Garrett pinned her easily with his body, grabbed her arms and pulled them overhead. Clamping her wrists together, he ground the back of her hands painfully into the rocks. With the other hand, he reached into her pocket, lifting out the flash drive. And her phone.

Logan's heart sank. No movement or lights turned on in the houses above. It couldn't end like this. She had to see Amy . . . and Ben. This just couldn't be happening!

With a smug grimace, Garrett pushed the full length of his body against hers, wisely keeping his face out of reach of her teeth, and stayed there while she tried to squirm away. Tiring of this, keeping one knee on her chest and her arms secure over her head, he opened his jacket with one hand, put the flash drive and phone into the inner pocket, then zipped them in securely.

"Thank You, Miss McKenna," he said. "If I had time, I'd teach you a lesson. I'd teach you how to behave. Unfortunately, I only have time to kill you."

That's all Logan needed to hear. Knowing she wasn't going to get another chance, with strength born of stark fear, she pushed him off and rolled to the right. Gathering her feet under her, she rose and lurched toward the forest. Garrett's hand shot out, grabbed the heel of her foot. Slippery with seaweed, she yanked it free and kept going. Searing pain shot down her leg, but stopping was not an option.

Frothing with rage, yelling all the things he would do to her, no longer the controlled, calm killer, Garrett came crashing in after her.

There were acres and acres of forest, but after her initial sprint, Logan had to slow her pace. There was no clear path and she couldn't run. She could barely walk. Desperately, she looked for a place to hide, but after the comparative light of the beach, she couldn't see anything. She tried feeling her way with her feet. The ground was different here, wetter. More moss. She must be near the stream, but it sounded funny, like it was far off.

Gingerly, she stepped forward. Before she could grab anything to stop her fall, her good leg shot out from under her sending her sliding down a steep embankment.

Now she knew where the stream was.

This was it. She couldn't move. Every inch of her hurt. Her body rotated on the way down, scraping and bruising every side. If she was meat, she'd be all set for marinade. Just slip in some butter and garlic. The only good part of this scenario was that she was so far down, Garrett would have a hard time getting to her. Or seeing her. She could only see a sliver of sky above her.

Dragging herself out of the water, Logan pulled herself toward the darkest corner she could find, a narrow opening between two massive tree roots. Pressed between their sheltering arms, soaked to the skin and cold, she held herself perfectly still, listening for the sound of footsteps.

56

Logan opened her eyes on a pale, gray world. She had no idea how she slept, but dawn had arrived. Slowly, grays began turning into greens and browns. Squirrels squabbled, blue jays called, robins warbled good morning.

Was it? She supposed so. She hadn't expected to live the night, and here she was. Stiff and very, very cold, but alive. Garrett must have given up the search. He had what he came for. She reached for her phone before remembering Garrett had that, too. She took inventory.

Her clothes were still wet through and stuck to her body in several places, with bloody mud. But she didn't feel faint so couldn't have lost too much. Just superficial scratches she hoped. Her head throbbed.

Slowly, she flexed her frozen fingers and moved her arms. When that proved successful, she attempted to stretch out her leg. A groan escaped her lips. Bad idea.

Maybe she'd just sit here until her body warmed up. She tried rubbing the tops of her thighs to get the blood going, but that opened up some of the wounds when the flannel pulled away where it had stuck to her skin. What a mess.

Her right knee was swollen to twice its size. She didn't think her webbed knee brace thing would even fit over it now, or do any good if it did. She was pretty sure she must have torn through whatever was left of that meniscus, or done some new damage altogether. She wished she'd taken Anatomy in college. She liked knowing what she was dealing with.

Gingerly, she put her hand up to the right side of her face, tentatively touching her cheek and brow bone. More dried blood from a cut over her eye. She was going to have a good shiner on that side. The rest of her seemed okay, just banged up.

Well, no one was going to come rescue her. She'd just have to suck it up and crawl out. She looked around for a likely spot. Something relatively shallow, with trees to grab onto so she could haul herself up. There was a good candidate a few feet to her right. Taking a few deep breaths, she attempted to stand, but this brought on a whole new level of pain and she involuntarily fell back down.

Okay then.

Logan gathered her courage to try again.

"Hello down there!" an older woman's voice called out, "Are you okay?"

A pair of intelligent gray eyes set in a soft, wrinkled face peered down at her, over the tree root. Logan had never seen a more beautiful face.

Parting some ferns, the woman looked down at Logan.

"Oh my! Wait right there! I'll be right back. Don't move!" she said, disappearing.

Like she could go anywhere if she wanted to. Logan felt relief flood through her body. She settled back down to wait for the cavalry. She didn't care how long it took. The woman had gone to get help and that's all that mattered.

VANISHING DAY

Logan was surprised when the woman reappeared almost immediately, a few feet farther along the bank, in the more open area Logan had been trying to reach. Clad in a cheerful, bright blue running outfit with matching, white stripes down the jacket and pants, a huge Alaskan Malamute sat calmly by her side.

Beautiful dog, but Logan wasn't sure exactly how this helped.

"What's your name, sweetie?" the woman called down.

"Logan," she said, "Logan McKenna."

"I'm Edna, and this is Bear," she smiled.

Hearing his name, Bear lifted up his snout and licked his master's hand. "Bear's going to get you out."

Turning the huge dog around, she said, "Lucky for you we were doing a beach swim day and he has on his long lead."

She unlatched a silver, metal carabiner from Bear's collar and reattached it to a thick, metal ring located on the blue nylon harness, unfurling a long, thick, white nylon rope. Bear and his owner matched. Next, the woman deftly tied a huge, complicated-looking knot on the other end, then tossed that end down to Logan.

"Can you reach it?" she asked.

Logan answered by grabbing the end. "Thank You!" she said.

It took a few tries, but between the two of them—Bear pulling and Logan crawling—the strong animal managed to haul Logan out onto the path with only minimal damage . . . and cussing. She apologized to the woman for the language. She also knew she must look like something from the Night of the Living Dead.

"Oh no, dearie," she laughed. "Don't you worry about that," she said, hooking a surprisingly strong arm under Logan's arm. "My Johnny served on a submarine. No one can out-cuss a sailor! That was Sunday School talk compared to him."

So that's how she learned to tie that knot.

"Thank you . . ." Logan managed, catching her breath. "What was your name again?"

"Edna. Edna Gamble," the woman said, untying the dog's leash, letting it drag on the ground beside him. "I think if you drape your arm over my shoulders and lean on Bear here . . . Bear, Logan, Logan, Bear . . . there, now you're properly introduced . . . we should be able to get you back to the house. We just started our walk. I'm just up ahead."

Edna continued as the strange trio proceeded, "Bear doesn't really need a lead. He's a good boy, but they have these rules, you know, in the Cove, for people whose dogs don't behave."

Logan made agreeable noises. Ben felt the same way about Purgatory, but considering she'd been lunged at a few times by an aggressive Doberman mix in the neighborhood back home, she had to agree leash laws were a good idea.

Once they were inside, Edna sat Logan down at the kitchen table, then went to the sink and ran some hot water. Edna's home was filled with furniture from the '60s, all Danish Modern, upholstered in bright blues with cheerful, yellow throw pillows. Pictures of her husband in his uniform, their wedding portrait, and a series of graduation and baby pictures, presumably of children and grandchildren, filled one wall.

Gently but firmly, Edna began wiping at the dried blood on Logan's face, being careful not to break open any wounds and start the bleeding again.

"What happened?" Edna asked.

Logan said she was out hiking, didn't realize it was getting dark, and slipped.

Edna didn't look like she bought that story but said nothing. A few minutes later, she leaned back to take a look at her handiwork. "Not bad, but that cut over your eye will need stitches, and we haven't even started on the bottom half of you yet," Edna said.

Her rescuer wanted to call 911, but Logan said she was fine, just wanted to get back to the place she was staying. Edna didn't have any dry clothes that would fit her, so she put a towel down on the front seat of her car to drive her back home as she was, torn, sticky, wet pajama bottoms and all. Logan said nothing was wrong with her that a good, long, hot shower wouldn't fix. But she insisted on Logan eating something first.

After forcing her to drink a very strong cup of coffee and an excellent, gooey peach-filled pastry, Edna finally agreed to drive her home. But only if she took her number, along with a baggie full of sterile gauze, Neosporin, and Band-aids—her own portable, mini-first aid kit. Next, she reached into the hall closet and pulled out a pair of crutches.

"This should hold you until you get yourself to a doctor. Which you should do as soon as possible," Edna scolded. "Tom used them last year after his hip surgery. They should be tall enough for you."

Logan thanked her again and promised to call if she needed Edna to drive her to urgent care. She wanted to go home and get into the shower, try ice on her knee first.

The chase through the forest felt like miles in the dark last night, but Rita's house was only a few blocks from Edna's. Houses were scattered mainly along four or five streets, but Rita's was on the back end of the community, at the edge of the forest. Two rights and a left—and they were there.

Edna pulled into the driveway next to Logan's rental car. Leaving the engine running, she got out and helped Logan up to the door, which was wide open. Edna raised her eyebrows and gave her a piercing look, but said nothing. Everyone was entitled to their secrets.

Sorry she lied again to this nice woman, Logan mumbled something about the lock on the doorknob not working . . . she'd have to tell Rita about it so she could get it fixed. Must have popped open after she shut it yesterday. Probably never fit right to begin with. Yes, she'd be sure and engage the deadbolt this time. She forgot yesterday.

Logan knew that sounded lame, but she couldn't think of a better explanation off the top of her head. She had no idea where Garrett was or what he might do. If she called the Oregon police, what evidence did she have that he, or anyone else, attacked and tried to kill her? He was long gone. He had the flash drive. Would he leave Lori alone now? Last she heard, Lori—or Lauren, as Garrett called her—was still in ICU. He couldn't get to her there. She hoped. Besides, he had what he came for. His precious files.

Logan didn't want to tell Lori that her husband had the flash drive. She'd gone to great lengths to keep it safe, and Logan felt like she'd failed to protect it. She wondered if Lori was out of the ICU yet. Bonnie said the doctors were keeping her just far enough under not to pull her tubes out, but not in an induced coma exactly. That far under would do permanent brain damage.

And Shannon. What was going to happen with that adorable little girl?

She thought about calling Detective Andrews, but he would just ask why she hadn't called earlier. Why had she hung onto the flash drive for several days, instead of turning it over to the police? She didn't have a good answer for that. And now, she lost it. She couldn't even prove it existed.

Good job, Logan.

What she had was Zip. *Nada. Nyet.*

Exhausted beyond belief, Logan hopped down the hall toward the shower.

57

Cruising north on the 101 through Lincoln City, Garrett itched to step on the gas, but didn't want to get pulled over. The bar rush was over, but you never knew. He passed Wells Fargo as he was leaving town. Five and a half hours to Seattle, maybe only five without traffic through Portland, and he'd be home. He adjusted his rear view mirror and checked for cops. All clear. The streets were deserted.

He didn't like leaving loose ends, but really, what was the McKenna woman going to do? Now that he had the flash drive, she didn't have anything on him. He checked for security cameras before he went in through the window. There were none. The only way into Little Whale Cove was through a gate, which had a camera aimed at the pass through, but that was easy. He just left his car in guest parking near the guard shack, which was unmanned that time of night, and walked in. Piece of cake.

Forty minutes after leaving Lincoln City, he pulled into Spirit Mountain Casino for gas. He bought a hat and some dry shoes at the twenty-four-hour gift shop, tossing Logan's phone in the dumpster on the way out. His pants and shirt were okay. He'd go home, shower, be in the office by 9:30 a.m. If his luck held.

He had the flash drive. That was the most important thing. When he got home, he'd have to go through it one document at a time, to see what she stole. Maybe it wasn't too bad. Whatever it was, he'd manage it. Everything was going to be okay.

Taking his phone out of airplane mode . . . he hadn't wanted it to ring while he was crawling into someone's bedroom . . . Garrett plugged it into the car charger and tapped on the voice mail icon. There were twenty-three voicemails waiting. The first few were from his assistant, Patricia, panicked at the police search. He started skipping through. Were they all from her? He didn't even listen to the rest of the last one, which sounded like her quitting. He scrolled past to the next number, not one he recognized. The message was short and clear.

"10:00 p.m. Ruth's Chris. Don't be late," the voice said. Garrett glanced at the clock on the dashboard.

Shit.

It was three o'clock in the morning. 10:00 p.m. had long since slid on by. Garrett banged his hand on the steering wheel. He felt sick. Just then the phone jangled in the plastic cupholder. Garrett looked down. Unknown caller. He tried to pull himself together.

"Hello?"

"Mr. Delaney, I am disappointed."

In me, in the universe, in the fact that the police were crawling all over my office, and probably at least some of your financial records . . . ??

The caller did not clarify. Or explain why he was up and not sounding a bit sleepy at 3:00 a.m.

"A man should take better care of his family, Mr. Delaney, and his business. As I'm sure you are aware, there was an unfortunate fire in your building earlier this evening. I'm afraid all the offices on your floor were destroyed."

A fire?

No. He was not aware. He'd been kind of busy this evening. This was unreal.

"Since your services will no longer be required, my associate is waiting for you at your home, to make sure the terms of our agreement are satisfied. Our business is at an end."

The thought of walking into his home, where that ugly, little man waited, smirking, probably sitting in Garrett's good chair, turned his stomach. In one day it was gone. All of it! His business, his money and, if he went back home, probably his life! Well, he just wouldn't go back. He rolled this new idea around in his head for a minute.

The hell with them!

The police, Mr. Yoshimoto's gopher, all of them! The juggling, the kowtowing, the obsequious crawling to the client he should never have taken on. All of it needed to go. He could see that now. What he needed was a simpler life.

Time to clear the decks! He had the cash. He had the passports. Only the Logan woman knew he'd been out here, but she didn't know where he was now, or where he was going. If she managed to survive the night, and identified him, the police would assume he'd return to Seattle. They'd be looking for him there. But there was nothing left for him in Seattle.

He could go to Mexico. Start a new life. Open a little bait shop. Maybe run a charter boat. Give sailing lessons. Their last vacation he landed a big marlin. He was good at fishing.

Garrett got back on the road. All he needed now was his family. That's all he needed. He could see that now. Lauren would come to her senses. Lauren, Shannon . . . they could all be together again, just like it was before all this got so crazy.

Lauren loved him. He knew he'd messed up. He'd show her he was going straight. No more big money schemes. He was going to be a good husband.

He grabbed his phone, pulled up GPS, and in the destination box, entered Tijuana, Mexico. All he needed to fix his life was his wife and daughter. This was going to work.

Hell, they're on the way!

58

Lori felt herself floating, drifting up toward consciousness. There was light, some muffled sounds. She still couldn't feel anything. It was like she didn't have a body. It was exhausting. Too much effort to fight her way to the surface.

She drifted in and out through ribbons of memories. She was back in Seattle. Before Jasper, before she and Shannon escaped.

She had fifteen minutes before Neal came looking for her. Fifteen minutes to make the call. The only reason she was alone now was because she told him she had a parent conference with Shannon's pre-school teacher. Instead, she was meeting with the people from House of Ruth. When she called the number the nurse gave her, they told her what to do. All she had to do was call. When she was ready.

She decided to wait until summer vacation. After Shannon was out of pre-school. The House of Ruth people had it all worked out. They'd obviously done this before. Her contact told her to make sure she had no appointments, work or personal, for the week she was leaving. That way no one would miss her right away and start looking for her.

This was not going to be a problem. Garrett made her quit her job years ago, and she had no plans with friends to cancel. Garrett had seen to that. Because of his increasing pressure, she gradually drifted away from all her friends. The only person she saw now was her mom, and not very often. Her mom knew Garrett was jealous. She wouldn't think it unusual if she didn't call for a week or so.

The bottom line was no one would miss her or come looking for her for weeks. Still, her neighbor, Rae McCluskey, may wonder. She was usually out gardening in the mornings and always said hello. Gave Shannon holiday cookies last Christmas, which Garrett made her throw away. She lied to Rae and told her they were delicious. They'd avoided her ever since. She was embarrassed. The woman had been kind. What must she have thought of her?

Lori's mind wandered again. She began to feel her body, although it was still too heavy to move. She tried to lift an arm and failed. The memories continued to flow, stronger now.

Vanishing Day finally arrived! Her heart raced. She felt so alive!

Early morning, the smell of coffee in her to-go cup. Windows rolled up. Hum of traffic on the highway. Shannon asleep on the seat next to her. Still slightly giddy with the success of their escape. She'd lowered the passenger seat as flat as it would go and tucked pillows and coats around her daughter to make her comfortable.

That's why she left. Shannon. Shannon laughing. Shannon beginning to lose that look of tight worry around her eyes. Her new job, her new friends, her nice neighbor.

Lori moaned.

The last night at the new house came pounding back. A sledgehammer of memories. Opening the door, seeing him there, fighting, Garrett going for Shannon, her leaping on his back . . . his fist coming straight at her face . . . blinding pain . . . falling.

VANISHING DAY

Where was Shannon? What happened to Shannon?! She had to get up and find Shannon! But her body wouldn't move.

◊ ◊ ◊ ◊ ◊

Except for the background harmony of blips and hisses, the ICU was quiet. Rhonda expertly moved through her routines, checked her patient's vitals, fluid and oxygen levels. Right now, her patient was resting peacefully. Nine days ago, she regained consciousness, but the doctors had to give her something stronger to keep her from pulling out her tubes. She kept trying to get out of bed. The team finally agreed to use physical restraints in case she woke when no one was there and tried again.

For the past week, the doctors kept her more or less under, so she could heal. There was no family to update. Officially, police had her down as a Jane Doe, but Rhonda called her by the name the EMTs said she went by, Lori.

Just as she did with all her patients, Rhonda talked to Lori every time she came in. When she ran out of local gossip, she even told her about her recent breakup with her boyfriend. Lori was a good listener.

The last thing she did before leaving was to go through a set of mobility and circulation exercises. Lifting Lori's right leg, she dug deep into the muscle tissue, stroking firmly up toward the heart, working her way all around the leg. Next came bending and stretching, then straightening the sheets. None of her patients ever got bed sores. She was just finished with the right leg and starting to work on the left, when she saw Lori's eyelids twitch. Holding her breath, she watched intently.

After a couple of false starts, they fluttered open, then looked directly at her. Rhonda smiled. Lori had beautiful, soft, brown eyes.

"Yes!" Rhonda shouted, beaming a huge smile, "It's about time you woke up! Welcome back to the land of the living!"

59

After scrubbing off the mud and grime in the shower, Logan looked in the mirror and assessed the damage. Using Edna's first aid kit, she was able to patch herself up well enough to not scare people. There was even one of those Steri-Strip things to hold the skin on her brow bone together where it split over her right eye, which was also starting to turn purple.

Lovely.

She released her wet hair from the scrunchy and tried to push some of the curls over to cover the bandage a little, but without bangs, it was pointless. Sighing, she figured she'd just have to live with it.

Other than the knee, none of her wounds were very serious. And even the knee pain she hoped would soon resolve itself with the whole RICE thing: Rest, Ice, Compression, and Elevation. Speaking of which, she needed to see if there was any ice in Rita's freezer, or better yet, a bag of frozen peas.

Pulling on underwear, some jeans and an olive-green, long-sleeved t-shirt she got out of her suitcase before her shower, Logan pushed her wet hair out of her face, positioned the crutches under her arms, and swung herself into the kitchen.

Girl's gotta eat.

Before she showered even, Logan had logged into Alaska Air to change her flight. She wanted to leave now, but the last flight out was booked. Next available was the one she was already scheduled to take in the morning. Probably just as well. She still had the two-and-a-half-hour drive to Portland, plus time to turn in the rental car, all of which took longer on crutches, so she resigned herself to sticking to her original travel itinerary.

It felt weird not to have her phone, but Rita had a landline, so before she went to bed, after locking up every door and window securely, she'd called Ben to apologize for not calling the night before. When he asked why she wasn't calling from her cell, she told him she'd dropped her phone in the woods somewhere and hadn't realized Rita had a landline until just now.

She would tell him the full story in person tomorrow, of course, when she got home, but not tonight! He'd be on the first flight up here if she told him now, and that was ridiculous. She was leaving in the morning. He couldn't get here before she could get there.

An hour later, hair mostly dry, ersatz ice bag tied around her knee, she sat enjoying the last of the wine out on the deck. Looking out into the forest, her run through those trees last night seemed surreal. How had she gotten mixed up in all this? She should have just handed that flash drive over to the police the minute she found it. Andrews would have it, and probably have figured it all out and had Garrett in custody by now. But noooo . . . she had to stick her nose into it. Again.

The next day, while waiting to board, Logan checked in with Bonnie. Bonnie said Shannon was fine and Lori was awake and out of ICU. They told her she could go home soon if they could release her into someone's care. Bonnie had, of course, volunteered to take her in, but Lori, although grateful for what she had done for her daughter, said she wanted to go home to her own place as soon as she was ready. Just her and Shannon. Get things back to normal as soon as possible.

So, maybe by tomorrow.

All this was good news. It meant she could tell Lori she found the flash drive, but didn't have it anymore. Hopefully, that meant Garrett wouldn't be bothering Lori again. He had what he wanted. What Lori did with that information, whether she chose to stay in Jasper or run again, was up to her. Her new friends would be there for her, though, if she decided to stay.

With the help of Edna's crutches and a handful of Ibuprofin, Logan finally hobbled onto Alaska Air Flight 105. The guy behind the check-in desk took one look at her shiner and handed her a new seat assignment.

"You definitely qualify for pre-boarding," he said with a straight face.

Logan was about to check her carry-on, but again the flight attendant took pity on her and hoisted it up into the overhead.

"Don't tell anyone I did that," she smiled. "We're not supposed to lift."

Logan wasn't about to get a gift horse in trouble. Instead, she mouthed a "thank you" and saluted.

She slept for most of the flight.

Two hours later, lowering herself onto the edge of a cement planter in front of the John Wayne statue at Orange County airport, basking in the welcome sun, Logan tucked her luggage behind her feet, and searched the steady stream of vehicles for Ben's truck. When it came into view, she almost cried.

"What happened to you?" Ben said, taking her things and helping her up.

She hugged him fiercely.

"You should go away more often," Ben said, hugging her back, tossing her bag behind her seat, and helping her up into the cab.

That was just one of the things she loved about Ben. He didn't overreact to trouble. Which was a good thing, because in the last couple of years, she managed to find trouble quite a few times.

He did demand a full explanation after they got home. When she got inside, Dimebox stalked past with his tail in the air, letting her know just how he felt about her being gone. Dimebox definitely had abandonment issues. Later, he would curl up next to her on the couch, but not until he felt she got the message.

Before she could unpack, Ben sat her down on a bar stool at the kitchen counter—there wasn't room for a table in her little hobbit– hole home—and proceeded to stuff her full of chili rellenos, rice, salad, and a couple of his infamous mojitos. The man could cook!

He'd planned on taking it all up to the deck, where they usually ate and enjoyed the sunset together, but the crutches, plus no railing on the outside stairs, precluded that idea.

"Using up the last of the rum," was his excuse when he made her the second mojito.

She wasn't complaining. The swelling in her knee had settled down, but still hurt like hell. With Ben's phone, she called the ortho's office and got an appointment for the next afternoon. Nothing to do until then but let the mojitos work their magic.

Between bites of her delicious welcome home dinner, Logan filled Ben in on the highlights of her trip—toning down the part about being chased through the forest by a violent maniac. If Ben was upset with her for not telling him sooner, he didn't waste time arguing about it. He thought she should call Detective Andrews, but saw her point about not having any evidence against her attacker. It'd be her word against his. Even though he wanted to go kill the guy himself, Ben reluctantly agreed it made some sense not to stir the hornet's nest.

Whatever she decided to do, he wasn't letting her out of his sight tonight or any other night. He had to work tomorrow but would get off early to take her to the doctor's and stay the weekend. She knew he was hoping to convince her to bring in the police and she promised to give it some thought, but reasoned that if Garrett wanted to hurt her, he would have come back last night at Rita's house in Little Whale Cove.

Changing the subject, she asked him to fill her in on his latest projects and all things Jasper, including the ongoing saga of Iona and Taylor's romance, which was apparently still going strong. She loved listening to Ben talk—just having him near. His voice, his eyes, the warm bulk of him. The way he absentmindedly rubbed the back of her hand with his thumb. All of it made her feel grounded. Safe.

Later, after Ben rinsed and stacked the dishes, she made room for him on the couch, and allowed him to kiss away all her boo-boos. Later, he carried her up the stairs, joined her in a long, hot shower, then doctored all the uninjured parts of her.

60

Officer Redart was at the end of his shift when the call came over the radio.

"Frank 92. Possible 288 in progress. Male, Caucasian, about 45, slim. On foot. Men's restroom. Fort Tejon Rest Area."

"Frank 92. On my way. 10-4."

Redart hoped the guy was long gone and he'd be able to make it home in time for his son's birthday party. It was this afternoon and he still had to pick up his gift, a Mongoose Legion L80 20" Wheel Freestyle. Josh was really into BMX. Good at it too. Practiced for hours. Redart had picked up a few extra shifts to pay for it. If his son was going to put that much effort into something, he deserved the best.

He cruised into the rest stop, parked and checked out the men's restroom, then, after announcing himself first, the women's side. All clear. No one there. Probably just someone's ex calling the cops on him, trying to get him in trouble. It's amazing what some women would falsely accuse the father of their children of. Just to pull his chain for dumping them. Or to bleed him for more money. Redart hoped never to be divorced. There was only one other car in the parking lot, out at the end, under a tree. Just to be thorough, he'd check it out before going in.

◦ ◦ ◦ ◦ ◦

Garrett jolted awake to an abrupt, loud rap on the glass. "Sir, open the window," a muffled, male voice said.

Garrett struggled up and tried to focus. He looked out the front windshield. No one there. Confused, he looked left, then right and about jumped out of his skin. A police officer's stern face looking in at him through the passenger side window. Obviously not happy Garrett wasn't responding quicker, he rapped on it again, harder this time.

"Open up!"

After a couple false starts, Garrett found the right button and lowered the correct window. It smoothly slid down and clicked into place.

"Yes, Officer? I was just resting my eyes for a minute," he said, unsure of the rules.

He blinked at the police officer's frowning face. He looked very official, shades and everything. Bright sun stabbed Garrett's eyes. What time was it? What did this guy want? He couldn't have been speeding, he wasn't moving at all. He was parked.

"License and registration," the officer said, straightening up.

While Garrett fumbled with his wallet and the glove compartment lock to get the requested documents, the officer leaned down again and asked, "How long have you been here?"

Garrett thought back. He didn't know if sleeping in your car at a rest stop was allowed in California. He didn't think it was in Washington.

"Just a few minutes, Officer. I just pulled over to use the

facilities and I must have dozed off," he said, waggling his empty Starbucks cup, then handing him his license and registration through the window. He was waking up now.

"Stay in your vehicle."

Okay.

Garrett remained in the Volvo.

The officer got back in his car, checking something. Garrett didn't like the look of this. He was in his car a while. When he finally got out and started walking back, he had a whole different body language. He approached the Volvo as if it might bite him, hand on his gun.

Not waiting to see what was going to happen next, Garrett started the car and peeled out. Cursing, Officer Redart ran back to his unit, got in, yanked the door shut, and floored it.

"Frank 92. In pursuit. Highway marker 38, moving south on I-5. Felony arrest warrant on a Garrett Delaney, Male, Caucasian, six feet, 175. White Volvo SUV Charlie, Alpha, X-Ray, nine, four, two."

Luck was in Garrett's favor. Two exits down, he swerved in front of a semi just in time to make Exit 40. He smiled as the cop car missed the turnoff. There was nothing around here but a big box discount store. Just in case the cop doubled back, he went inside. He didn't want to get back on the freeway just yet.

Once inside, he looked around to get his bearings. Man, were there some weird people in here. He didn't know the last time he'd been in a Walmart. Lauren did all the shopping. The only stores he frequented were a couple favorite, high-end department stores and his golf pro shop. After checking out the Halloween aisle full of plastic skeletons, pumpkins, and bags of candy, he wandered into men's clothing. Grabbing some pants and t–shirts, he ducked into a dressing room. He had no intention of trying on this garbage. He just needed time to figure out his next move.

As long as he was hiding out in here, he checked his phone for messages. There was only one. It was short.

You are not here.

The terrifying calm with which these few words were spoken almost undid him. But of course he wasn't there. Why would he voluntarily go home to meet up with Yoshimoto's goon? Like a shark, he needed to keep moving. What was it the nature shows said? You stop swimming, you die.

He waited another half hour until a sales clerk knocked on the flimsy door frame of the dressing room and asked if everything was okay in there. A few minutes later, holding a bag containing a pair of pants and a t-shirt he wouldn't be caught dead in, Garrett stood a few feet inside the exit doors of the garden center. He looked out at his car for another fifteen minutes before walking over to it, then ventured back on the road. He dropped his new clothing in a trashcan on the way out. A homeless guy ambled over and peered down into the can to see if there was anything worth retrieving in it.

On the way out of the massive parking lot, Garrett pulled over to the side farthest away from the store, near a newly landscaped berm. Small, stiff plants poked up in a neat pattern out of bare dirt. He parked, got out, and emptied the rest of his Evian onto the ground. Looking around first, he bent down and mixed it up with a takeout spoon from the car, then smeared the resulting mud on his license plate. He eyed his handiwork.

Not bad.

For the next hour, Garrett kept an eye on his rearview mirror. So far so good. He wanted to push it, but needed to keep within the speed limit until he got there. Jasper was still eight hours away without stops. He'd need toothpicks to prop open his eyelids if he drove straight through, but he didn't have the luxury of stopping.

His phone rang again. Same number. He ignored it and pressed on the gas, then dialed it back to sixty. He adjusted his speed to be just slightly slower than the cars in the fast lane. The last thing he wanted was to get pulled over.

61

Ben took Logan to the doctor. The news was as good as could be expected. She would need surgery, but not until the swelling went down. They sent her home with a Cortisone shot and another prescription for pain pills she wouldn't fill. It was now almost lunchtime and she was feeling much better.

Bonnie brought burgers, plus food to help stock Lori and Shannon's fridge for at least a week, including a chocolate and strawberry brownie cake Mike made. The three of them went over after they ate. Ben checked the house several times. Finding no boogiemen hiding in the closets or under the beds, he gave the all clear. They put the food away, then made a huge Welcome Home sign for Lori's arrival and hung it over the door so she'd see it first thing.

Bonnie left to go back home and collect Shannon and Haley, while Ben went to Hoag to pick up Lori and her mother, who hadn't left her side since she flew in this morning. Grandma had taken the first flight to Orange County as soon as Lori was able to call her. At first, she had worried about Garrett finding out, but Lori told her all that was over. She wasn't running anymore.

The house looked great. The social worker agreed it was best for Shannon to not see everything as it was the terrible night she saw her mother almost killed by her father, so everyone chipped in to erase all traces of the violence the little girl had witnessed.

Anonymous volunteers from the House of Ruth put up fresh curtains and brought in a new end table and lamp to replace the broken one, painted one wall a pretty, soft sage green. A bright tropical print slip cover brought the old couch back to life. A soothing, abstract seascape now hung over the fireplace. The House of Ruth people wouldn't be at the party, but told Logan to make sure Lori knew she had a home there for as long as she needed one. Everyone wanted them to stay.

Bonnie brought a huge arrangement of fresh flowers displayed in a graceful, hand-blown, glass vase donated by Howard Miller. Narrow at the bottom, it swirled to an open top, resembling an Easter lily. Founder of the glassblowing school connected to the Otter Festival, Miller kept in touch with Logan after she helped identify the killer of one of his students a couple of years earlier.

When Lori got out of Bonnie's SUV, Logan wasn't sure what to expect. The young mother had been so brutally attacked only a few weeks ago, almost dying as a result, but her wounds had healed well. With Logan's freshly blossoming black eye, crutches, and stitches, she knew she looked the worst of the two. Luckily, Shannon didn't seem traumatized at the sight of either of them.

The little girl, who had been waiting on the porch with Bonnie, scrambled off her seat and flew across the front yard straight into her mother and grandmother's open arms, almost knocking both of them over. Family hug—not a dry eye in the house. Or yard.

Shannon wouldn't let go, so Lori carried her into the house and sat down at the kitchen table. Shannon, safely ensconced in her mother's lap, excitedly pointed out the Welcome

Home sign and balloons. Logan and Ben set out the food and everyone stood or sat around visiting. The social worker, who arrived late due to another call out, warned them that Shannon might be clingy and insecure for a while, but she needn't have worried.

After the first few minutes of sitting on Lori's lap, Shannon popped her thumb out of her mouth, jumped down to chase a balloon, and asked Grandma for more 'chockit' cake. She and Haley were out on the porch sword fighting with Logan's crutches right now. Kids were amazingly resilient.

Juan stopped by with a collection of cash Lori's co-workers had taken up for her at the restaurant. He reassured her that her job was waiting when she felt well enough to return to work. Ned and Sally brought Quinn, along with their instruments. Quinn immediately joined Shannon and Haley on the porch. Ben brought Purgatory, who, after allowing the kids to mob him with kisses, immediately plopped down on the porch and went to sleep.

The party wound down with the sun. Ned and Sally lifted a sleepy Quinn into their car and headed home around 7:30 p.m. Tomorrow was a school day. Sally was taking Mavis's class and Ned was coming over to work with Logan in the office first thing in the morning.

First thing in the morning to Ned meant 11:00 a.m., so Logan knew she had plenty of time to wake up, eat a leisurely breakfast, get ready and hoist herself up to the Fractals studio office over what used to be her garage before he got there. She might even have time to grab a cinnamon roll ...

With Rita's support, and her part time work at the New School, Fractals was fully funded for this year, but it was time for the next round of grant writing. The 2017/2018 school year would be here before she knew it. Begging for money was the least favorite part of her job, but after the excitement of this last week, she was almost looking forward to spending the day plowing through some dull paperwork. At least she'd get to spend the day in a bright, sunny, warm office vs Wednesday's location, huddled in the dark and wet, freezing, wedged between two tree roots, with a violent maniac after her.

Logan and Ben cleaned up the kitchen and Ben took out the trash while Lori and Grandma put Shannon to bed. Logan wondered if the little girl would have any trouble going to sleep, but when Lori stepped back into the kitchen, she waved her arms in the air in a silent cheer.

"Out like a light!" she stage whispered.

"I'm just going to sit with Shannon for a while," Mrs. Stanton said, going back into her granddaughter's room.

Lori's mom was so loving and warm, it made Logan wish her own mother had been even remotely like that. Sometimes she wondered why she seemed incapable of loving her husband or her child, but most of the time she just accepted that particular hole in her life. It wasn't something she dwelled on often.

She squeezed out the sponge and dried her hands on a dishtowel, one of a dozen flour-sack ones Bonnie brought when she saw Lori didn't have any.

"Didn't know where everything went, so we just left things drying in the rack. Hope that's okay," she said.

"Oh no, that's fine," Lori said, "I didn't even know I had a dish rack. I can put those few things away in the morning."

Gripping the back of one of the kitchen chairs, she looked up at her new friends, "I can't tell you how much I appreciate everything you've done. For me, for Shannon. If you hadn't arranged for her to stay with your friend, Bonnie, and Haley— Shannon just loves that girl—my little girl would have wound up in some awful foster place with strangers."

Tears welled up in her eyes and her voice choked, "I just can't ever thank you enough."

Ben nodded, coughed, and stood there, holding his cake pan. Logan wiped her hands on her jeans, then hopped over to give Lori a hug.

"We're just so happy you're okay and you and Shannon are home again," Logan said.

"Ben," Lori said, turning toward him, "do you mind if I talk to Logan for a few minutes . . . alone?"

"No, of course not," he said, "Logan, do you mind bringing Purgatory with you? My hands are kinda full."

Logan knew Purgatory would trot obediently by Ben's side, hands full or not, but she understood. He was leaving the dog to guard. Just in case. But he didn't want to alarm Lori or bring back any bad memories for her. When the back door shut behind him, Lori motioned for Logan to sit down with her at the kitchen table.

"Want any cake?" she said. "I think there's some left in the fridge. I'm going to have seconds."

At the mention of cake, Purgatory lifted his head and looked hopeful.

Logan never turned down cake.

62

With Purgatory sated and draped over Logan's feet under the table, they got down to business and polished off the last bit of Mike's cake. Purgatory had at least two more slices.

Once they'd licked the last bit of frosting from their forks, Lori looked up and finally asked, pointing at Logan's eye, "Did Garrett do that to you?"

"Yes," Logan said. "Well, indirectly."

There hadn't been a chance to get into this with everyone around for the party.

"He broke into the house I was staying at looking for the flash drive you hid in the dog toy, but I heard him at the window. I got away, but then he chased me through the forest. I'm so sorry, Lori. I tried to keep it away from him, but he got it. I just couldn't hang onto it."

"That's okay. It wasn't yours to protect. I am sorry I brought all this into your life. I didn't intend to leave it there for long. I was going to tell you about it. I just knew I had to get it out of the house where Shannon was."

Logan nodded. She had so many questions. She knew what was on it, but why were those files so important? Did Lori put them there? What did they mean? Why was Garrett so desperate to get them back? What would he do with them now?

Lori took a deep breath, then spoke again, answering some of her unasked questions.

"I can't even begin to tell you how it all started. When I met Garrett, he was a good man. Bright, funny, romantic, and very loving. I know that's hard to believe now. He was so male. Or what I thought a male should be. Strong, take charge. But after we married, things changed. It's an old, tired story, I know. I can't believe I let it go so far, get that bad."

"I had a good job, you know," she said somewhat defensively, as if expecting Logan to judge her. She straightened up in her chair. "I managed the accounting department for one of Garrett's clients. He was just starting out then. When he walked into the office, I'd never seen anyone so handsome. Gave me the full court press. Swept me off my feet."

Lori pushed her fingers through her hair, pulling the skin tightly back from her face.

Logan just listened. She wasn't judging. After all, she'd fallen for Jack and never knew he cheated on her for years.

Lori looked up, as if the explanation for all those years was hidden above the kitchen cupboards.

"Then, well, he just seemed angry with me all the time. I knew he was not happy about something, and it was up to me to guess what it was. I had to drag it out of him at first, but then he'd just drop comments all the time. I had too many friends, the wrong friends, friends who were a bad influence on me. Work was taking too much of my time away from home. I couldn't be a good wife and work, too. So, I stayed home. When I did what he wanted, it was always wonderful for a while. He started making more money and gave me, and Shannon when she came along, everything.

"Then came the blowups. Never predictable, although in hindsight, they really should have been. I was on edge all the time. I never knew when he was going to blow, and when he did, it was always my fault."

Lori looked at Logan, begging for understanding. Logan let her talk. She didn't think Lori had ever had the opportunity to completely unpack it all, to understand it herself. She'd probably been too busy surviving. First at home, living with an abusive spouse, then running away, trying to establish a new life for herself and her child.

"I remember the first time he hit me. It shocked both of us. He was so sorry and said he'd never do that again. If I just hadn't made him so mad. Worn that dress," she sighed. "One of his friends complimented me on it and it made him furious. He insisted I was coming onto him, but I wasn't! I didn't even like the guy.

"Anyway, over time it happened more often and got worse. He just lost control. But I knew he loved me, and in spite of everything, part of me loved him. I wanted to help him. I thought if I could just be better, perfect enough, we could go back to how it used to be, when we first got married.

"I don't know how or when it happened, but all of a sudden, I woke up one day and realized I was alone. Completely alone and in prison," she said, "In hindsight I can see it's all textbook. So obvious, but when you're in it, things aren't so clear," she said.

"So, you don't want to hear my whole sob story. I just wanted to explain about the files. I tried to get away before, but I always went back, or he found me and dragged me back. Threatened me with losing Shannon."

She rolled her eyes, "Stupid. I know!"

"I knew if I were going to get away and stay away I'd need insurance—some kind of leverage.

"Garrett is a hedge fund manager. Good at it, too. But the economy tanked, we got overextended, and he got greedy. I suggested we sell the house—we didn't need all that, but he refused. Little by little, he started making riskier investments and eventually took on some shady clients. I didn't know all this until after I saw the files. Garrett often worked from home and when I was in his office one day, his laptop was open and it was all there. I used to do the books, so I knew what I was looking at.

"He was money laundering. I was married to a criminal! It gave me the guts to leave. That and the fact that I knew Shannon would be next.

"Anyway, with this kind of dirt on him, I thought maybe he would finally let us go, leave us alone. So I copied the most damning files onto a flash drive, made my plans, and left."

"How did he know you had the flash drive? How did he find you? Is that what he came for that night?" Logan asked.

"I'm not sure how he knew we were in Jasper, but I called my mom. I'm guessing he had her phone bugged and traced the call. He's had Neal put trackers on my car before. He was my driver. My babysitter, really. But Neal was a nice guy. Garrett had power over him. He was out on parole. One call from Garrett and he'd be back in prison. He had to do whatever Garrett told him to do. I'd like to believe he wouldn't have helped him otherwise.

Lori remained quiet for a minute, then continued.

"When Garrett came to get us, to bring us back, he thought we had no choice and would get in the car peacefully. I told him I wasn't going back this time and made the mistake of telling him I had some leverage. When he saw I meant it, that I was never coming back, he went to get Shannon. When I tried to stop him, that's when he lost it again with me."

They both sat there, silent, witnesses to Garrett's fury.

"I should have told you about all this, but I didn't know who I could trust," Lori said. "I'm sorry I got you into this."

She looked at Logan again, as if seeing her for the first time. "You look awful!"

Logan laughed, breaking the tension.

"Oh! I didn't mean that the way it sounded. It's just that your eye and everything," she said, gesturing toward Logan's face.

"That's okay, Lori, I've looked in the mirror. He did a number on my face, but I'll heal. And my knee would probably have needed surgery eventually anyway. Might as well get it over with. It's all good."

The two women reached across the table simultaneously and Logan squeezed Lori's hand, then got down to the problem at hand.

"The question is, what will he do now?" Logan asked. "Are you and Shannon going to be safe? Now that he has the flash drive, do you think he'll be back?"

"I don't think so. Even Garrett must know when he's beat," she said. "He knows I'll never go back. No, I think now that he has the files back, he'll just get back to keeping that client of his happy and making more money."

"Then," she said, pushing her chair back as she got up, "he'll probably go out and find another little chickadee to impress and keep under his thumb."

"Don't you want to press charges for the assault?" Logan asked.

"No, I realized in the hospital that I don't need the flash drive. The assault is what I have over him now, I can always press charges later, within whatever the statute of limitations is on that. I'll have to check. As long as he steers clear of me and Shannon, I'll leave it be. I'm not into revenge."

Logan hoped Lori wasn't being too optimistic. She didn't think it was revenge to make sure the guy got what was coming to him. Logan's first instinct was to nail the bastard and press charges herself in Oregon for Garrett's attack on her: breaking and entering, assault, attempted murder, or whatever she could throw at him, but she'd never been in this exact situation before. She'd have to talk with Rick. He knew a lot more about what these guys did—how they reacted—than she did. She didn't want to further enrage him.

It might make him come after Lori again. Or her.

She wanted to ask Lori if she was planning on keeping her new name or going back to her old one. If she reclaimed her actual identity, she'd also get her college degree, driver's license, and social security number back. The works, her whole life. But it was late and they were both tired. Plenty of time for all that.

They talked about Shannon some more and how she was doing, then Logan yawned.

"Past my bedtime, Lori," she said. "Better get this guy home."

She nudged Purgatory's shoulder with her toe. "Come on, big guy, your Daddy's waiting for us."

Pushing herself up from her chair, standing on her left leg, Logan tucked her crutches under her armpits, and let herself out the back, reminding Lori to lock and latch it behind her. Ben had installed deadbolts for her on both front and back doors.

63

A blood-curdling scream jolted Logan awake. It was still dark. Since he had an early morning job, Ben had gone home already, taking Purgatory with him. Grabbing her crutches, Logan hopped as fast as she could down the stairs, trying not to fall and break her neck.

The screaming came from the front, not the back, of Lori's house, so Logan threw the deadbolt on her front door and, hoping her knee brace would be enough, tossed her crutches and flew down the sidewalk. She knew she was probably doing more damage to her knee, but the Cortisone shot gave her mobility and she took it.

The action was centered on Lori's front porch. The porch light lit up the scene. The Welcome Home sign fluttered wildly above the door. Three people were locked in a deadly embrace. Shannon was hanging onto Lori, who gripped her daughter as tightly as she could, desperately trying to hold on. Mrs. Stanton flailed at Garret's head, but Logan watched, helpless, as Garrett unpeeled the little girl's arms from around her mother's neck, ripping her away from Lori, then sprinted across the front lawn with the little girl in his arms. Engine running, a Volvo was waiting at the curb, driver's side door open. Garrett threw Shannon in across the front seat, jumped in after her, and screeched away from the curb.

Grandma swore and Lori crumpled onto the porch, letting out an unearthly wail.

Logan dialed 911 just as Ben and Purgatory came running around the corner. Ben had a gun.

Wow! She'd have to ask him about that later.

It seemed to take forever, but Detective Singh, someone Logan hadn't met before, was there in just over five minutes. He addressed himself to the distraught mother, now sitting inside at the kitchen table, being comforted by her mother.

"Don't worry, Mrs. Delaney . . ." Singh began.

"Please don't call me that. I want nothing to do with that last name. It's Wright, Lori Wright."

Her mother squeezed her shoulders. They were all in this together. They'd face it together as a family. And Garret was definitely not part of that family anymore. They had finally gotten Lori to calm down enough to function. Logan hoped she could keep it together. She remembered how panicked and desperate she felt when Amy went missing at sea in a storm, with a murderer on the loose, only a year ago.

"Okay, Ms. Wright, I understand," Singh said, speaking directly to Lori. "I just wanted to assure you that everything is being done that can be done to locate your daughter and bring her safely home. We've issued an Amber Alert. An arrest warrant is already out for your . . . for Mr. Delaney . . . and all cars are out, including Detective Andrews and Diaz, but we need your help."

"Okay. What can I do?" Lori said.

"You gave us the make and model of the car your husband was driving, the Volvo, but do you have any idea where he may be taking her? Do you have any property here? A vacation home, perhaps, or another place Mr. Delaney has been or may feel safe at?"

"No, nothing. We live—lived . . . in Seattle. We've never been here before. I don't think Garrett has, but he travels some for business. I don't really know . . . That's why I chose Jasper," she said, fighting back tears, hands clenched in front of her on the table. "I didn't think he'd find us here."

She began to sob.

Logan went to the living room and brought back a box of tissue. Lori blew her nose.

"Okay, let's go over this again," Singh said. "From the time you first saw him . . . What did he do, what did he say? Did he explain why he took Shannon?"

"I didn't let him in this time. He didn't knock. If he did, I didn't hear him. We had both gone to bed. Mom was in my room and I made up a bed on the couch. He must have tried the door and then gone around the house until he found a way in. Both doors were locked and all the windows were shut, but I hadn't put the wooden dowels in all of them. Shannon's window. She must have taken it out to play sword fight with. That's her new thing. He just lifted it up and let himself in. Like I said, I was in the living room when he walked in from the back with Shannon in his arms, still asleep, her head on his shoulder."

"I'd never seen him like that. Crazy look on his face. His hair was sticking out on one side, his clothes were all dirty and the look on his face. It was just manic looking," she said. "My heart just stopped."

"What happened next?" Singh asked, checking his note pad.

"Like I told you before, he started talking crazy, but all calm like everything else he'd done hadn't happened. He had this awful smile. Told me he had gassed up the car, it was waiting for us all outside, we were going now, it was all going to be great. Better than ever. He just kept rambling on. He grabbed my arm, pulling me toward the porch.

"That's when Shannon woke up and started screaming. Mom came out to help. Shannon tried to squirm away from him, latching onto my neck. And then, once he tore her loose, he took her."

Lori hung her head.

"She screamed all the way to the car," her mom added, stroking Lori's hair.

"And they headed north or south on PCH?" Singh asked.

"South, they turned left. South," she said softly, all hope gone from her voice.

o o o o o

The golden arches were a godsend. Garrett pulled off the freeway. Next to the McDonald's was a strip mall with a darkened thrift store and a shoe repair place. All closed. He pulled around back and parked behind the dumpster. Checking quickly around the car, he got out, locked Shannon in, and jogged across the street to the McDonald's. Hopefully, it wouldn't take long. Happy Meals were Shannon's favorite. One of those should shut her up.

It didn't.

She started screaming again the minute he got back. He tried several times to shove a Chicken McNugget into her mouth, but she spit it out each time, then gagged, throwing up all over the seat and him. Thrashing wildly, she kicked over her drink and now he was covered in vomit and root beer.

"You ungrateful brat!" he yelled, slapping her across the cheek.

Shocked into silence, Shannon just stared at him, then started screaming again, this time even louder. Enraged, Garrett got out and stomped around the car. This is what they did to his daughter! Turned her into a brat. Scared to death of her own father! All he wanted was to take care of her. This was all Lauren's fault—and that bitch of a mother she had.

Probably half under the influence of that Logan woman. He knew Lauren would have seen reason and come with him to Mexico so they could all be safe together if it wasn't for her nosy neighbor getting involved. She must have poisoned them both, corrupted his family, turned them against him!

He yanked open the door and grabbed Shannon out of the car by one arm, holding her away from him, avoiding touching her soiled pajamas. Throwing her into the bushes, he tossed what was left of her Happy Meal back in her direction. Then, using some wipes he had in the glove compartment, he mopped out the seat as best he could, removed the floor mat where much of the root beer had spilled. Shaking, he dumped them on the ground and slammed the door shut.

"There. All yours! Let's see how you do on your own, Miss Independent!"

Feeling rather pleased with himself, he got back into the Volvo and, spitting gravel, sped away from Shannon's cries. He was through with women. Of all ages.

Mexico, here I come!

He managed to get over into the correct lane before the light turned red. He still had a few more hours to the border, didn't want to get popped when he was so close.

His phone buzzed as the car in front of him made it through the yellow. Text message. He reached down to shut it off, but before he did, the phone rang loudly and he accidentally answered it. The voice was cold and very familiar coming through the car's audio system.

"What's the matter, Mr. Delaney? Didn't Shannon like her Happy Meal?"

✿ ✿ ✿ ✿ ✿

The RAV4 full of teenagers going to a beach party barely missed broadsiding the Volvo as it rolled through the intersection. The driver swerved to the left. As the Toyota went into a 90 degree spin, the girl in the passenger seat screamed. Inches from her face, bloody brains were sprayed all over the Volvo's window. They belonged to the man missing part of his head, slumped over the steering wheel.

64

NOVEMBER 24, 2016, THANKSGIVING DAY

Iona and Taylor were the first to arrive. Iona handed Logan an insulated, nine-by-thirteen casserole carrier with handles.

"Cheesy-Jalapeno Enchiladas, my specialty. They may need to be warmed up a little. We drove in from my place. Holiday traffic is hell this time of day. Four hundred degrees for ten minutes ought to do it," she said.

"Better put a warning sign on those," Taylor said, before exiting out to the patio. "They'll singe your eyebrows at thirty feet."

"It's true! I like my food hot and my men hotter!" Iona laughed.

In the last couple of months, Logan and Ben had gone out with the unlikely pair a few times. She got to know Iona better, as a person, not the stern head of security at the Otter Arts Festival.

She learned Iona was a breast cancer survivor, for one thing, which explained her "grab life by the horns" attitude.

"Beating cancer gives you a remarkable perspective," she told Logan one night. "You take no shit, no prisoners, and just do what feels right in life."

Logan couldn't disagree. The only thing she'd survived lately was knee surgery and that was enough to make her not take her health or anything else for granted. Although still going to physical therapy twice a week, she'd ditched the crutches and was pretty much back to normal. She offered to ship them back to Edna in Oregon, but she said to keep them.

"You never know when you might want to go hiking again at midnight," she deadpanned.

Someday Logan would have to tell her the truth about what happened.

Bonnie and family were already seated at the picnic tables outside with Amy and Liam. Ben, as usual, had gone all out. Brined turkey, roasted sweet potatoes, shredded Brussels sprouts with bacon. They had to do without the fry bread, because Lisa and Thomas were up in Idaho, but Logan picked up some baguettes and Paul brought crescent rolls.

In Southern California, you could still enjoy most Thanksgiving dinners al fresco. Amy had invited Cheryl, an associate of Liam's from New Jersey who didn't have any family in town. She brought cherry pie. Cheryl was Liam's supervisor at Scripps Aquarium in La Jolla, where he was doing post doctoral work in Marine Botany.

"I'm still in shock," Haley was saying. "How did he ever get elected?"

"Well, I for one voted for him!" Cheryl said. "I like him."

When everyone looked at her like she had lost her mind, she said, "I know. Everyone says he's crazy, but all the other choices were same-o, same-o. And who needs more of the status quo? Nothing is getting done. It's a complete logjam in Congress.

Things need to be shaken up. It couldn't get any worse!"

Logan wasn't sure she agreed with that. Just look at history. Countries didn't last forever. On the timeline of history, the United States of America was only a blip. A lot of civilizations had gone under after being on top a lot longer.

"Not much any of us can do about it, anyway," Liam said, ever the peacemaker. "You've got all these checks and balances here, right? It's not like he's an emperor. American presidents can't do whatever they want. Someone will keep a lid on him."

Bonnie rolled her eyes, "Okay guys, no politics or religion around the Thanksgiving table. We need at least one peaceful meal."

The election results were all anyone had been talking about all week. Rose called and was in apoplectic shock. Rita wasn't far behind, but calmer about it. Ben was pretty much apolitical, which Logan hadn't decided was good or bad.

In her mind, there were no easy answers. The only way anything was going to change was to get money out of politics, and how that was ever going to happen, she had no idea. She decided to help Bonnie change the subject.

"Haley, how are the applications coming?" she asked.

After seeing firsthand what Shannon went through, Haley had decided to become a child psychologist or social worker. She got to sit in on some of Shannon's therapy sessions and was in awe of Shannon's counselor and how much she helped her work through everything. Haley piled on extra credits in order to graduate with her class and meet all the requirements for the colleges she was applying to.

"Okay, but I'm having a tough time with some of the essays," she said.

"I know your Mom has it covered, but if you need a second pair of eyes on it, let me know," Logan offered.

Haley thanked her and then got up to check on something in the house. Logan grinned and gave her a thumbs-up.

Gina, the director of the Sea Otter Center and Amy's boss, came in with her assistant, Dennis. Amy had been working with them at the Center and doing so well Gina was considering putting her in charge of elementary school field trips. Amy loved baby humans almost as much as baby otters.

Bonnie asked Logan about the school board's big Fractals report instigated by her nemesis, Dr. Metterson. He was just looking for ways to make the program and by default, Logan, fail.

Logan raised her glass of Sauvignon Blanc, "Passed with flying colors!"

"Hear! Hear!"

"*Slainte!*" Liam raised his with the traditional, Scottish toast.

Logan couldn't prove direct correlation that Fractals was improving test scores on the big, standardized end-of-the-year exams, but second–year Fractals students outperformed students not enrolled in the program by more than 14 percent. Several of the board members, one of them a retired engineer, who were at first skeptical of the connection between music and increased development in the brain, visited campuses where her program was being run and shared their support with her privately.

"Those kids look happy—and they stay happy all the way through Calculus, Organic Chemistry and Physics! Which more are grasping. Now that's progress! That has to be good for kids!"

Lori and Shannon made it just in time for dinner. What a difference two months made!

65

Dressed in a crisp, white, cotton blouse and navy capris, Lori's new, short haircut made her look like an entirely different person. Glowing and happy, she didn't need much makeup, but indulged in a mani-pedi for the occasion. Her feet clad in slim leather sandals, one ankle sported a small, discrete tattoo.

She told Logan last week she applied to officially change her name to Lori Wright from Lauren Delaney, and already had two job offers from local businesses. The House of Ruth people were working with her to purchase the house she'd been staying in. She didn't have it yet, but it looked like Garrett's life insurance was going to pay out. That would definitely help. She was even talking about setting up an online accounting business, so she could spend more time with Shannon.

Shannon, black curls bouncing, was adorable in her navy and white sailor dress. Shirley Temple reincarnated, she was all dimples and smiles, a far cry from the frightened little girl dropped off anonymously at the ER of the local hospital, scraped and bruised, her dress ripped and covered in vomit. Because of the Amber Alert, she was quickly identified and after being cleaned up, and treated for minor abrasions, reunited with her very grateful mother and grandmother.

Grandma Stanton, after staying as long as she could to get in as much Shannon time as possible, was back in Washington state. They wouldn't be separated long, though. Lori said they were going up there for Christmas.

Enrolled in pre-school now, Shannon was always bringing Logan and Ben macaroni necklaces or pictures she drew of Purgatory or them. When she spotted Ben, she let go of her Mom's hand and ran over to tell him all about something. He scooped her up, gave her a hug, nodded sagely at whatever it was she said to him, then set her down to go play with Purgatory, who was waiting patiently for her attention.

The huge dog and the little girl spent a lot of time together over the last two months. Purgatory was a big part of her therapy after what she went through at the hands of her father.

No one mentioned Garrett anymore, but Rick filled Logan and Ben in on the details of his demise a couple of weeks ago when he and Paula came over for dinner. He said Detective Andrews was pissed Delaney got shot before they could arrest him.

Singh, a rookie detective, went over the CCTV footage at higher magnification, and did indeed find the black Jeep that matched up with the partial plate Logan got. Turns out it belonged to a friend of Delaney's—one that also had a private plane he borrowed occasionally, which, coincidentally, Medford reported had some damage to it that could easily have been caused by a heavy weight hitting it, like a body being tossed out of the airplane over the Pacific.

In coordination with the Seattle Police Department, Rick said Detective Lutrell did a financial autopsy on Delaney's banking and crypto records. They had him dead to rights on everything, even before he went rogue. They even matched the DNA collected from under Lori's fingernails from the first attack. The feds were particularly interested in one of Delaney's primary clients, a Mr. Yoshimoto. Logan remembered that name coming up frequently on the flash drive files she had seen but didn't understand at the time.

It would have been so much more satisfying to arrest Garret, Rick said, but since he was fairly well off, he probably would have walked anyway, or gotten off with a slap on the wrist.

"Even with Logan witnessing him kidnapping his daughter, and Lori testifying against him in court?" Ben asked.

"Yep. Happens more than you know," Rick said. "You can shoot somebody in the street at high noon with a dozen witnesses, and a good lawyer can get you off. Say the sun was in your eyes and you were aiming at a squirrel."

"Amazing!"

"So, in a way, maybe whoever it was who got him did everyone a favor," Rick said. "At least he won't be around to bother Lori or Shannon anymore. Or you, Sis."

Couldn't argue with that. She'd certainly slept better the last few weeks, knowing her attacker was dead. No one knew for sure, but it was assumed one of his criminal clients got to him first. Rick said Andrews didn't have time to cry in his beer. He already had five more cases piled on his desk, which brought the grand total to thirty-two. He was working these with Singh. He and the younger detective seemed to get along well, and Diaz was out for foot surgery.

○ ○ ○ ○ ○

While the guys cleared the table, the girls went inside.

Bonnie put four pink candles in the cake and found some matches. Haley got the ice cream out—'chockit' of course—and put it on the tray with a metal scoop, some napkins, bowls and plates. The surprise had been hard to keep.

"Do you think she knows?" Logan asked.

"Nope," Lori said. "Bonnie had Mike keep him under wraps at the firehouse for me. All the guys at the firehouse fell in love with him—didn't want to let him go. They just brought him over, brought him in the front so Shannon didn't see him. And you can't hear anything from outside."

As they mounted the stairs, they could hear Shannon's surprise whining to be let out. Not much more than a ball of thick, wavy, white fur, the puppy waddled over and started to nose Lori's hand through the wire door.

"Are they ready out there?" Logan asked, grabbing the bag of dog treats and toys she'd kept hidden in her closet the last couple of months. Turns out Lori told the truth about one thing. Shannon really did have a birthday coming up. It just happened to fall on Thanksgiving this year.

Haley went to scout things out.

"Yeah, Ben's got her on his lap right now," she reported. "They've got all her presents piled next to her and everyone's sitting around in a circle on the blanket, over on the grass."

Lori lifted the carrier by the handle on top, stepping carefully down the stairs. Logan thought to throw a dishtowel over the carrier to help quiet him momentarily.

The procession wound its way out onto the patio.

"Close your eyes, Shannon!" her mother said.

Shannon, wiggling with anticipation, did as she was instructed. Lori walked into the middle of the blanket, knelt down and unlatched the wire gate of the carrier. Just as Shannon's eyes flew open, three pounds of puppy love launched himself out of the carrier and bounded joyfully right to Shannon, licking her face and arms and legs, turning himself inside out with delight at the new turn of events in his life. Shannon threw her arms around his neck, hugging him tight.

"What kind of dog is that?" Cheryl asked. "He's big! How old is he?"

"He's called an English Cream Golden Retriever. He's only eight weeks old," Lori told her, not taking her eyes off her daughter and her new puppy.

"He's so cute! Look at those polar bear paws!"

Purgatory padded over and lay down at Ben's feet. He accepted being upstaged by the newcomer. You can't compete with a cute puppy. He yawned widely.

Just wait till the first time you poop on the floor . . .

"What's his name, Mommy?" Shannon asked her mom.

"He doesn't have a name yet. He's whatever you want to call him," Lori said.

Shannon furrowed her brow in concentration while she considered this monumental task.

"I want to call him Cloud!" she said, ". . . or Snowball! . . . or Marmarrow!"

Logan laughed. The dog would probably have fifteen names before the end of the night. Logan's eyes teared up. She hated it when she got all sappy, but it wasn't often that the universe came together like this.

Ben came over and put his arm around her. They stood comfortably watching the puppy attempt to lick and jump on everyone at once, then chase his tail and do it all over again.

"You're enough," he said in a low, but clear voice, pulling her close. "You're more than enough."

Logan wasn't sure she heard him right. She lifted her face and searched his eyes.

A couple of months ago, Logan thought she was going to lose Ben over the issue of having children. She already had a grown daughter and didn't want to start a new family now.

"You're sure?" Logan asked, almost wishing she hadn't.

Ben ran the back of his hand down her cheek, smiling into her eyes.

"I'm a lucky man, and I know it."

Words weren't adequate to express her feelings, so Logan hugged him back fiercely. She felt the same way. She knew how lucky she was to have Ben in her life. And her daughter's. He'd walked Amy down the aisle last year. Ben was part of their family.

It was all Logan could do to keep her mouth shut. This would be the perfect time to tell him, but she'd been sworn to secrecy. In a few months, Ben was going to get all the baby time he wanted. Amy and Liam were expecting. The baby was due in March. And if it was a boy, they were going to name him Benjamin Liam Buchanan.

ACKNOWLEDGMENTS

A heartfelt thank you to everyone who gave of their time to answer my innumerable questions and put me back on the right path when I wandered. This book is better because of you.

Crimes Against Persons Detective, Corporal David Gensemer, of the Laguna Beach Police Department, gave me a glimpse into the workings of a detective bureau in a small, beach town similar to Jasper, CA.

In attempting to understand the dynamics of spousal abuse, I am grateful to Dr. Patricia D. Rozee, professor emeritus of Psychology and Women's Studies at California State University at Long Beach, California for her expertise on violence against women. Our interview was enlightening and the research materials she provided, invaluable, in clarifying the often misunderstood causes and effects of spousal abuse. Thanks also to Carrie Askin, LCSW, for her Psychology Today article, "Five Reasons People Abuse Their Partners." Reporter and Advocate for domestic violence victims, Amanda Kippert, also provided front-line insights.

Much appreciation to my Alpha and Beta Readers, whose

insightful observations improved the story, and Sandra McClintock, for polishing the manuscript.

Many thanks go to Kim Peticolas for bringing these new editions of the Logan series to life. Her powerful cover designs and sleek interiors are awesome!

Dr. Joseph C. LaDurantey, retired Police Chief, fellow author, and Managing Director of the Vollmer Institute, helped me portray police procedure and dialogue authentically.

Congratulations to the Name-a-Character contest winners, Janie Greene-Livingston for Rae McCluskey, Marilyn Lafiura for Edna Gamble, Marcia for Neal Everly, and Alisha Henri for Lucas Kai. I tried not to make any of them too dastardly, as some, I discovered, were named after family members.

Residents of the real Little Whale Cove will notice I changed street names and some of the topography to protect privacy and enhance the danger in one of the chase scenes. And the characters are, of course, entirely fictional.

If I have forgotten anyone, please forgive. All remaining errors are mine.

As always, my eternal gratitude goes to my husband, John, who understands when the Logan light is on. Headphones firmly clamped on my head, sounds of ocean waves crashing on rocks blocking out all other sound, he gives me the luxury of being ensconced in Logan's world, oblivious to the demands of eating, sleeping, laundry, or ringing phones. Honey, you're the best!

ABOUT THE AUTHOR

A self-admitted book addict, Valerie Davisson was the kid with the flashlight under her pillow, reading long after lights out. After a life of travel, she now lives on the Oregon coast with her husband, John, and their new puppy, Finn. When not working on her latest book, she's probably in the kitchen, cooking up a storm for family and friends.

Enjoyed the Book?

If you enjoyed this book, please consider leaving a review on Amazon or Goodreads. And be sure to check out the rest of the Logan McKenna series.

Shattered (Book 1)

Forest Park (Book 2)

Devil's Claw (Book 3)

Safe Harbor (Book 5)

Want to know more about Valerie Davisson or her next book? Make sure to visit www.valeriedavisson.com and sign up for her newsletter.

Made in the
USA
Middletown, DE